FIGHTER FRED

BOOK 2

THE FIGHTER FRED SERIES:

Fighter Fred and the Dungeon of Doom
Fighter Fred and the Wombat Wilderness
Fighter Fred and the Evil Temple of Evil

OTHER BOOKS BY JASON A. HOLT:

The Dragonslayer of Edgewhen
The Artificer of Dupho
The Klindrel Invasion
The Burglar of Sliceharbor
The Bladesman of Darcliff
Galaxy Trucker: Rocky Road

Visit jasonaholt.com.

FIGHTER FRED
AND THE
WOMBAT WILDERNESS

JASON A. HOLT

Fighter Fred and the Wombat Wilderness
Jason A. Holt

This is a work of fiction. All of the characters, organizations, locations, and events are either products of the author's imagination or are used fictitiously.

This is not a Dungeons & Dragons® product. Dungeons & Dragons® is a registered trademark of Wizards of the Coast. Although some Dungeons & Dragons rulebooks are briefly quoted or paraphrased for purposes of satirical commentary, no relationship between Fighter Fred and Wizards of the Coast is implied.

Published by the author.
JasonAHolt.com

paperback ISBN: 978-1-950841-03-5
epub ISBN: 978-1-950841-02-8

Not all who wander are lost.
But their chances of becoming lost on any particular day are one in three.

CHAPTER ONE: IN WHICH FRED MOPES.

THERE'S A CERTAIN SORT OF STORY that begins with the main character moping around in his pajamas. Fred would never start a story that way. *So there I was, moping around in my pajamas, when suddenly, I had a brooding thought!* No. No one would listen to a story that started like that.

And yet, that was how Fred started every day.

Fred was not, by nature, a moper. Fred was a fighter. In fact, the building in which he moped every morning was known as the Fighters' Guild.

The building was square, four stories tall, with walls of stone. From the outside, it resembled a keep. Inside, it resembled a barracks.

Fred moped on the uppermost floor, sitting on his bed. The bed sat in a long row of similar beds. Beside the bed stood a rack holding his plate mail armor. His belt and scabbard hung from a knob on the corner of his headboard. The fighters always kept their swords handy in case the building was suddenly attacked. No one in Basetown was likely to lead an assault on the Fighters' Guild, but it was an adventuring town, and adventurers are always ready to be attacked.

Fred was an adventurer. Or at least, Fred had been an adventurer, not long ago. Actually, how long had it been since his last adventure? Fred tried to do the math, but it had been over a week, and Fred wasn't sure how calendars worked.

Maybe Fred wasn't an adventurer anymore. Maybe he was just a moper. He could join the Mopers' Guild. He could sleep with his pajamas hanging on a rack beside his bed in case a cry rang out in the middle of the night exhorting him to jump out of bed and mope.

Wait, that didn't make any sense. If professional mopers kept their pajamas on a rack, what would they wear in bed?

This puzzle distracted Fred for several minutes. (He really wasn't very good at moping.) He had narrowed the possible answers down to "a second pair of pajamas" or "nothing" when a comrade-in-arms came up the creaking stairs.

The comrade-in-arms was his friend Yellin' Helen. Her head appeared first, wearing a pensive expression. Next came her torso wearing a frumpy woolen sweater. That was good; it wouldn't have made sense the other way around.

She paused there, visible only from the waist up, with her attention focused on Fred. Her expression grew more pensive. Her sweater grew more frumpy.

She exhaled a sigh that said, *Fighter Fred, I was really hoping for more from you … but I'm not surprised.* That's a lot to say with a sigh, but Fred had been on lots of adventures with Helen, and he knew what her sighs meant.

Helen continued her climb into the top-level barracks, revealing herself to be a woman in a skirt and not a mermaid or a centaur. Of course, if she'd been a centaur, she would have sounded more hoofy and not like a woman climbing stairs in thick wool socks. Unless she wore socks on her hooves. Were centaurs even allowed up the stairs?

"There's still time to get breakfast," she said.

Right. Breakfast. That was what Fred was supposed to be doing. Instead of moping.

"I'm not very hungry," he said.

"Maybe you'd *be* hungry if you ate some breakfast."

"I ate breakfast yesterday."

"At noon."

Fred thought about it. Had he really moped around until noon? "I suppose."

Helen crossed the room and opened the trunk at the foot of her bed. "I'm going out to look for an adventure. Wanna come?"

"Maybe later."

"Just a one-shot," she said. " 'A hill giant has been terrorizing neighboring farms.' 'An old woman asks you to find some herbs in the forest.' "

Fred didn't say anything. Helen slipped out of her skirt and sweater and put them in the trunk.

" 'A merchant asks you to deliver a letter across town.' "

"Don't take one of those," said Fred. "No merchant hires a fighter to deliver a letter unless it's addressed to a werewolf or something."

Helen slipped into her armor—two pieces of plate mail just big enough to conceal her brand-name underwear.

"Well, I have special skills that make ordinary merchants trust me to deliver letters to other ordinary merchants."

"Which skills?"

Helen strapped her humongous sword to her mostly-bare back. "I'm a barbarian, Fred. I can't read."

"Oh, right."

"Want to come? You can pretend to be my little barbarian brother."

"Maybe next time."

"Right. Next time." Her lips tightened, as though she had something else to say—something she was holding back.

She let her breath out with a sigh. This sigh said, *I'll let you get away with this for one more day, Fighter Fred, but next time ... next time I don't know what I'll do.*

Fred thought about giving in, then, while Helen was putting on her leather adventuring boots. He didn't want to mope around the Fighters' Guild forever. And an adventure with Helen would be fun. Maybe.

But what if it wasn't? What if no adventure would ever be fun again? Could he allow himself to relax and enjoy it, or would he always be haunted by the image of Paul the thief standing in a flame-charred corridor holding a sword that he had just driven into his friend's gut?

This brooding thought held Fred's attention as Helen's boots clomped across the floorboards and down the stairs. By the time he snapped out of it, she was gone.

He should have gone with her. An adventure with Helen would have been just the thing to set him right again. Helen was smart. She would never lead an adventure that ended with party members killing each other.

Helen had warned him about the thief. For that matter, the *thief* had warned him about the thief. Paul had always acted like he wanted to kill them and claim their share of the treasure, but Fred had assumed it was just an act.

What was it Twilight had said? *We become what we pretend to be.* Fred should have seen it coming.

Fred should have stopped it from happening.

Fred's last adventure had nearly ended in a giant fireball. Somehow, everyone had survived, but they were in no condition to fight. As soon as the thief had realized this, he'd stabbed Mak-Thar the mage and claimed his share of the treasure. Then Twilight the elf had killed the thief—partly out of revenge, partly out of self-defense—leaving Fred and Twilight as the only survivors.

Well, not quite. It turned out that the elf was actually the servant of some moon goddess of life and rebirth or something, and he arranged to have the mage reincarnated in the body of the party's mule. So the thief was the only party member who hadn't returned. Fred should have hated the thief for what he'd done. Fred should have been glad that Twilight had killed him. But Fred thought maybe there had been a way the whole thing could have been prevented.

Helen said if she'd been on the adventure she would have just kicked the thief out of the party. He was determined to be a bad guy, and the only way to deal with him was to get rid of him.

That's what Helen thought, but Fred saw it differently. Deep in his heart, he felt that if he had been a little wiser, if he had known what to say and when, he could have convinced the thief to find his better self. In Fred's mind, the adventure had ended badly not because the thief had decided to be evil, but because Fred had not realized he needed to convince the thief to be good.

Fred blamed himself. Every morning. In his pajamas. It was getting monotonous.

Helen's boots clomped partway back up the stairs. This time she stopped with only her head showing, leaving open the possibility that she might be one of those snakes with a woman's head. What were they called? Mak-Thar would know.

"The elf who stares at my chest is here to see you."

Fred hadn't seen Twilight since the adventure. They'd both rested up a few days at a village tavern, and then Fred had come back to Basetown alone.

Fred wasn't sure he wanted to see Twilight again. It might bring back too many memories. On the other hand, if his goal was to avoid memories of his last adventure, then maybe he should stop brooding about it every morning.

"Send him up."

Helen made her tight-lipped face again. When she had decided what she wanted to say, she said, "Nuh uh. Only guild members are allowed upstairs. If you want to talk to him, you have to come down."

Fred rose to his feet with a sigh. This was his own sigh, so he didn't need to interpret it.

He shuffled across the floor in his bunny slippers—made from real rabbit fur with the ears left on.

"You're coming downstairs in your pajamas?"

"Well, I don't own a toga."

"You're grumpy this morning." She turned back down the stairs. The clomping of her boots was probably proof that she wasn't a snake. Good thing, because snakes probably weren't allowed upstairs.

Fred paused to be sure that seeing Twilight really was something he wanted to do. After a moment's thought, he decided that he wasn't sure, but he shuffled down the stairs anyway.

* * *

By the time Fred made it to the bottom floor, Helen had already left the building in search of adventure. Twilight stood waiting for him in the guild's entryway.

"You really *do* have pajamas and bunny slippers!"

"Hi, Twilight."

It was good to see the elf again. Twilight was dressed for adventure. He wore comfortable boots decorated with images of birds in flight. His form-fitting doe-hide leggings looked clean and recently scrubbed. He wore several layers of bright clothing under a sensible grey traveling cape. A bow was slung over his shoulder. His sword, his knife, and various pouches hung from his belt. A compact pack on his back gave the impression that he was prepared to set off into the forest on a moment's notice.

"Oh, Fred. I am indeed glad to see you again. I feared you would already be off on another adventure."

"Nope. Still here."

"And are you well?"

Fred shrugged. "I'm all healed up."

Twilight gave him a scrutinizing look. "All healed up in body, at least."

"I've been using the ointment you gave me."

"You look like you need ointment for your soul."

"Do you have some?"

"No, Fred. I was speaking metaphorically."

"Oh. It sounded like the common tongue."

Twilight smiled. "I have missed your company, Fred. Not that Mak-Thar is an inadequate companion, but he has been rather moody."

"Has he been moping?"

"One could say that."

Maybe Fred and Mak-Thar could start a Mopers' Guild. That was about the only guild Basetown didn't have yet.

"In truth," continued Twilight, "I am actually here on Mak-Thar's behalf. He is having some difficulty adjusting to his new situation, and I thought you might be able to cheer him up."

"Oh, is that all you want?"

"Why, yes. Were you expecting something else?"

Fred looked closely at the neckline of Twilight's sparkling white tunic and saw a fine silver chain. Fred recognized that chain from the last adventure—it held the Amulet of Spring.

Twilight had risked his possibly-immortal elven life to obtain the amulet, and now he was apparently wearing it under his tunic against the skin of his slender elven chest. Fred realized that he had expected Twilight to show up and ask for help returning the amulet to the elves. If Twilight just wanted him to cheer up Mak-Thar ... well, Fred didn't know if he was disappointed or relieved.

"I'd love to see Mak-Thar," said Fred. "Tell him to come visit anytime."

"Fred, he's a mule. They won't allow him inside the building."

"Are you sure? It might be okay as long as he doesn't come upstairs."

"Fred. Would you come out and talk to him? Please?"

"You want me to go outside?"

"Yes. Mak-Thar is outside."

Fred looked at the solid wooden door that separated the Fighters' Guild from the world. When was the last time he'd been out that door? He hadn't been outside at all, had he? He'd just come home, climbed the stairs, traded his armor for his pajamas, and started moping.

It was probably time to stop.

"But I'm in my pajamas."

Twilight clapped a hand onto Fred's shoulder. "Any man who has the strength to hold off a horde of giant spiders while Mak-Thar calculates the blast area of a fireball also has the strength to change out of his pajamas."

Fred had been telling himself that every day. Maybe it was time to listen.

He sighed. "I guess you're right."

CHAPTER TWO: IN WHICH MAK-THAR IS PERMANENTLY A MULE FOR NOW.

A FEW MINUTES LATER, Fred was tromping down the stairs wearing his boots and armor. His scabbard no longer hung from his bed; it was belted to his hip.

Did getting dressed make Fred feel better? No. His heart was still moping.

But getting dressed made Fred act better. He wore his armor with an easy grace. He moved through the building like he belonged there. The cook came out of the kitchen to give him a smile, a pat on the back, and a cold turkey leg. Fred was already gnawing on the bone by the time he opened the door and stepped outside.

"Wow. Has the sun always been that bright?"

"Yes, Fred. Welcome back to the land of the living."

Twilight was being sarcastic. Mak-Thar was the one who had died and been reincarnated. Fred had just been moping.

Mak-Thar stood in the street at Twilight's side. He was a mule. Before Mak-Thar's reincarnation, the mule had been named Evenstar—because of a star on its forehead and because that was just the sort of name a person like Twilight would give a mule.

Evenstar had been an average mule with a calm and easygoing temperament. But now that Mak-Thar had been reincarnated into Evenstar's body, Mak-Thar's emotions showed through.

Mak-Thar was downtrodden. His ears drooped. The line of his back sagged. His hind legs stamped disconsolately in the dust of the street.

"Hi ya, Mak-Thar. How's it going?"

Mak-Thar gazed at Fred with misery in his eyes. "I've been suspended from the Mages' Guild."

"Oh," said Fred. That sounded uncomfortable. "Suspended by what?"

"He means they've kicked him out, Fred."

"No mules allowed?"

"No mules allowed," said Mak-Thar. "Or, to put it more precisely, they have said that, since I cannot do magic, they can no longer consider me to be a mage."

"You can't do magic?" This was news to Fred. "But you were the one who told us how to divide the treasure. You even knew the prices we'd get when we sold the used battle axes."

Twilight rolled his eyes. "He can still do *math*, Fred. He just can't wave his arms and wiggle his fingers."

"No fingers, no magic," said Mak-Thar. "Sad, but true."

"Oh," said Fred. "Isn't there some sort of mule magic you could learn?" Fred imagined Mak-Thar kicking his hind feet and waving his tail.

"No one at the guild could teach him," said Twilight. "Because none of them are mules."

"Oh, right."

"The Mages' Guild says I have to be a fighter now."

"Really?" Fred couldn't imagine Mak-Thar as a fighter, not even if the Fighters' Guild voted to allow mules upstairs.

"Yes," said Mak-Thar. "It's logical, I suppose. I attack as a two-hit-die monster and save as a fighter of the second level."

"Yeah, I see what you mean." Fred had no idea what Mak-Thar meant. Logic in the Mages' Guild was always full of numbers and empty of common sense.

"Do you think he could be a fighter?" Twilight asked.

"Well …" said Fred. Everyone always said that a fighter was the easiest type of adventurer to be. And certainly the members of the Fighters' Guild represented a wide range of body types and intellectual ability. But one thing they had in common was a certain temperament. And the best way Fred could think of to describe that temperament was that it was the opposite of Mak-Thar's. "… Maybe."

"Oh, whom are we kidding?" said Mak-Thar. "We all know I'm not a fighter. We all know that I have always solved problems with my wits and not my muscles. Suddenly being able to eat grass and carry four thousand gold pieces has not changed that."

Fred looked at Twilight. "Yeah. That's kind of what I was going to say."

"There must be some way to turn me back into a mage again," said Mak-Thar. "I can't adventure as a mule."

Twilight placed his hand on the mule's shoulder and said, "Mak-Thar, when I asked Selene to intervene on your behalf, she chose this form for a reason. You were not reincarnated as a mage. You were reincarnated as a mule. You must find a way to live with that."

Mak-Thar turned his sad eyes on Twilight. "Are you sure? Maybe she just meant this as a penance. Maybe she just wants me to donate a thousand gold pieces to her temple before she restores me to my original form."

Twilight shook his head sadly. "Alas, that is not our way."

Fred asked, "Well, have you asked the sage?"

"Why?" asked Mak-Thar. "Does Basetown have a new sage?"

"No. It's still just Sage the Sage."

"Wait," said Twilight. "The town sage is actually *named* Sage?"

"Yeah," said Fred. "It's an amazing coincidence!"

"It's not a coincidence," said Mak-Thar. "It's someone's idea of a joke, and I don't find it very funny."

Twilight looked confused.

"She's not even a mage," said Mak-Thar. "She's just a half-pint."

Twilight said, "Half-pints are a simple people, but surely a half-pint who has lived many years can be the source of much folksy wisdom."

"She's the source of much folksy side quests," said Mak-Thar.

"Well, she does like to give out quests," Fred admitted. "But what do you expect? This is Basetown."

" 'Go to the heart of the volcano and bring me back a silver tea set,' " said Mak-Thar. " 'Then visit the lair of the red dragon and steal the matching cutlery.' "

"I assume you are jesting," said Twilight.

"I jest you not," said Mak-Thar. "And that's the price for something simple, like 'Where can I find a plus-one sword?' If you need to remove a curse, she's ten times worse."

"That rhymed!"

"The gift of Selene is not a curse!" said Twilight. "It is a sacred opportunity to better yourself and gain a deeper understanding of the interconnectedness of all living beings!"

"Sure it is," said Fred, trying to smooth things over. "Mak-Thar knows that. He's grateful to be alive. Aren't you, Mak-Thar?"

"I believe I have stated as much many times."

Fred decided that meant yes. "But we can't really know how long Selene wants him to be a mule, can we?"

"What are you talking about?" asked Twilight.

"Well, she's a goddess," said Fred. "And aren't goddesses supposed to be mysterious?"

Twilight said, "When a servant of Selene speaks of 'mysteries', we are referring to knowledge that cannot be obtained in the ordinary way—an enlightenment or an insight."

"Uh huh," said Fred. "So do you have enlightenment about how long Mak-Thar needs to be a mule?"

"Why do you keep saying 'how long'?" Twilight asked. "Mak-Thar *is* a mule. It's permanent."

"Sure," said Fred. "It's permanent *for now*. But how long does it have to *stay* permanent? Do you think she'd get really mad if we tried to change him back?"

"Change him back? I know of no way to do so."

"That's why we go visit Sage the Sage," said Fred. "She might know how to change him back. Then after a heroic quest—"

"With a ridiculous number of side quests," said Mak-Thar.

"A heroic quest ..." said Twilight. And Fred knew he had him.

Twilight rubbed his chin and nodded. "Yes. I suppose after actions that are sufficiently heroic, it might be possible for Mak-Thar to become a man again."

"And then he could be a mage again," said Fred.

"Would that make you happy?" asked Twilight.

18

"Yes," admitted Mak-Thar. "Even though I know that half of Sage's side quests are pointless."

"Let's go visit the sage," said Fred. "She's a cute little half-pint. You just have to like her."

"Actually," said Mak-Thar, "half-pints have only moderate racial reaction bonuses, which leaves open the possibility that we can react to her neutrally, or even with great skepticism."

"This is what I've been dealing with for the last ten days," said Twilight. "I'm so glad to have you in the party again."

"Thanks," said Fred. "I'm glad to be back ... I think."

CHAPTER THREE: IN WHICH TWILIGHT DOESN'T GET RELIGION.

WHEN FRED HAD FIRST ARRIVED IN BASETOWN, it had held three guild houses, two temples, and a bank. And of course, there were also the usual taverns and adventuring supply stores that you found in every town. Year by year—and sometimes month by month!—the town had grown. Here's an alchemist who will identify that mysterious potion. Here's a sage who can answer difficult questions.

Sage the Sage had set up shop after Fred had joined the Fighters' Guild, but before the first of the big growth booms. A few months later, there was an animal trainer who could show you how to raise and train a baby hippogriff. A weaponsmith who specialized in silver weapons showed up just in time for the big wererat outbreak. A few months after that, the town got an engineer who could help high-level adventurers build keeps and towers and castles. A week later, Basetown got three real estate agencies, and there was no turning back.

The town had grown a lot since Fred had first seen it, but it still had the feel of a new settlement. Most of the buildings were made of wood. The streets were still unpaved.

There was new construction at Temple Square. One of the

oldest taverns had been torn down and most of the vegetable market had been torn up to make room for the stone foundations of a new temple.

In front of the construction site, a cleric was shouting, "Church of Law! Join the Church of Law! Free curse removal for new converts!"

"Church of Law?" asked Mak-Thar. "What's that?"

"We could ask," said Twilight.

They approached the construction site. When the shouting man paused for breath, Twilight said, "Greetings, gallant brother of the Church of Law. We see you are newly come to this town. Would you kindly describe to us your spiritual path?"

"I came on a path from the south," the cleric replied. "But soon the Church of Law will spread all over the land."

"And what's your alignment?" asked Mak-Thar.

"My Law! It's a talking mule!"

"I'm a reincarnated mage," said Mak-Thar. "I've only been a mule for ten days."

"And were you reincarnated against your will?"

"No."

"Then I'm afraid I can't help you. If you aren't cursed, I can't remove it."

"I apologize for being unclear," said Twilight. "We did not stop to … um … take advantage of your promotional offer. We simply wanted to know more about your belief system."

"I believe in Law."

"Which law?" asked Twilight.

"Any law."

"Any law is a good law?"

"Good and evil are irrelevant," said the cleric. "The important thing is to have rules."

"That's exactly what I believe!" said Mak-Thar. "You must be neutral, like me."

"Absolutely not. The practitioners of the Church of Law are lawful."

"Lawful?" asked Mak-Thar. "Is that some new alignment?"

"Lawful and chaotic," said a woman in a black cloak, who seemed to have appeared from nowhere. "Two new alignments coming soon to a town near you."

"What are you doing here?" demanded the cleric with the booming voice. "This is consecrated ground!"

"Hm," said the woman.

"This is the lawful side of the Temple Square. We have a building permit! No chaotics allowed."

"But we don't follow the rules," said the woman in the black cloak. "That's how you can tell we're chaotic."

"Of all the indignities! I shall call for the city guard!"

"Good luck," she said. "They're across the square, playing dice in the tavern I just bought."

"Thou wily temptress! They won't be happy when they learn you plan to tear down their tavern to build your abominable temple."

"Eh, that was last week's plan. Now I'm planning to expand the tavern and turn it into a casino. That will bring in more converts than any temple could."

The lawful cleric sputtered with indignation.

Mak-Thar said, "But *The Adventurer's Guide* recognizes only three alignments: good, neutral, and evil."

The woman in the black cloak smiled. "Change is coming, little talking mule. Some people follow the rules. Some people write them."

The man glowered. The woman looked smug.

Because Mak-Thar and Twilight seemed to have run out of questions, Fred assumed they had gotten all their answers. He set out across the square, and one heartbeat later, the elf and the mule did the same.

"Worshipping the law for law's sake," said Twilight, shaking his head. "No good can come of that."

"Well, if he's neutral enough," said Mak-Thar, "no evil can come of it, either."

In front of a domed building decorated with dove frescos, a round-bellied woman was chanting, "Temple of Good. Temple of Good. Y'all come home to the Temple of Good. Blessings for the worthy, healing for the rest. We're Basetown's oldest temple and we're still the best!"

They passed a tiny stone chapel in the middle of the square. A sign outside said, *We're neutral and we don't care.*

Mak-Thar hesitated. "Since I'm neutral, I suppose it would be in character to stop and give them a donation."

"Especially since you are about to embark on a quest," said Twilight.

"But if any neutral deity even exists," said Mak-Thar, "it would be unable to intervene without compromising its own divine principles."

"A theological conundrum," Twilight agreed.

"Well, I'm indifferent," said Mak-Thar. "And I can't reach my coin pouch."

"I'll donate for you," said Fred.

"Oh, would you? My gold is in the third saddle bag on my left. Two coins should be sufficient."

Fred reached into the indicated bag on Mak-Thar's back and found two gold pieces. He dropped them into the iron lockbox below the sign that said, *Eh, thanks, I guess. Your generous donation helps pay the salary of the chaplain who empties this lockbox.*

"Are you sure neutrality is about indifference?" asked Twilight. "I thought it was supposed to be all about maintaining a cosmic balance."

"I don't know," said Mak-Thar. "I suppose it could be about balance, but I'm not a cleric, so I don't really care."

Twilight asked, "Are all human religions so vague?"

"*The Adventurer's Guide* presents alignments as generalities," said Mak-Thar. "That allows the rules to be seamlessly integrated into any setting."

Twilight rolled his eyes. "Or it allows a town to embrace the generalities and completely fail to deliver any sense of setting whatsoever."

"Basetown is a very good setting for adventures," said Mak-Thar. "It has everything we need at the prices specified by *The*

Adventurer's Guide. Any time a setting attempts to have so-called 'character', that really just means it has a set of arbitrary restrictions that prevent players from exploring all of the game space."

"I have no idea what you just said."

Fred had no idea what either of them was saying. He had once divided the world into thinkers and fighters, but he was beginning to suspect that Twilight might actually be a third thing. Maybe Twilight was a talker. Fred had never adventured with anyone else like him.

As they walked through town, Mak-Thar and Twilight continued to argue, which attracted a few stares from people who weren't expecting to see a talking mule.

Ha! This was *Basetown.* You should expect *anything.*

As they passed a tailor shop, Fred heard the tailor say, "Yes, I heard that a band of orcs has been attacking sheep farms in the east. That's why wool is getting so expensive."

A short while later, they passed a beggar who said, "Alms for a poor refugee? My village up north was destroyed by evil cultists."

Fred dropped a gold piece into his cup.

As they passed the tavern at the end of the block, the door opened and an angry dwarf tossed a thief onto the street. He shouted, "That's what you get for telling lies! A magic portal has opened in the south? It leads to a strange dimension? Who ever heard of such nonsense?"

Twilight said, "These random snippets of conversation seem suspiciously informative."

"Just ignore them," said Mak-Thar. "This neighborhood is notorious for its adventure hooks."

"Adventure hooks are metaphorical," said Twilight. "You can't just find them in a particular neighborhood."

"That used to be true," said Mak-Thar. "At one time, if you wanted to hear rumors, you had to go into a tavern and buy a drink. But now they're getting desperate."

"They?" asked Twilight. "Who are 'they'?"

"I wish I knew," said Mak-Thar. "Obviously, it's someone

with enough money to hire rumormongers, but I can't figure out what their game is. Perhaps the region's local governments think it's cheaper to solve their problems by attracting adventurers rather than by equipping and maintaining a police force."

Basetown certainly had plenty of adventurers to attract. Adventurers had always outnumbered locals for as long as Fred had lived here, but now the adventurers *were* the locals. Most people moved about in groups of five or six—and most groups had at least one cleric, one thief, and one mage. Armor and weapons were everywhere. Sacks bulged with gold pieces.

"You know," said Twilight, "if every adventuring party spends like we do, a town can probably *make* money by attracting adventurers."

"Good point," said Mak-Thar. "I've read essays explaining how the capture of a dragon hoard can lead to—"

"A battle of five armies?" asked Twilight.

"Worse," said Mak-Thar. "It can lead to massive inflation. Fortunately we have price controls in *The Adventurer's Guide.* Otherwise prices would run amok."

"We're here," said Fred.

"Are we?" asked Mak-Thar. "It's so hard to tell without a map."

They stood outside a humble-looking cottage with a picket fence and an herb garden. A sign on the door said *Sage.* And underneath, in tinier letters, had been added *the Sage.*

"Honestly," said Mak-Thar, "I'm sure she's built her entire business on a case of mistaken identity."

"Well," said Fred, "I think they have a sage in Watergate."

"Ugh," said Mak-Thar. "Watergate is over a month's journey from here. I shudder to think of the side quests. I'll have to take my chances with Sage."

CHAPTER FOUR: IN WHICH MAK–THAR NEGOTIATES WITH SAGE THE SAGE.

FRED KNOCKED ON THE DOOR of Sage's cottage. A cheerful voice answered, inviting them to come in.

Fred opened the door and entered the room that served as Sage's office, parlor, library, and herbarium. Bundles of drying herbs hung from the rafters. A perfectly-ordinary-looking-but-possibly-magical broom stood in the corner. Shelves were lined with tomes and potions and jars of pickles.

At first glance, the room was what you would expect. The second glance was disorienting. The front door, the coffee table, and the six chairs for customers were all normal-human sized, but the far side of the room was normal for half-pints. That is, Sage's chair and writing desk were half sized. The door to the kitchen was designed for someone only three feet tall. The worst part was that the walls diminished to keep the proportions the same. The back wall was only four feet high, so the kitchen and the writing desk and everything else at that end appeared to be normal height and twice as far away.

The room made Fred feel like he was inside an optical illusion. Well, okay, Fred actually thought he was inside a "tickle illusion", but Fred knew what Fred meant.

Fred was followed by Twilight and most of Mak-Thar. (To avoid crowding everyone, Mak-Thar stopped with his hind hooves still on the doorstep.)

Sage emerged from the kitchen and said, "Have a scone. They're fresh."

They were so fresh that they were steaming. The curly-haired, middle-aged half-pint was carrying them on a pan that she had to hold with oven mitts.

Fred took a scone, sat down in a chair, and helped himself to the honey that was sitting in a pot on the coffee table.

"Your mule doesn't want to wait outside?" she asked.

"I'm your customer," said the mule.

"Ah," she said. "That explains it. Care for a scone? Or should I fetch a bowl of oats?"

"My forage for the day has been adequate, thank you."

"I see. You're a bit stuffy for a mule."

"I have been a mule but a short time. I used to be a mage."

Twilight took a scone and sat down beside Fred, holding the scone as though he didn't know what to do with it. "He has been reincarnated by the goddess Selene."

"Oh." Sage made a quick sliding motion with her baking pan and sent a scone sailing through the air to land neatly on her writing desk. "That's a little unusual, isn't it? Don't reincarnated people usually come back as people?"

"You're the sage," said Mak-Thar. "You tell us."

"Well, you're as cheeky as a mule."

Sage went into the kitchen and came back with a tea set. It was silver. With matching cutlery. Mak-Thar gave Twilight a meaningful look.

Sage set the tea set on the coffee table and filled two cups and one saucer.

"Thank you," said Mak-Thar. He took a slurp from the saucer.

Sage said, "I assume you're here because you are having difficulty with your love life."

Mak-Thar sprayed his tea across the room. "What?"

Sage giggled and went to the kitchen to fetch a rag. "It's no use. Mules can't have babies. Scientific fact."

"This is not about my love life!"

Sage came back and began daintily wiping tea splatters off her walls. "I know, but the joke was worth it."

"Well!" said Mak-Thar. "If you're done having fun at my expense, could you tell me if there's a way for me to become a mage again?"

"Um, and a man again," said Fred. "I don't think he wants to be a magey mule."

"Yes," agreed Mak-Thar. "And a man again."

"Possibly," said Sage. "Yes, I might know just the thing. It will return you to your true form. But are you sure a mage is your true form?"

"Of course I am."

"And yet, you have all the manners of a mule."

"Oh," said Mak-Thar. "Yes, yes. You are very witty."

"That's why I'm the sage, and you're the ... customer."

"Yes," said Mak-Thar. "About that. I am, of course, very desirous of learning more about this thing you say can return me to my true form—"

"I'll need a little favor first."

"Yes, I'm sure you will, but I would like to propose—"

"My niece's birthday is coming up. I can think of nothing that would please her more than entertainments performed by a talking mule. She lives in a village three weeks to the southeast. Now along the way—"

Mak-Thar said, "HEE-HAW!"

Twilight dropped his scone. Sage raised an eyebrow.

"If I may interrupt," said Mak-Thar, "I understand how you would like this to go. First you'll send me on an errand to entertain your niece. Along the way, you'll want me to drop off a remedy for someone's sick grandmother."

"Sick goat," said Sage.

"Then at your niece's village, the mayor will complain of ogre trouble—"

"Orc trouble."

"—and request our help solving that problem. On the way back, we shall meet a messenger boy who says that Sage has left Basetown and requests that we meet her at a dark inn on a remote road on a stormy night."

"It could be a clear night," said Sage. "I don't control the weather."

"There, you will reveal the secret remedy that I so desperately need, but there will be a devilishly complicated caveat—"

"Is that like a catch?"

"Yes."

"Then yes."

"And so it will go," said Mak-Thar, "round and round, until we have done every errand you can think of."

"I help people; I give them an opportunity to help me. That's how the sage business works."

"Yes," said Mak-Thar. "That's how the sage business *would* work *if* we lived in a world that had not discovered currency. But thanks to this miracle of economics, it is no longer necessary to trade favors for favors incessantly in circles until the end of time."

Sage shrugged. "Only until I get a more pliant client."

"That rhymed!" said Fred.

"Sage," said Mak-Thar, "wisest of the half-pints in Basetown, please consider my counteroffer. According to *The Adventurer's Guide*, hiring a sage costs two thousand gold pieces per month. That is a rate of roughly seventy gold pieces per day. Telling me how to regain my original form will take you five minutes. Even so, I am willing to pay you for the whole day *if* we can do this without any side quests."

"Seventy gold pieces?" Sage asked.

"Yes," said Mak-Thar. "A whole day's wages for five minutes' work. In fact, I will gladly round it up to an even one hundred, just so long as we are clear that there shall be no side quests."

"Let's round it up to five hundred."

"Five hundred?"

"I can't let orcs crash my niece's birthday party. I'll need to hire some other adventurers to protect her village."

"Oh. Well, I see your point. Fortunately, I have the money saved up, and I am willing to pay this price, but only if you guarantee that there will be no side quests."

"Yes, okay, no side quests," said Sage. "But *you* have to promise to be polite to me."

"If my words or demeanor have offended, I sincerely apologize," said Mak-Thar. "I also apologize for besmirching your walls with your delicious tea, but—"

"But that was my fault. I'll own up to that. Okay. You've got a deal."

Mak-Thar said, "Fred? Would you, please?"

"Hm? Oh."

Fred got up and took Mak-Thar's pouch of gold pieces out of his saddle bag. "Um ... five hundred is kind of a lot."

"I can count it," said Sage. "Hand it over."

Fred handed it over. Sage spilled out some coins and began making stacks.

"The remedy you seek is in the waters of a magic spring. Those who drink from this spring regain their true form."

Fred thought that sounded good.

"That sounds bad," said Twilight.

Sage smiled. "Your elf-friend is wise. For some, the spring is a blessing. For others, it has been a curse."

"Please excuse me for interrupting," said Mak-Thar, "but do you mean the kind of curse that can be removed by a Remove Curse spell?"

"She means 'a bad thing,' " said Twilight. "If your soul is ugly and twisted, your body will become ugly and twisted. If you care only for money, you could be turned into a greedy pig."

Sage paused in her counting of the money. "Pigs are no more greedy than any other animal. That's just an expression."

"Oh."

Sage resumed counting. "Regardless, the elf has the right idea. When I say 'true form' I mean 'true form'. That's the cravat."

"Caveat," said Mak-Thar.

"That's the caveat."

"Well, I'll just have to risk it. I don't know what else I can do. Where is this magic spring?"

Sage asked Twilight, "Would you close the curtains, please?"

Twilight arose and did so. The room became darker. As the elf returned to his seat, the half-pint put her hands on the coffee table, leaned forward, and murmured, "He who would drink from the magic spring must first journey north into the Wombat Wilderness."

"Um," said Mak-Thar, "why all the dimness and murmuring?"

"Hush!" said Twilight. "This is the dramatic moment when she gives us our quest!" To the half-pint, he said, "Please go on."

Sage murmured, "In the wilderness you will find furbearing wombats. Skin them, cure their hides, and sew them to make warm robes."

"This sounds like a side quest," said Mak-Thar.

"The magic spring is high on the side of a snowy mountain. You will need wombat parkas to keep warm."

"Oh very well. Though why we can't just buy some robes in town, I don't know."

Twilight raised his hand.

"Yes?" asked Sage.

"I'm not sure we know how to make wombat parkas."

"Can you sew?" she asked.

"Of course," said Twilight.

"I'll sell you the wombat parka pattern," she said. "Fifteen gold pieces." And she counted it out from Mak-Thar's pouch.

"Wonderful," said Mak-Thar.

"Was that polite?" Sage asked.

"Um … it is wonderful that you are so generous with your knowledge, oh wise one."

Sage giggled. "Now, where was I?"

"In the Wombat Wilderness," said Mak-Thar. "Hopefully very close to the magic spring."

"Not yet," said Sage. "Next you must journey through the desert and seek Herman the Hermit."

"We agreed there would be no side quests."

"The mountain with the magic spring can be reached only by crossing a cursed bridge. Herman alone knows its secret."

"He won't tell you?" asked Mak-Thar.

Sage shook her head. "I've been trying to negotiate a licensing deal, but no luck."

"Very well," said Mak-Thar. "Is there a particular place we can find Herman the Hermit, or do we just wander around the desert shouting his name?"

"If your need is great and if your quest is worthy, Herman will find you."

"Wonderful," said Mak-Thar.

"Or if you prefer, I could sell you a map."

"How much?"

"Fifteen gold pieces."

"Done."

Sage fetched a map from her writing desk and laid it on the coffee table. Then she counted out fifteen more gold pieces.

"Once you leave the desert—"

"There's more?" asked Mak-Thar.

"One more. Once you leave the desert, you must journey south to the village of Mucho Caliente."

"Wait. Due south? Doesn't that take us back into the Wombat Wilderness?"

"No," said Sage. "To get to the desert, you go around the end of the Impassable Mountain Range. Herman and the village are on the opposite side, and for that half of your journey, you'll be going south."

"Well, I'm glad we made that clear," said Mak-Thar. "This would all be a lot easier if we had a map."

"Hm," said Sage. "Actually, I *do* have a map ..."

"Fifteen gold pieces?" asked Mak-Thar.

"Fifteen gold pieces."

"Very well."

Sage fetched another map from her writing desk and laid it on the coffee table. It was covered in hexagons.

"So Basetown is here," said Twilight, pointing to a hexagon with a little town in it. "And the magic spring is ...?"

Sage finished counting out fifteen gold pieces and then put her stubby half-pint finger on a hexagon almost next to Twilight's. "Here. On this mountain."

"Isn't that due west of Basetown?" asked Twilight.

"You can't go due west," said Mak-Thar. "The map is in hexagons."

"What?"

"Due west would put you on the line between two adjacent hexagons," said Mak-Thar. "That's not allowed. You have to go northwest or southwest."

"I'm sure it would be fine as long as we didn't tell the cartographer," said Twilight.

"It would not be fine," said Sage. "It would mean your doom. To the southwest lies the Bottomless Gorge. It's a very long drop."

"We could follow the contour of this mountain and pass north of the gorge," said Twilight.

"You could," said Sage, "if you want to find out why it's called the Impassable Mountain Range."

"I see," said Mak-Thar. "So you are recommending we go around the Impassable Mountain Range by traveling many days north and then many days south."

"It's less likely to lead to certain death," said Sage.

"But supposing we were to fly?" asked Mak-Thar.

"Interesting idea," said Sage. "How do you propose to make a mule fly?"

Mak-Thar flipped his ears. "Ah. I see what you mean. Flying magic usually applies to creatures 'human-sized or smaller'."

Sage nodded. "I don't know how a mule can fly across the Bottomless Gorge. Of course, someone else might know. I hear they have a good sage in Watergate."

"We're not going to Watergate," said Mak-Thar. "Please finish explaining your recommended route."

"Where was I?" asked Sage.

"We had just visited the hermit," said Twilight. "And then there was something about a village."

"Ah yes." Sage put her finger on a hexagon next to the one with the magic spring. "You must journey to the village of Mucho Caliente. On the slopes above the village grows a certain kind of pepper known as the chili. The villagers harvest this pepper and make from it a potent red powder."

"And you want us to bring you back a bottle of it," said Mak-Thar.

"No! I promised there will be no side quests. This chili powder is for you. The road to the Cursed Bridge is guarded by a fierce white dragon. If you can trick her into inhaling this chili powder, it will neutralize her ferocity, and you shall be able to pass in safety."

"Why can't we just kill the dragon?" asked Mak-Thar. "*The Adventurer's Guide* says that of all dragons, the whites are the weakest. We should be able to take it on if we recruit a few more mid-level fighters."

"She has eggs," said Sage.

"Even better," said Mak-Thar. "We can sell the eggs and turn a profit."

"Who would buy dragon eggs?" asked Fred. He was imagining some sort of giant omelette.

"Lots of people," said Mak-Thar. "The hatchlings can be trained and raised to become flying mounts."

"Oh."

"That sounds foolishly ambitious," said Twilight. "Dragons are a long-lived species. Raising a hatchling could take fifty years before it's strong enough to fly, much less carry a rider. And incubating the eggs could take centuries."

"But I'm sure there's a way to get a dragon as a flying mount. Would someone get out my copy of *The Adventurer's Guide*?"

Sage said, "Listen, mule. Do you want to regain your true form or not?"

"I want to regain my true form."

"Then get the chili powder and outwit the dragon. That's the way this quest is done."

"Well, I suppose outwitting the dragon *is* more in character for me."

Sage nodded decisively. "That's it, then. In the forest, get the wombat pelts. In the desert, meet the hermit. In the village, buy the chili powder. The villagers will show you the road to the dragon, which you bypass with the chili powder. Then you cross the Cursed Bridge using knowledge gained from the hermit. Follow the path up the mountain, wearing your wombat parkas if you get too cold. Near the top, you find the spring. Drink. True form. Done. No side quests. Have I met my end of the bargain?"

"Well," said Mak-Thar, "it sounds like a full-blown wilderness adventure to me. But under the circumstances, one has to expect a little adventuring—at least for the sake of game balance. Very well. I am satisfied."

Sage swept the coins off the table and caught them in her skirt. She carried them into a back room and came back with the pattern for the wombat parkas.

At Mak-Thar's request, Fred folded the pattern and the two maps together and tucked them into Mak-Thar's copy of *The Adventurer's Guide*, which was stowed in one of his saddle bags. Fred also stowed Mak-Thar's money pouch, which was now much floppier and not nearly so heavy.

As they took their leave of Sage the Sage, Mak-Thar was careful to say his farewell politely. Then the three brave adventurers headed back down the street toward the Temple Square.

After about a minute, Twilight asked, "Mak-Thar, how much does one gold coin weigh?"

"A tenth of a pound."

"That's what I thought. So five hundred gold pieces ..."

"Would weigh fifty pounds."

"And she just carried away fifty pounds of gold in her skirt?"

"Fifty-four point five pounds," said Mak-Thar. "Those half-pints are stout little fellows."

CHAPTER FIVE: IN WHICH MAK-THAR AND TWILIGHT NEARLY GET THROWN OUT OF A TAVERN THAT THEY DO NOT ACTUALLY GO INTO.

"SO," SAID MAK-THAR as they hiked through Basetown, "it seems we shall indeed be facing a wilderness adventure."

"A heroic quest," said Twilight, and Fred could tell that he very much enjoyed saying those words.

"Well, even if we don't attempt to slay the dragon, we'll still need more than two party members."

"Two?" asked Twilight. "I'm sure Fred will come as well. Won't you, Fred?"

Yeah, Fred pretty much had to come along. The whole mess was his fault in the first place. Mak-Thar was a mule because he'd been reincarnated. He'd been reincarnated because he'd been dead. He'd been dead because the thief had stabbed him. And the thief had stabbed him because—

Well, Fred still wasn't quite sure why. But maybe the thief hadn't known any better. Maybe if Fred had said, *Hey, Paul, by the way, stabbing your friends is wrong*—maybe then the thief wouldn't have done it, and Fred could have been in the tavern right now, telling everyone about the look on Mak-Thar's face when he realized his party was about to be engulfed by his own fireball. That would have been really funny if they had all come back alive.

But the thief was dead and Mak-Thar was a mule. It was all Fred's fault.

"Fred?"

"Of course I'll come," said Fred.

"There," said Twilight. "You see? We are three."

"I was counting you and Fred," said Mak-Thar. "I wasn't counting myself. The Mages' Guild has declared me to be an NPM."

"Oh dear," said Twilight. "This sounds like another silly rule from your *Adventurer's Guide*."

A street urchin ran up to them and said, "They say Jean Peabody's husband was found naked and raving in the woods. No one knows what happened to Jean."

"Thank you," said Twilight. "We already have a quest." They kept walking.

"It's not a silly rule," said Mak-Thar. "It's a legal fact. Talking animals are NPMs."

Twilight sighed. "And do, please, tell us what these initials stand for."

"Non Party Member," said Mak-Thar, obviously surprised that Twilight didn't know. Of course, the last time that Twilight had known a rule in *The Adventurer's Guide* had been *never*, but Mak-Thar had a tough time understanding that not everyone likes to read rulebooks for fun.

Mak-Thar flapped his ears and said, "Party members can be human fighters, human thieves, human clerics, human mages, dwarven fighters, half-pint fighters, and elven fighter-mages. All other characters are NPMs."

"So you're not in the party?" Fred asked.

"I am," said Mak-Thar. "But as an NPM."

Twilight said, "So you're a Non Party Member party member."

"It's not as complicated as you make it sound."

"Didn't you tell us that all Non Party Members are monsters?"

"By definition, yes," said Mak-Thar. "But the rules refer to NPMs as 'monsters' primarily in the context of combat. If you choose to interact with them verbally, they are denoted as NPMs."

Fred waited for the thief to say that Mak-Thar's mom was an NPM, but the thief wasn't there.

"So you're in the party, but you're not a member," said Twilight.

"Precisely. In fact, you could think of me as a half-member. I get only half the usual experience points, because I am not participating in the decision making."

"You're not?"

"No. I'm your mule. I just follow you around and do what you say."

"I'll believe it when I see it," murmured Fred.

"Furthermore, when treasure is divided, I am entitled to only a half-share. Although, of course, my morale statistic will be higher if you offer me a full share."

"Your morale statistic," said Twilight.

"Yes. Higher morale makes me less likely to abandon the party in times of danger."

"But it's *your* quest," said Twilight.

"Yes," said Mak-Thar. "That should definitely give me a strong morale bonus. You can probably get away with paying me only half a share."

Twilight said, "Mak-Thar, you are a sentient being who can make his own decisions regardless of any statistics published in *The Adventurer's Guide*. You are *not* an NPM. No one is!"

A woman carrying a basket of apples said, "There are so many refugees in town since that evil temple was established in the north." Fred wasn't sure who she was talking to—maybe the apples.

"Look," said Twilight. "Do you think *I'm* an NPM?"

"Are you a fighter-mage?" asked Mak-Thar.

"No. I am a servant of Selene."

"Then according to the Mages' Guild, you're an NPM."

"But *you* don't think so," said Twilight. "*You* think I'm a real person."

"*I* think you're getting around the core rules by using a rules supplement. You don't seem to be doing anything particularly abusive, so it doesn't bother me to acknowledge you as a party member. But *I* am hoping to be reinstated by the Mages' Guild. If I want to be in the Mages' Guild, I have to play by the rules as written. Therefore, I am an NPM."

"You're impossible, that's what you are."

While his friends argued, Fred had been leading them to a very particular tavern. He needed to find Yellin' Helen.

Mak-Thar was right. They shouldn't go wandering off into the Wombat Wilderness without some help. Mak-Thar was having an identity crisis, and there was no way of knowing how he would hold up in a fight. Twilight was pretty good in a fight, but he insisted that his goddess didn't want him to wear armor. And Fred was more of a dungeon crawler than a mountain man. He'd been on wilderness adventures before, but only when someone very competent had been in charge—someone like Yellin' Helen.

Helen was a barbarian. She knew stuff like how to hunt and where to camp. And she knew how to organize a party. With Helen in charge, Fred wouldn't have to worry anymore. The hike would be hiked. The quest would be quested. Helen would see to it that things got done.

Whereas if Mak-Thar or Twilight was in charge, most of the quest would be spent debating questions like "What's an NPM?" and "Do oak trees really exist if I can't find them on the encounter table?" To put it bluntly, if the elf or the mule was in charge, Fred would have to be in charge—and that had gone very badly. Fred needed Helen.

The tavern was called the Bloody Axe. It had no sign above the door—just an axe embedded in the outside wall. The blood on the axe always looked recent. This was marketing aimed at a very specific clientele.

"I think you should wait outside," Fred told his friends. "And, uh, if you plan to argue some more, maybe stand far enough away from the door that no one inside can hear you."

The mule and the elf looked perplexed, but they didn't try to follow him inside.

Taverns are quiet in the mornings, but in an adventuring town, they are never without customers. The Bloody Axe was about half full, with an equal mix of dwarves and barbarians.

The barbarians wore furs and loin cloths and leather boots. If they wore armor, it only covered the body parts that had to be covered for modesty's sake. Any one of them could have walked into a medical academy and immediately gotten a job as a model of the muscular system.

The dwarves sat at separate, shorter tables murmuring in their own language. They wore so many layers of armor that they probably had chain mail underwear. They accessorized with weapons—so many weapons. If Fred had tried to wear an axe, a war hammer, a dagger, and a crossbow, he wouldn't know how to sit down.

When Fred walked into the Bloody Axe, all conversation ceased and everyone turned their eyes to him. Two heartbeats passed. Then everyone pretended that nothing had happened and went back to their conversations again. They all spoke quietly, being very careful to not disturb their fellow patrons.

Helen liked to come here after a hard day's work. She would sit at the end of the bar and drink an ale or two. No one was sitting at the bar now.

Well, okay, that guy in the skunk-fur kilt and horned helmet was sitting at the bar, but that guy was *always* sitting at the bar, passed out face down and burping.

Fred climbed onto a barstool upwind and waited until the barman asked, "What can I do for ya?"

Fred gently plonked two gold pieces on the bar and quietly slid them across to the barman. "Have you seen Yellin' Helen today?"

"Yeah. I told her there was a shopkeeper on Turnip Street who was complaining of strange noises coming from his attic."

"Oh," said Fred. "Well, that shouldn't take long."

If he'd been alone, he would have bought an ale and waited for her. As it was, he was with Mak-Thar and Twilight—who had already found something else to argue about:

"Look, apples are a highly durable fruit, but they won't last all winter and into the following spring. Her apples weren't even wrinkled."

The patrons nearest the door stopped their conversation and frowned.

"Well, perhaps they were wax," said Mak-Thar's voice, outside the door, but not as far outside as Fred would have liked.

"Why would she carry wax apples?"

"They're just a prop," said Mak-Thar. "She's been hired to give out adventure hooks. The apples help her look the part."

"I think the apples were enchanted. And perhaps she's been enchanted, too. Who was she talking to, I'd like to know!"

Now patrons at other tables were looking at the door and frowning. Some of the dwarves were starting to grumble.

Fred said, "If Helen comes in, tell her Fred was looking for her. Thank you."

The barman nodded.

Fred headed for the door—but not in a hurry. No, Fred walked with the confident stride of a man who wanted everyone in the tavern to know that he was going to take care of their problem, and there would be no need for any of them to get up and hit someone with an axe.

"We aren't going to attempt to disenchant the NPM rumor-monger," said Mak-Thar. "It's an irrelevant side quest. In fact, it's not even a side quest. The side quest was related to whatever it was she was telling her apples!"

Fred stepped out of the tavern and shut the door gently behind him. Mak-Thar and Twilight were still standing where he had left them and not where he had advised them to be. He opened his mouth to suggest that they start walking, but just then, a new person entered the conversation:

"Hi! Are you guys going on an adventure?"

She was an elf, sharply dressed. Her leather boots had that funny turned-down cuff thing at the top. (Did boots need cuffs? Fred had never been able to figure that out.) Her leggings were so tight you could see her kneecaps. Her hips were hidden by a flouncy little chainmail skirt. Her torso was encased in shiny black armor.

The armor was womanly without being even vaguely bra-shaped. Fred had no idea how that was done. It must have taken an elven blacksmith fifty years to create a suit of flat-chested armor that looked feminine.

She wore a sword, a longbow, a quiver of exactly twenty arrows, and a smart little backpack that told the world she was ready for adventure, or at least a spunky day hike.

The total effect was intriguing. She looked amazing! And she spoiled it all with her next words:

"My elf is so cool you won't believe it. You just *have* to take her along."

"Excuse me?" asked Twilight.

"Okay, get this. I maxxed out her armor class, so she's great in combat. But she can also cast, like, any spell in the book. *And* she's got these magic boots that make her silent enough to be a thief. So whatever you guys need in your party, I got you covered. What do you say? Can I play with you guys?"

"This is not a game," said Twilight. "We are about to embark upon a very dangerous quest."

"Right! Right! Roleplaying! I'm a great roleplayer. And the best thing about my elf is that she can, like, fit into any party. I'll show you. Tell me what you need."

Fred said, "I think we need to move across the street."

"Okay," said the enthusiastic elf. "Sure, I'm a team player."

She did not move across the street. None of them moved across the street. Fred *needed* them to move across the street. The grumbling inside the tavern was getting louder.

"Elves *are* versatile," said Mak-Thar. "Given my unfortunate situation, we certainly need a spellcaster."

"Right! A mage! My elf is a great mage. She gets full bonuses to experience points."

"But who is this elf you claim to possess?" asked Twilight.

"Huh?"

"You keep saying 'my elf'. I assume this means you, but I have no idea why you insist on referring to yourself in third person."

"I'm not following you," said the elf.

Something heavy slammed into the door of the tavern. From the metal bit that managed to penetrate all the way through to their side, Fred judged it to be an axe.

"Would you follow me?" asked Fred. "We really do need to cross the street."

"Sure!" said the new elf. "Does that mean I'm in?"

"You're in, you're in," said Fred. "Now let's go."

Now Fred *was* walking somewhat rapidly. If the doors burst open and a mob of angry dwarves and barbarians trampled them underfoot, it would be all his fault. He should have known Mak-Thar and Twilight couldn't be trusted to stand around outside a place like the Bloody Axe. And this new elf—well, that was just bad timing, he supposed. You ran into all kinds in Basetown, and running into her kind at this particular time was just a case of bad luck.

"So, like, what do you guys do?" asked the elf who referred to herself as *my elf*.

"I'm a fighter," said Fred.

"I used to be a mage," said Mak-Thar. "But now I'm a mule."

"Really?"

"Um," said Twilight, "you do see his ears, right? Did you think it was a clever disguise?"

"But how can you be a *mule*? That's not a character class."

"I'm an NPM for now," said Mak-Thar. "Our hope is that I can be returned to my true form. In fact, that is our current quest. Thank you for your offer of assistance. Allow me to introduce myself. I am Mak-Thar the Magnificent."

"I'm Fred," said Fred.

"I am Quin-Quong-Long-Hilorilon," said Twilight.

"Queequeg-what?"

"It means 'The Sound Made by a Lark's Wing at Twilight,' " said Twilight. "Have you forgotten your mother tongue?"

"Uh ... what?"

"He lets us call him Twilight," said Fred. "Maybe you can just call him that."

"Okeydoke."

They continued on down the street. Fred could no longer hear any noise from the Bloody Axe, so it seemed that disaster had been averted.

"So now you could tell us your name," Fred suggested.

"Oh! Right! Roleplaying! Okay, get this. My elf has, like, the coolest name. You're gonna love this. Ready?"

They were ready.

"Nightshaaade!"

"Nightsha-a-ade?" asked Twilight. "With three *A*s?"

"No. Just Nightshade. With one *A*. Although, I'm thinking maybe it would be cooler if I added a *Y*."

"I wouldn't overdo it," said Mak-Thar.

"Right. Right."

Oh, thank goodness! There was Helen!

Fred stopped and checked the immediate vicinity for any businesses that catered specifically to the homicidal. Relieved to see that there were none, he said, "Okay. I'd like you three to wait here a minute. *Right here.* Not anywhere else. I'm going to go get us a party leader."

CHAPTER SIX: IN WHICH HELEN AGREES TO JOIN THE PARTY AND LEAD THEM ON A HEROIC QUEST AS SOON AS MAK-THAR GETS DONE SHOPPING.

YELLIN' HELEN SAUNTERED ALONG THE STREET with her humongous sword resting on her shoulder. Her bare legs were scratched and bleeding. She wore a half smile, and her eyes were filled with that lazy sort of intensity peculiar to certain alley cats and to fighters who have just won a battle but are not too tired to win one more.

People moved out of her way. No one mentioned that Farmer Brown's pigs have gone missing and a neighbor reports glimpsing a strange creature out in the woods. Wherever she was going, she was guaranteed to arrive unmolested. Probably, she was heading for the Bloody Axe, where she would fit right in.

Fred did not put himself directly in her path, but he moved to a place where she would see him.

Helen's half smile became a real smile, washing the danger out of her eyes. She sheathed her sword in her back scabbard and clapped Fred on his armored shoulder.

"Fred! You got dressed!"

Had he really been moping that bad?

Okay. Yeah. He'd been moping that bad.

"Hi, Helen. Good to see you again."

"Yes. It's been nearly two hours."

"Well, I suppose," Fred admitted. "But a lot has happened since I saw you last."

"You went on a one-shot?"

"I agreed to go on a wilderness adventure."

"Good for you!"

"Helen, I was wondering … Well, I'm not very outdoorsy, you know. We could really use your help."

"You want me to be your native guide?"

"Huh?"

" 'Me see big scat. Smell like owlbear been here. Walk quiet. Don't step there.' "

"No, nothing like that. It's just always nice to have another fighter around, that's all."

Helen tilted her head sideways and looked Fred in the eye. "It's been a while since we've adventured together. Where are you headed?"

Fred tried to remember. "A forest, a desert, and a snowy mountain, I think. Probably in that order."

"Oh, it's one of those 'Go get the thing and bring it back' quests."

"No. More of a 'My friend was reincarnated as a mule and I feel sort of responsible so I'm taking him to a magic spring that will change him back' quest."

"A quest that actually has a point? Even better!"

"So you'll come?"

"I'll come. Which tavern are we leaving from?"

"How about the Boar's Head?"

"Ravens ate their sign. They changed the name to Pig Skull Country Pub."

"That's a terrible name!"

Helen shrugged. "It's better than Hideous Mass of Flesh-Eating Maggots Country Pub, which is the sign they would have had if the ravens hadn't come along."

Fred tried to imagine the sort of clientele who would want to grab a bite to eat at Hideous Mass of Flesh-Eating Maggots Country Pub. He decided Pig Skull was just fine.

An urchin walked up to them and said, "A shopkeeper on Turnip Street has been hearing strange noises in his attic."

Helen shook her head. "Not anymore he isn't. I took care of that."

"Oh. Sorry. Um, how about Jean Peabody? Has anyone figured out why her husband was found naked and raving in the woods?"

"He's obviously a were-something," said Helen. "But as far as I know, no one has gone to check."

"Okay. Thanks. I'll mong that rumor for a while." He set off.

Helen said, "This town just gets crazier and crazier."

"So what was in the attic?" asked Fred. "Was it the old 'We sound like bats but we're actually harpies' trick?"

"Thank goodness, no. It was 'sounds like bats but actually rats.'"

"That rhymes!"

Twilight approached them and said, "Hello, Helen."

"Oh look! It's the elf who stares at my chest."

"I'm not staring, okay? I'm just short. It's not my fault that your chest is at my eye level."

"I know," said Helen. "But you're fun to tease."

"It's only fun for you," said Twilight. "Anyway, I didn't come over here to stare at your chest. I came to look at your legs."

"Where's Mak-Thar?" asked Fred.

"He and Nightshade decided to go shopping."

"Oh," said Fred. "Do you think they'll remember he's a mule?"

Twilight rolled his eyes. "Who knows?"

Twilight knelt in the dust at Helen's feet.

Helen was surprised. "You were serious about looking at my legs!"

"Yes. What bit you? Beavers?"

"Rats," said Helen.

"Just rats?" asked Twilight. "Or 'rats comma giant'?"

"Rats comma giant," agreed Helen. "Look, this is real sweet of you, Twilight. It almost makes me sorry for teasing you. Before you get out your herbally things, let me find a place to sit down."

Fred was afraid Helen was going to suggest the Bloody Axe, but she just moved out of the street a little and sat down on a convenient hitching post. Twilight got out his herbally things and started cleaning her wounds with moss.

"Helen has agreed to come with us," said Fred.

Twilight said, "Well … at least that will give me a chance to monitor these wounds for signs of infection."

Helen said, "I bet you say that to all the girls."

"There's five of us now," said Fred. "Do we need a sixth?"

"We're just going to walk a long way and then climb a mountain?" Helen asked.

"It's a heroic quest," said Twilight. "But yes, you have the gist of it."

"Five should be fine, then. It's not like we're going to be facing off against a dragon."

"Actually …"

They told her the whole thing, then, while Twilight cleaned, disinfected, and bandaged her wounds. Then Twilight went to tell Mak-Thar and Nightshade about the plan to meet at the Pig Skull Country Pub.

* * *

Fred and Helen returned to the Fighters' Guild to pick up the special equipment that they used on wilderness adventures. Helen's special equipment was a small, furry satchel that she wore over one shoulder. Fred's special equipment was a walking stick that he kept in the trunk at the foot of his bed.

"That's it?" asked Helen. "You came back to the Fighters' Guild for a stick?"

"It's a very good stick," said Fred. "I've had it since I left home. Do you think I'll need my bundle?" He showed her a square piece of cloth.

"What would you bundle in it?"

"Eggs," said Fred. "I set out into the world with nothing but this stick and a bundle of eggs."

"How did you keep it from turning into a linen omelette?"

"I'm pretty good at carrying eggs."

"Maybe you should bring your loot sack," Helen suggested.

That was a good idea. You never knew when you were going to run into a heap of gold pieces. For some reason, everyone always assumed that Fred was the best person to carry the treasure. Fred put the linen square away and pulled out his loot sack. Then he changed his mind and packed his linen square inside his loot sack. Now he was ready for gold pieces *or* eggs.

So with his walking stick in hand and his loot sack over his shoulder, Fighter Fred set out on a brave journey to the Pig Skull Country Pub, where he and Helen waited for the others to show up.

After they had each sipped their way through two ales, Helen asked, "Do any of your friends know how to find this place?"

CHAPTER SEVEN: IN WHICH OUR HEROES BRAVELY SET OUT INTO THE WOMBAT WILDERNESS.

TWILIGHT SHOWED UP about ten minutes later to say that Mak-Thar and Nightshade were waiting outside. Fred and Helen paid their bar tab and went out with him.

"We would have been here earlier," said Twilight, "except that Mak-Thar insisted on visiting every shop in town to see if they sold a street map."

Mak-Thar put his ears back. " 'A little tavern on the north

side of town' is very vague directions. I'm sure that if we had found a map, we would have arrived much sooner."

"Helen," said Fred, "meet Mak-Thar the Magnificent."

"I used to be a mage," said Mak-Thar. "And now I am a beast of burden."

"I can see that."

They all could see that. Mak-Thar was loaded with sacks and saddle bags. He had let Sage think she had cleaned him out, but he must have had more gold stashed somewhere to finance his heroic shopping expedition.

"And I'm Nightshaaade! I'm sort of like an elf, and sort of like a ninja. You wouldn't believe my stats."

"Oh," said Helen. "Um, pleased to meet you."

"This is Yellin' Helen," said Fred. "She's my buddy from the Fighters' Guild. She's agreed to lead us on this adventure."

"Yes," said Mak-Thar. "About that. As we were walking over here, I was thinking about our personnel, and I believe I have determined a marching order that will optimize our combat tactics. It places our strongest fighters on the most likely attack vectors, while fully utilizing my observational capabilities. As a mule, I have 360-degree vision."

"Are you sure you're not a mage?" asked Helen. "Because that sounded *exactly* like the sort of thing a mage would say."

"I am now unable to do magic," said Mak-Thar. "However, the transformation has left my mental faculties undiminished."

"So what you're saying," said Helen, "is that you aren't a mage anymore, but you're still a smart—"

"If I may interrupt," said Twilight. "I'd like to ask everyone on this heroic quest to not say the *A* word. Mak-Thar was put into Evenstar's body thanks to the grace of the goddess Selene. Such coarse humor would be disrespectful."

Helen's mouth fell open.

"Yeah," said Nightshade. "That's really bad taste."

"Besides," said Mak-Thar, "those jokes don't make any sense. I'm not a donkey. I'm a mule."

Helen said, "So you're half—"

"He's half *donkey*, yes," said Twilight. "But that does not mean he should be the object of vulgar puns."

"But they're so *easy!*" protested Helen.

"Nevertheless," said Twilight, "I must insist."

"So I can't say he's being a silly—"

"No."

"What if he makes an—"

"A fool of himself? He does that quite frequently, I'm afraid. Still, no."

"What if he falls into a pit?" asked Helen. "Can I say, 'Mak-Thar, get your ... self out of there!'?"

"Hmm," said Twilight. "Well, we should leave some room for friendly jests. What do you think, Mak-Thar? Can we allow it?"

"I suppose," said Mak-Thar. "But it's not funny if I've broken four ankles."

"I think we're agreed, then," said Twilight. "Do we have anything else we need to consider before we head north?"

Fred shook his head. "I think we're ready to go."

"Yeah," said Helen. "Let's haul Mak-Thar out of this town."

* * *

And so they set off. Helen took the lead. Fred walked beside her, tapping his walking stick against the road.

Mak-Thar followed behind and complained to Twilight that no one wanted to use his optimal marching order.

Nightshade said, "I'll guard the rear! My elf is super sneaky, and she can hide in the bushes."

"What good will that do?" asked Twilight.

"If anyone ambushes us from behind, I'll ambush them first!" Nightshade drew her bow, dropped into a crouch, and scuttled into the grass that grew beside the road.

"But there aren't any bushes here," said Twilight.

"There's always bushes," said Nightshade. "Even deserts have bushes." She maintained her crouch and kept up with the party by hopping backwards.

"She's going to get tired," Fred said to Helen.

"She's going to get cramps," said Helen. "Where did you find her?"

"On the street."

"Figures."

"She was begging to come," said Fred. "And she's very enthusiastic."

"Yes. Very."

"I'm going to find some berries," said Nightshade.

"This is the season for roots and onions," said Twilight. "Berries won't be ripe yet."

"I'll find some wild onions," said Nightshade.

"We aren't even in the wilderness yet," said Twilight.

"We're not?"

"This is still farmland."

"Technically," said Mak-Thar, "any adventure outside a town and not in a dungeon is a wilderness adventure."

"Yeah," said Nightshade. "I'll go steal some farmer's onions."

"Whatever for?" asked Twilight.

"For practice! I'm learning to be a thief."

"Elves can be thieves?" asked Helen.

"Technically, no," said Mak-Thar.

"But I have these sneaky magic boots," said Nightshade. "And I have scrolls that let me cast Invisibility and stuff. So, like, I can totally be a thief for you guys. Just say the word."

"I don't think we need you to rob any poor, innocent farmers at this time," said Twilight.

"Well, okay, but I told Mak-Thar I'd forage so we don't run out of food."

"We aren't going to run out of food," said Helen. "There's plenty of game in the Wombat Wilderness."

Twilight added, "And I know many species of edible plants which are actually in season right now."

"Well I hope you guys find something," said Nightshade. "Because Mak-Thar's afraid you're going to eat him."

"What?" asked Fred.

Helen chuckled. "I wondered what was in those sacks you're carrying. Iron rations?"

"Three months' worth," said Mak-Thar.

"So we have three months of iron rations," said Helen, "and you're afraid that we'll get so hungry that we'll stop to roast the party mule while we're still in sight of Basetown."

"It could be a long trip," said Mak-Thar. "I didn't think you'd eat me right away."

"Look," said Helen, "I may be a barbarian, but that doesn't mean I'd eat a *mule*. Not without mustard."

Twilight said, "I think Fred has told you how our last adventure ended. I suppose Mak-Thar is still feeling a little anxious."

Nightshade shook her head sadly. "I can't believe a party member just stabbed you like that. I would *never* stab a fellow party member. Let's make a pact, okay, guys? Let's all agree that, no matter what happens, we aren't going to kill each other."

Helen said, "Um, Nightshade, that's supposed to go without saying. We don't need to 'make a pact.' It's part of the code."

"Part of what code?" asked Mak-Thar. "There's nothing about a code in *The Adventurer's Guide*."

"It's so basic that you shouldn't have to write it down," said Helen. "Watch your buddy's back. Never leave your wounded behind. And always split the treasure evenly. Don't they teach this stuff in the Mages' Guild?"

"We don't have any unwritten rules in the Mages' Guild," said Mak-Thar. "They can't be rules until they are written down."

"Okay," said Nightshade. "So if you all promise not to eat Mak-Thar, I'm going to climb a tree so I can scout ahead."

"We're in farmland!" said Twilight.

"Okay. I climb a barn."

* * *

Fred and Helen had been wrong—Nightshade was not the one who got tired. Nightshade couldn't stick with anything long enough to get tired.

She scouted ahead. She guarded the rear. She guarded the left flank. She guarded the right. For twelve seconds, she guarded both flanks by looking both ways while standing on Mak-Thar's back.

Whenever they passed a tree, she climbed it. Whenever they passed a bush, she hid in it.

At one point, she offered to practice her thieving skills by attempting to pick their pockets as they walked. Helen said, "Absolutely not!" and Nightshade pouted for a full minute before she wandered off into a wheat field to forage for something that Twilight said couldn't grow there.

Fred was relieved when they finally reached the forest. Nightshade immediately found some mushrooms (Twilight conceded that they were edible) and after that, instead of scouting and guarding and climbing trees and foraging, Nightshade was able to focus on just scouting and guarding and climbing trees.

"At least here we have actual trees to climb," said Twilight. "Although, really, the only thing you can see by climbing a tree is leaves."

Because of the late start to the day, and because the walk through the fields had actually been quite long, Helen called a halt after they were only an hour into the forest.

"Okay," she said. "We're in the Wombat Wilderness now. I think we should stop before it gets too dark to set up camp."

Nightshade said, "I'm an elf, so I can see in the dark. But I'm, like, totally okay with stopping when you guys need to. I'll climb a tree to make sure our camp is safe."

Twilight rolled his eyes.

Mak-Thar asked, "Could someone get the map out of my saddle bag and make a tick mark at the place where we camp?"

"I'll make the tick mark for you," said Twilight, "*after* we get your saddle off your back. Why I allowed you to overload yourself, I have no idea."

"I'm not overloaded," said Mak-Thar. "Mules can carry four thousand gold pieces."

"And miscellaneous rations weigh only eight pounds," said Twilight. "Yes, I know. Nevertheless, I think it's time for a little rubdown."

"A rubdown?" asked Mak-Thar.

"Don't think about it too much," said Twilight. "You're a mule, remember?"

Mak-Thar sighed. "How often I wish I could forget!"

Helen asked, "Fred, would you break off some standing deadwood that we can use as fuel for a fire?"

"I can do that!" said Nightshade. "I know all these cool cantrips."

She waved her fingers and pointed at a nearby tree. A small dead branch snapped and fell to the ground.

"I've got one for breaking things, one for making things change color. I know one for unbuckling things—really funny when you use it on somebody's belt to make his pants fall down. Oh, and there's one that can transform a small object into any other small object."

She picked up an acorn, closed her hand around it, then opened her hand to reveal a wooden button.

Mak-Thar was incredulous. "You memorized cantrips?"

"Yep!"

"The Mages' Guild doesn't *allow* cantrips!"

"Um, I've got a different guild? In another town?"

Mak-Thar said, "There is only one Mages' Guild and *The Adventurer's Guide* is its law!"

"Well maybe my elf knows, like, special elf magic or something. Anyway, she has cantrips."

"Are they contagious?" asked Helen.

"What are cantrips?" asked Twilight.

"Well, speaking purely theoretically," said Mak-Thar, "because, you understand, this particular rules supplement is forbidden, so of course I have never read it ..."

"Of course," agreed Twilight.

"Yes. Well then, speaking purely theoretically, a cantrip is a zero-level spell that one learns from one's master during apprenticeship and then discards in favor of higher-level spells."

"But you don't have to discard them," said Nightshade. "You can fit, like, eight of them in one spell slot."

"Four," said Mak-Thar. "The rules supplement I did not read clearly says four."

"Well, I remember it as eight."

Mak-Thar said, "Even at four, it's overpowered. A first-level mage has only one spell slot, but the cantrip rules would allow her to cast *four* spells!"

"At once?" asked Twilight.

"Per day," said Mak-Thar.

"Oh," said Twilight. "Honestly, four spells per day doesn't sound like much."

Mak-Thar said, "She's only supposed to be able to cast *one*."

That had always bothered Fred. Imagine if the Fighters' Guild had run things that way! *Sorry, Fred, you're first level. You're only allowed to attack the goblins once today. You'll get a new attack tomorrow, if your higher-level friends can keep you alive that long.*

Not that mages were *useless*. Sometimes a Fireball spell was exactly what the party needed. But first-level mages never knew anything useful like Fireball. They knew Magic Missile, which was basically equivalent to one shot with a bow, and then they were done.

Try joining a mercenary band as an archer, and then say you'll shoot your bow only once per day. See how far that gets you.

Nightshade said, "Well, my elf has three spell slots. So that's, like, twenty-four cantrips, if I want."

Mak-Thar said, "You told me you were first level!"

"I am," said Nightshade. "But if I'm going to adventure with higher-level characters, I need to have *some* advantages, right? Who wants to be Vanilla Elf?"

Fred thought *Vanilla* would be a nice name for an elf.

"We all start out as vanilla characters," said Mak-Thar. "Over time, we learn and grow. That's what makes the game so special."

Twilight stopped doing his mule rubdown. " 'Game', Mak-Thar?"

Mak-Thar made a flapping sound with his nostrils. "Very well. That's what makes *life* so special."

While Mak-Thar had been expounding, Helen had built a firepit. Fred realized he ought to find those dry sticks that Helen wanted, so he set off into the forest. The sun was setting, and the light under the tree canopy was already growing dim. Helen had stopped to make camp at just the right time, which was one of the many reasons Fred had brought her along.

He was glad Helen was here to kind of keep a handle on things. He was a little worried about Nightshade. He wasn't quite sure what she was.

She was obviously magey enough to argue with Mak-Thar over the rules, but she also carried a sword and wore armor. This was normal for elves. (Twilight didn't wear armor, but Twilight wasn't normal for anyone.) Fred supposed the thing that bothered him was the way she tried to be a thief, too. Maybe he was overreacting. Maybe he was still thinking about the *last* adventure, when the party had been betrayed by the thief. That really wasn't fair to Nightshade.

She was nothing like Paul. Paul had been mean to people, but Nightshade was always trying to get them to like her. Paul had been in a hurry to get to the dungeon; Nightshade just wanted to be busy—even if she wasn't going anywhere. Nightshade was cheerful and fun to have around ... so why did she remind him of Paul?

My elf has three spell slots. That was it.

What did that mean? What sort of person talked that way?

Mak-Thar, presumably, knew what spell slots were. Fred assumed that they were some sort of pocket that mages sewed inside their robes. But Mak-Thar didn't talk about them in mixed company. (By "mixed", Fred meant "fighters and mages".)

And most importantly, Mak-Thar would never refer to himself as "my elf"!

Well, no. Because he wasn't an elf. But Fred knew what his

point was, and that wasn't it. The point was—what had Twilight said? Bird person? She talked like a bird person? Fred couldn't remember. Anyway, Nightshade talked about herself like she wasn't really there.

That was it. That was the bit that reminded him of Paul. She thought she was something that she was pretending to be, instead of being something she was pretending she was.

Hm. That was almost insightful, but the more Fred thought about it, the more it seemed like it might actually be gibberish. Fred decided to give up on figuring out Nightshade for now and focus on fetching dry sticks. That was the sort of thing he could handle.

He really didn't know her well enough to make any judgments, yet. Adventurers can't truly know each other until they've shared their first battle.

CHAPTER EIGHT: IN WHICH MOST OF OUR HEROES FIGHT THEIR FIRST BATTLE.

THEY FORAGED for supper. Nightshade found more mushrooms.

Twilight found some young shoots. He promised, "If we wrap them in wet leaves and roast them for twelve minutes, they shall be quite tasty."

They weren't tasty, but it didn't matter because Twilight hadn't found very many of them, so Fred only had to be polite for three shoots.

Actually, none of the foraging mattered because Helen came into camp packing an entire deer.

"You just walked out into the forest and found a deer?" Twilight asked.

"That's a critical success on the Hunting Table," said Mak-Thar.

"How can you hunt without a bow?" asked Nightshade.

Helen didn't find their comments worthy of an answer. She

just sent Fred out for more wood and started roasting the venison.

As Fred returned with more wood, Nightshade was saying, "Well, Twilight and Nightshade don't eat the deer, because elves are vegetarians."

Twilight said, "Okay, in the first place, I'm sitting right here, so I don't need you to tell Helen what I will and won't eat. And in the second place, elves are *not* vegetarians."

"There's no *rule* about it," said Nightshade. "We can be vegetarians if we want."

"If we *want*," said Twilight. "But that's different from a blanket statement like, 'All elves are vegetarians.'"

"I didn't say '*all* elves'. I just said 'elves'."

Twilight said some elven cuss words.

"Okay, fine," said Nightshade. "My elf eats some dead deer meat to be polite and thanks you very nicely."

"Um," said Helen, "does that mean you want me to cut you off a slice?"

"Yes, please."

"It's still kinda rare," said Helen. She hacked off a bloody hunk of warmish muscle and passed it to Nightshade.

"Thank you," said Nightshade.

"Even *I* like it cooked a *little* bit," Helen mumbled.

After a while, the meat got hot, and Helen cut off a slice for herself. And not long after that, the meat was cooking, and Helen was slicing off bits for everyone.

Well, everyone except Mak-Thar.

Twilight said, "Oh, Mak-Thar! I hope we have not repulsed you."

"I hope you don't feel left out," said Fred.

"No, I'm perfectly fine," said Mak-Thar. "Honestly, I was just thinking of how convenient it is that I can eat grass all day and don't have to worry about the hunting and foraging tables. High-level wizards are wasting their time when they create magic items like Luther's Bountiful Picnic Blanket. What they should really be doing is researching an item that allows the bearer to eat grass."

"A Girdle of Grazing?" asked Helen.

"Perhaps a Ring of Rumination," said Mak-Thar. "Honestly, it disturbs me when *The Adventurer's Guide* refers to magical belts as 'girdles'."

"Wait," said Fred. "You mean a Girdle of Giant Strength is just a magic belt?"

Helen laughed. "You thought it was a magical undershirt to hold in your tummy?"

"Well ... yes."

"Oh," said Helen. "That reminds me. I have to do a certain number of product placements per adventure."

"Product placements?" asked Nightshade.

"For my sponsor," said Helen. "Here goes. 'Nycadaemon Knickers: putting the *bra* in bravery.'"

"Putting the what where?" asked Mak-Thar.

"Helen's a professional underwear model," said Twilight.

"Ah," said Mak-Thar. "Well, that would explain the plate-mail bikini. Helen, I've been meaning to ask you, if it's not a personal question ..."

"Yes?"

"What is your armor class?"

Helen gave Mak-Thar a confident and reassuring smile. "Don't worry. Mages ask me that all the time. My armor is technically plate mail, but it has an armor class equivalent to chain mail. In exchange, I get the movement and stealth advantages of leather armor, as long as I'm not in a situation where the glare off the metal might give me away."

"Really!" Mak-Thar was impressed.

"Yeah," said Helen. "Of course, the truth is that I just fight fast and try to kill everything before it can hit me. But according to my sponsor: chain-mail armor class, leatherlike stealth."

Nightshade said, "I have stealthy plate mail, too, because it's elf armor."

Twilight rolled his eyes.

Mak-Thar asked Helen, "So when you say your armor is technically plate mail, that applies to ... what exactly?"

"Called shots," said Helen. "I still get full plate-mail bonuses against called shots."

"Well," said Mak-Thar, eyeing Helen dubiously, "I guess your armor does protect your *heart*, at least."

"And my bladder," said Helen. "Although, not even kobolds would attempt a called shot to the bladder."

Nightshade asked, "Um … is this conversation weird to anyone else? Because to me, it sounds kind of weird."

"It's weird," agreed Twilight. "But I'm just glad to see Mak-Thar acting like himself again. Mak-Thar, I think this is the most cheerful I have seen you since we divided treasure."

"It feels good to be *doing* something," said Mak-Thar. "And I'm very grateful that you have all come along. Sage didn't promise much treasure—assuming we don't try for the hoard of the white dragon. I hope you all get enough experience points to make it worth your while."

"What a touching and rules-oriented sentiment," said Twilight.

Nightshade said, "My stats are cranked so high that I get full XP bonuses from whatever. So I'm up for anything."

Helen gave Fred a look that said, *I can't believe the way she talks. Are you sure you had to bring her along?* (Fred knew how to interpret Helen's looks as well as her sighs.)

They sat around the fire for a while, chewing on venison. When the silence had stretched too long, Helen said, "Fred, tell us a story."

"Oh. A story." Fred loved telling stories. When was the last time he had told one?

Fred realized he hadn't told a story since coming back from the Dungeon of Doom.

"Tell them the story of the gorgon's cave," said Helen.

"Oh, you know that one already."

"But they haven't heard it."

"All right." Fred took a deep breath. How did that story start?

Why was he wondering about how to start? Fred had always started his stories at the beginning and stopped at the place where he could get the biggest laugh. He shouldn't have to think about it.

"You know," said Fred, "I don't really feel like it right now."

"Oh," said Helen.

Twilight reached into his backpack and pulled out a slender wooden flute. "Perhaps this shall ease our spirits."

The elf played a haunting melody that told of flowers withering in the summer heat and innocence lost. Fred wasn't sure how he knew what the song was about—he just knew.

"Very nice," said Helen. "What's it called?"

" 'My Funny, Lazy Butterfly.' "

Well, Fred was close.

"I liked it, too," said Mak-Thar. "I wonder if I can give myself a plus-one bonus to morale."

"Sure," asked Twilight.

"Go for it," said Helen. "Knock yourself out."

"My elf reaches into her backpack and pulls out a guitar," said Nightshade, without actually reaching into her backpack and without actually pulling out a guitar.

"A guitar?" asked Twilight. "Elves do not play the guitar."

"Do you have proficiency in guitar?" Mak-Thar asked. "Each musical instrument uses up one proficiency slot."

"Oh. Well in that case, never mind. My elf scouts around camp looking for wolf tracks."

"Let us know if you find any," said Twilight.

And Nightshade actually did get up and start wandering around, although it was now quite dark, which made it hard to tell if she was actually looking for wolf tracks.

"Is anyone still hungry?" Helen asked.

None of them were. Helen fished a leather thong out of her satchel and hung the remainder of the venison in a tree. "Let the sagas sing that our brave band journeyed one entire day through the Wombat Wilderness without eating the party mule."

Mak-Thar put his ears back. "Technically, it's only been eight hours. And speaking of time, I have figured out the optimal organization of our watches. As a mule, I have extraordinarily keen hearing. That makes me the obvious candidate for the middle watch, when the night is darkest. Because Helen went on an adventure this morning, she is the one most likely to suffer fatigue penalties, so she should *not* have first watch."

"I'll take first watch," said Nightshade.

"I'm getting to you," said Mak-Thar. "We are fortunate to have two elves in the party. Because elves do not sleep, we shall be able to—"

"Elves don't sleep?" asked Nightshade.

Twilight shook his head. "Elves don't sleep. How can you not know this?"

"Well, I'm *sorry*, okay? It's not like I have the entire *Adventurer's Guide* memorized."

"But you're an elf!"

"Yes, yes," said Mak-Thar. "Now as I was saying, we shall be able to split the night into two elf-watches. Each elf-watch is equal to a standard watch plus one-half. In other words, one elf shall watch for half the night and the other for the other half. Twilight, am I correct in assuming that you *do* need four hours of meditation, but you do *not* need time to memorize spells?"

"I don't cast spells. I am a—"

"Yes, yes. You are a servant of Selene. Nightshade, on the other hand, is acting as the party's mage on this expedition. She will need to meditate and memorize spells in the morning. Since she cannot combine this activity with guard duty, I will ask her to take the first elf-watch and Twilight to take the second elf-watch, when Nightshade is memorizing her spells."

Twilight grumbled, "If she doesn't know her spells already, I don't see how an early-morning cram session is going to help."

"So our watches are now determined," said Mak-Thar. "Fred and Nightshade shall have the first watch. Fred shall wake me for second watch. Nightshade shall wake Twilight for second elf-watch. And I shall wake Helen for third watch. Any questions?"

"I'm already asleep from listening to you plan watches," said Helen.

"You wish to suggest an alternate plan?"

"No, Mak-Thar. We'll do it your way. Good night." And Yellin' Helen lay down in the dirt and leaves near the smoldering camp fire.

Twilight said, "Wait, that's it? That's your bed? You just lie on the ground and 'Poof! Dreamland'?"

Helen opened one eye. "How are *you* going to get to sleep?"

"Elves don't sleep," said Twilight.

Helen closed her eye. "Well, then … good night."

Mak-Thar announced, "I shall sleep standing up. It is easier on my knees. And it should give me a reaction bonus, although mule reaction bonuses are not, of course, specified in *The Adventurer's Guide*."

"What an appalling oversight," said Twilight. "Perhaps you can request a rules revision."

"I'm still trying to make sense of the revised and expanded edition of *The Bestiary*," said Mak-Thar. "I hope they *never* change *The Adventurer's Guide*."

"My elf sleeps standing up, too."

Twilight said, "But elves don't sleep!"

"Oh. Right. Can I meditate standing up?"

"Yes," said Twilight.

"Yes," said Mak-Thar. "But not right now. You have first watch."

* * *

Fred took first watch with Nightshade, as ordered. He kind of wanted to swap stories with her and get to know her better, but he was afraid their conversation might keep Mak-Thar awake. It didn't matter, because Nightshade didn't stay in one place long enough to talk to. She kept running around camp and climbing trees.

Fred sat beside Helen—who started snoring right away—and warmed his hands against the embers of the dying fire. This was going pretty well. He didn't exactly know how many hours were in a "watch", but that didn't matter, because he didn't have any way to measure the hours. For a while, he sat and thought about his friends. Then he sat and wondered whether this adventure would give him any good stories to tell. Then he sat and thought about nothing.

When he heard *himself* snoring, he figured that had probably been long enough for one watch. He woke himself up enough to go wake Mak-Thar. (As a mule, Mak-Thar really *could* sleep standing up. It was kind of cool.) And then Fred spread his loot sack on the ground and lay down near Helen.

Her snoring reminded him of the Fighters' Guild, and he dreamed he was back in his own bed, lying in his pajamas. It was not the most exciting dream, but it made him feel peaceful and secure. It seemed to go on for a long time, but it ended very abruptly with a noise that sounded like—

"HEE-HAW!"

Do you know what reaction bonuses are? *Fred* didn't know. But if someone was quick on the draw, mages would say, *Oh, he has reaction bonuses.* So Fred knew that reaction bonuses were something he wanted to have. And he was feeling that, in this particular situation, he did not, in fact, have them.

The thing about being the person who does not have reaction bonuses is that it takes you a while to figure out what's going on. Mak-Thar was braying. Twilight was shouting, "Arise! Awake! To arms! To arms!" But Fred was confused, and so he was hearing Twilight shout, "Two arms! Two arms!"

And he couldn't tell if Twilight was giving advice ("Fight with two arms!") or if he was crying out in horror ("This horrible creature has two arms!").

Whatever it was, Fred couldn't see it. He was on his feet with his sword in hand—because even if his brain wasn't reacting, his hands and feet knew what to do—but the thing about nighttime in the forest is that it's dark. Fred wondered why Mak-Thar called them "watches" when it was impossible to see.

Behind him, Helen was moving and grunting. Her sword was striking metal. Her armored butt bumped his armored butt, and he realized that he and Helen were fighting back to back. (Because that sounds more heroic than fighting butt to butt.)

Suddenly, a ghastly white shape appeared before his eyes and swung a longsword at his forehead. Fred blocked, stabbed, and realized that his stab had gone through his opponent's ribs without hitting anything. He disentangled his sword from the skeleton's ribcage, twisted to let a thrust slide across his armor, and finally just punched the skeleton in the skull.

Bone cracked, and the skeleton went down.

Mak-Thar cried, "Twilight, you can turn undead!"

"What?"

"You can turn undead!"

"No I can't! And anyway, I don't want to become undead."

"*Turn,*" repeated Mak-Thar. "As in turn them away. Just show them your holy symbol, and they'll run away!"

And above the clamor of sword-on-sword and hoof-on-bone, Twilight shouted, "But servants of Selene do not carry holy symbols, because inert objects are without value when compared with the everyday living creatures which always surround us and shape our path!"

"Then say some mystic words!" Mak-Thar demanded. "You're supposed to be the cleric."

"Look, I can't just wave my arms and say, 'Skeletons, begone!' It's a lot more—"

The clamor of sword-on-sword and hoof-on-bone stopped. Twilight stopped shouting, and now the sound they heard was the rustling of bony feet running away through the ferns.

In a quieter voice, Twilight insisted, "It's more complicated than that."

"Yes, I'm sure it is," agreed Mak-Thar.

"The, um, the grace of Selene ..."

"Yes," said Mak-Thar. "I'm sure there's a way to work this into your paradigm. Aren't you lucky that it's the start of your watch and you have the rest of the night to figure it out?"

Chapter Nine: In which our heroes try to figure out what happened to Nightshade.

THERE'S A CERTAIN SORT OF STORY that starts with a man waking up with rotting leaves in his mouth. Fred wasn't keen on those sorts of stories. If you start a story with a man waking up, then you're kind of obligated to talk about how he brushed his teeth and shaved his whiskers. Unless your listeners are *really* fascinated by male hygiene, it's hard to make a story like that interesting.

Fred spat out the leaves, sat up, and wiped the cold dirt off his face. He was no longer in his pajamas. He was now encased in fifty pounds of very cold iron. And he couldn't help thinking that the days that had started with him waking up in his pajamas had definitely been better.

Morning light slipped between the tree trunks, and a patch of it illuminated Helen, a smudge of ash on her cheek, crouching by the fire and gnawing the venison off a leg bone. Fred wondered if that was how all underwear models started the day.

Fred looked around to see who was still asleep. No one else was there.

"Want some breakfast?" Helen offered Fred the opposite leg bone.

"Sure. Thanks."

Fred didn't want breakfast. His stomach wasn't awake yet. His eyes were awake and blinking. His back was waking up and asking to be stretched. But his stomach just rolled over in his belly, pulled a pillow over its head, and said, "Mmrrff."

Well, it didn't *really* say, "Mmrrff," of course. But if it had said something, it would have been the sort of thing you say to someone when you want them to know that you don't want to say anything.

Fred sat holding the venison leg, rotating his spine, listening to the crunch of his vertebrae resonating through his armor. After a minute or two, he stood up, still not taking any bites of his breakfast.

Fred surveyed the campsite. Bones lay everywhere. That was the nice thing about fighting skeletons—the battlefield always looked impressive once it was over.

"Mak-Thar picked up all their swords?" he asked.

"He made Twilight pick them up and put them in a sack."

Oh, right. Mak-Thar didn't have hands anymore.

Fred bit into the leg of venison. It tasted good.

"Nnnrgghhh …" said his stomach. (Not really.)

"Thanks for breakfast," said Fred.

"Any time," said Helen.

Fred hoped it would be every time. If Helen ever failed to find them food, they would have to eat iron rations—so called because, if you boiled them in an iron pot, you would feel inspired to dump the rations and eat the pot.

Fred didn't ask where Mak-Thar, Twilight, and Nightshade were because he knew that mornings usually begin with answering a call of nature. And yet, as his brain began to wake up, he realized that calls of nature usually don't take so long—assuming one hasn't been eating iron rations. Also, it seemed unlikely that the three of them would go answer a call of nature *together*. Especially since one of them was a mule, who could get away with answering whenever and wherever nature called.

Fred was still puzzling on this when Helen said, "Mak-Thar and Twilight went to look for Nightshade."

"Where's Nightshade?"

Helen rolled her eyes. "If we knew, no one would need to look for her."

Fred thought back to the skeletons. "Was she in the fight last night?"

Helen shrugged. "It was kind of dark."

She did not seem particularly concerned.

A twig snapped, and Mak-Thar came plodding through the trees, ears twitching with frustration. Walking beside him was

Twilight, looking worried.

"We can't find her anywhere," Twilight said. "Mak-Thar can't smell her body. I fear the skeletons have abducted her."

Helen tossed her venison bone into the fire. "She'll turn up."

"How can you be so certain?"

"I know her type," said Helen. "She's not hurt. She just has misted."

"She's misted?"

"No, no," said Helen. "She *has* misted. It's something you have. You know, like warts or lice."

Twilight looked offended. "I assure you, I have neither warts nor lice."

"Not *you* you. I mean *you* as in somebody else. Tell him, Mak-Thar."

The mule blinked. "Tell him what?"

Helen looked from one face to another. "You mean none of you guys have ever adventured with someone who flakes out and disappears for a while?"

Fred shook his head.

"No," said Mak-Thar.

"This is my second adventure," said Twilight.

"Really?" said Helen. "Okay. Well, some people are flaky. And Nightshade is flaky enough to be a snow storm. The smart thing to do is just set out along the road like we normally would. If she really wants to adventure with us, she'll turn up."

"That seems very reckless and unkind," said Twilight. "I know if *I* were abducted by skeletons, I'd want you to come looking for *me*."

"But you haven't been," said Helen. "And neither has Nightshade."

Twilight turned to Fred with pleading eyes. Why was he looking at Fred? *Fred* wasn't going to contradict Helen.

"Skeletons don't usually abduct people," said Fred.

"Oh, really?" said Twilight. "And do they usually attack people at night, less than an hour away from the nearest farm?"

"Yeah," said Fred.

"Yep," said Helen.

Mak-Thar said, "That does, indeed, sound like their modus operandi."

"Well excuse me for being the naive little elf boy, but where I come from, if a horde of skeletons shows up, it's a big deal!"

"Oh," said Helen. "Yeah, well, not around here."

"Yeah," said Fred. "If you're a day's walk from Basetown, you can pretty much expect to be attacked by *something*."

"The only surprising thing," said Mak-Thar, "was that our cleric took so long to turn undead."

"I wish you'd stop using that word that way," said Twilight. "A word like 'repel' or 'scare off' would cause less confusion."

" 'Turn' is the official nomenclature, and it is well defined in *The Adventurer's Guide*, as you would know if you had read the pages I asked you to read."

"But I don't *need* to learn your rules for being a cleric. I'm following a different path!"

"We're not following any path, yet," said Helen.

"We should track the fleeing skeletons," said Twilight. "They must have attacked for a *reason*. And now that Nightshade is missing ... well, doesn't it seem likely that she was the reason?"

Mak-Thar shook his head. "Monsters don't attack for *reasons*. They attack randomly, based on the appropriate encounter table. Any attempt to assign meaning post hoc is just a manifestation of the desire to process the world by imposing narrative structures."

Twilight said, "The world *is* narrative structures."

Helen said, "Twilight, you're making way too much of this. Mak-Thar, I can't understand half the words you say."

"I'm just saying that a skeleton attack, in this context, is not necessarily a hook for a side quest. It seems much more likely that this is a random encounter."

Fred did not want to gang up on Twilight, but he knew the other two were probably right. "Sometimes we just get into fights, Twilight. That's why it's called an adventure."

"I can't believe you all think we should just leave without

knowing whether Nightshade is dead or alive."

"Well, did you check her tree?" Fred asked.

"What tree?" they all asked.

"It was black and had branches." Fred looked around. "But now I don't see any black trees."

"Fred," said Helen patiently, "was it black because it was nighttime?"

"Maybe so," Fred agreed. "She went up when we started our watch. I don't know if she came down."

"I don't think she participated in the combat," said Mak-Thar.

"Me neither," said Helen.

"Was it a deciduous tree or some sort of conifer?" asked Twilight.

"I'm not sure," said Fred. "Which one of those has branches?"

"We need to search the trees systematically," said Mak-Thar. "There's a pouch in my fourth saddle bag on my left that has pieces of chalk. We can use it to—"

"There she is," said Helen. "Either that, or it's a giant squirrel."

"There's no such thing," said Mak-Thar. "At least, giant squirrels aren't listed *The Adventurer's Guide*. I suppose it would be possible for a squirrel to drink a Potion of Giant Growth."

Fred looked up through the branches. The thing in the tree was quite high up, but Fred was pretty sure it was Nightshade. He was pretty sure that no one in town would sell shiny black armor to a giant squirrel.

On the other hand, look at all the stuff they had sold to a talking mule.

"Nightshade?" he called. "Our watch is over. Would you like to come down?"

"She won't come down," said Helen. "She has misted."

"It's okay!" Fred yelled to the top of the tree. "I had lice when I was a kid. We won't think any less of you."

"She can't hear you," said Helen.

"Should one of us climb up and get her?" Twilight asked.

Helen sighed a sigh that meant, *I'm being very patient, even though you are a complete idiot.* "No. We should just go on down the road. If she really wants to adventure with us, she'll catch up."

Fred didn't like the way Nightshade was sitting in the tree. She was so still.

He asked, "Is it all right if I go up and get her anyway?"

"Sure, Fred," said Helen with a sigh that meant, *That's exactly the sort of thing I should have expected from you.*

The tree was no longer black, but it still had branches. Fred started climbing. Fred was not particularly good at climbing, but the branches were in places that made it easier for him. He arrived at Nightshade's perch and examined the body.

No, wait. She was breathing.

"She's breathing!" Fred yelled down to the others.

"Is she wounded?" asked Twilight.

She didn't look wounded.

"I don't think so," Fred yelled. "Should I try to wake her?"

"It won't work," called Helen. "If you want to bring her along, you'll have to carry her down. But honestly, it would be better to just leave her."

Fred tried to pick Nightshade up. He wasn't sure how to lift someone when he was standing in a tree.

"He might need rope," Mak-Thar said. "If he tries to carry over sixteen hundred coins of weight, he'll be unable to move."

"When Nightshade wakes up, I'll tell her you think she's fat," said Helen.

Mak-Thar said, "No, but she does have weapons and armor. And Fred has his own armor. I wish I could remember how much plate mail weighs."

Fred rolled the elf onto his shoulder. She flopped against his back. Fred climbed down. In a minute, his feet were once again firmly planted on cold dirt and rotten leaves.

Twilight stared at him in awe. "How did you climb down using only one hand with an elf on your back?"

Fred shrugged, causing Nightshade's armor to clink against his shoulder plate. "I just pretended she was a sack of treasure."

Twilight said, "Well, set her down and let me take a look at her."
Fred set her down. Twilight looked at her.

"Is she enchanted?" Fred asked.

"She's asleep," said Helen.

"Elves don't sleep!" said Twilight.

"No one sleeps through a battle," said Mak-Thar.

"It's not a normal sleep," said Helen. "But it's not an enchantment either—not the kind you can dispel. It's just a symptom of misted."

"You keep saying that word," said Mak-Thar, "and I feel like you must be saying it wrong, because I've never heard of this disease."

"Well, I don't know exactly what it's supposed to be called," said Helen. "The mages said something that sounded like 'misted'. Anyway, she's not going to wake up. We can bring her along if you want, or we can leave her here and she can catch up later."

Twilight shook his head. "This doesn't seem like a safe place."

"Or we can put her back in the tree," said Helen.

"I should be able to carry her," said Mak-Thar.

Twilight looked dubiously at all the stuff already on Mak-Thar's back. "How?"

"I anticipated that one of you might become incapacitated and it might be necessary to carry you for some distance. Accordingly, I made sure that my default load was low enough to allow me to add sixteen hundred coins. If Fred can carry her, I can carry her."

And so they loaded Nightshade onto Mak-Thar's back and headed down the road.

After a while, Fred realized that his stomach was awake, and he fed it the rest of the leg of venison. Then he found a twig and brushed his teeth.

When they stopped at a stream to fill their waterskins, he shaved his whiskers, but since it didn't lead to an amusing story, he never told anyone about it.

CHAPTER TEN: IN WHICH OUR HEROES FIGHT RANDOM MONSTERS.

THE ROAD THROUGH THE FOREST turned into a trail. By noon, the trail had turned into a path. About an hour later, the path faded away and they were simply walking through the woods.

It really felt like an adventure now! Fred cheerfully tromped along with his walking stick thumping into tree roots or sinking into mats of decaying leaves.

After about ten minutes of following Helen through the trees, Mak-Thar asked, "Are you an experienced guide?"

"Very experienced," said Helen.

"But she's not a guide," said Fred. "She's a friend."

"I wasn't going to suggest that you give her only half a share of the treasure," said Mak-Thar, completely missing the point. "I was simply wondering if she counts as an experienced guide for purposes of getting lost."

"Definitely," said Helen. "I've been lost hundreds of times."

"Oh," said Mak-Thar. "Well, *The Adventurer's Guide* says we can't be lost if we are following an experienced guide. If we're following someone who has been lost hundreds of times, then our chances of getting lost on any particular day are one in three."

"We just go north," said Helen.

"That *is* what the sage said," Mak-Thar agreed. "But the first step in getting lost is not knowing which way is north."

"Can't we follow the moss?" asked Fred.

Helen said, "No, Fred. Moss just sits there."

"I'm sure Fred was referring to moss growing on the north side of trees," said Twilight.

Fred hadn't been entirely sure what he had been referring to, so he was glad that Twilight knew.

"Isn't that just a myth?" asked Mak-Thar.

"Not entirely," said Twilight.

Good thing it wasn't. Any myth about moss growing would be a pretty boring myth. *So there I was, growing on a tree, when suddenly* … Yeah, that wouldn't work. If the high point of your life is having someone pet you so they can tell which way is north, then you probably can't get many free drinks out of your stories.

Twilight was saying something about complex relationships between aspect, slope, dew point, and other things Fred didn't understand. The elf concluded with, "But even so, we can infer that the mossy side is losing less water to evapotranspiration, and hence is probably more northerly."

"Ah!" said Mak-Thar, delighted that Twilight had managed to explain something as simple as moss in such a complicated way. "That sounds very good. Here is what we shall do, then. Helen, you will continue to guide us."

"Oh, good. I was so worried about job security."

"And Twilight, you will use your Woodcrafting skill to verify that we are continuing to head north. The chances of you *both* getting lost are only one in nine."

"You're overthinking this," said Helen.

"That's how you can tell he's still Mak-Thar," said Twilight.

Helen said, "Being lost is no big deal, okay? You just keep going until you're found again."

"I am glad that strategy has worked for you in the past," said Mak-Thar. "But since I brought only three months of rations, and since I am theoretically edible and you may have brought mustard—"

"I was kidding."

"Nevertheless, I would prefer not to lose time going in circles."

"Relax," said Helen. "We're going straight."

* * *

Actually, they weren't going straight at all. They were wiggling around trees. But whenever they wiggled left, they made up for it by wiggling right the next time. Fred was pretty sure Helen wasn't going in circles. To go in a circle, she would have to go all the way around a tree, and if she did that, she would run into the hind end of Mak-Thar.

And so they wiggled their way through the afternoon and into the evening, when Helen told them it was time to set up camp. She found a nice spot and started a fire.

Twilight unloaded Nightshade from Mak-Thar's back and set her near enough to the fire to keep her warm, but not close enough to roast her. Then he unloaded the rest of Mak-Thar's stuff.

As soon as his saddle was off, Mak-Thar found a bare patch of ground and rolled over on his back. Waving four hooves in the air, he looked ridiculous, but happy.

While Mak-Thar rolled, Twilight checked Helen's rat bites.

"I think the bandages can come off," he said. "You seem to be healing without infection. Although, I'm not sure how the skin discoloration will affect your modeling career."

"Oh, that will clear up with time," said Helen. "Anyway, I mostly pose for woodcuts. The wood carvers know how to flatter me."

"Ah," said Twilight. "Trick carving?"

"Yeah," said Helen. "None of those woodcuts are real."

Twilight looked at Nightshade snoring by the fire. "And now for my next patient. How long do you think Nightshade will be, um, 'out'?"

Helen shrugged. "Who knows? There's a guy at the Bloody Axe who's been asleep for two years."

"That guy with the horned helmet and the skunk kilt?" asked Fred.

"Yeah," said Helen. "He fell asleep in the middle of an adventure. His party hauled him back, gave his share of the treasure to the barkeep, and left him sleeping there."

"No one can sleep for two years," said Twilight. "Not without food and drink."

"He's in a tavern," said Fred. "There's plenty of food and drink."

"It sounds like an enchantment," said Twilight.

"It's not an enchantment," said Helen. "It's just the consequence of extreme flakiness."

Mak-Thar, who was now back on his feet, asked, "Did his party try casting Dispel Magic?"

Twilight asked, "Did anyone try to kiss him?"

"He's wearing a *skunk kilt*," said Helen.

"You know," said Fred, "no one has tried kissing Nightshade."

Helen thought about this. "I can't decide whether kissing a sleeping party member is sweet or creepy."

Twilight rolled his eyes. "Don't read too much into it. It's just a routine medical procedure."

He gave Nightshade a peck on the cheek. She stayed asleep.

"Well at least she didn't turn into a frog," said Helen.

"You can't break enchantments with a kiss," said Mak-Thar. "That sort of thing only works in fairy tales."

Twilight pointed to himself and Nightshade. "We're fairies."

"Yes, well, you tell very misleading tales."

Fred said, "I thought fairies were little glowing people, one foot tall."

"Those are pixies," said Mak-Thar. "But they don't glow; they just turn invisible."

Fred asked, "If they're invisible, how do you know they don't glow?"

Mak-Thar blew air through his flapping nostrils. "I think it's time to determine the night's watches."

So Mak-Thar told them all what to do again, but it didn't matter, because nothing attacked them.

* * *

The next morning, Fred woke up in cold armor and they wandered through the forest some more. That day, they got attacked by hobgoblins. That night, they were attacked by a tiger. On the following day, they were attacked by giant glowing beetles.

* * *

As Twilight sewed up the gash that a giant beetle's giant mandibles had left on Mak-Thar's rump, he said, "Okay, I'm beginning to see what you mean about random encounters."

"Thank you," said Mak-Thar. "It is very good of you to admit I was right about something."

"They're just so frustrating!"

"Aw, come on," said Helen. "That was fun."

"Fun?" asked Twilight. "Being attacked by insects big enough to eat your head is fun?"

"Um? Yeah."

"They were only three feet long," said Mak-Thar.

"And yet if the beetle had clipped this artery, you could have bled to death."

"But he didn't," said Helen. "So it was fun."

"Perhaps it was fun for you," said Twilight. "But it had no story impact. Have you grown as a person because you whacked off an insect's head? Has being bitten on the butt helped Mak-Thar become a better mule?"

"Actually," said Mak-Thar, "the beetles' glowing glands can be harvested. We can pack them along, and they will illuminate our camping sites for the next six days."

"Oh," said Twilight. "So the acquisition of limited-warranty lighting fixtures counts as story impact now?"

Fred said, "Look, Twilight, sometimes the story is in how you tell it. I mean, sure, on the one hand it was just another beetle battle. But *anything* can make a good story if you tell it right."

"Really?" said Twilight skeptically. "Okay, then. Go ahead. Tell me a good story about that battle."

Fred thought about it. What was the funniest or most unexpected thing that had happened?

"Um, I'm not sure I can do it off the top of my head. I don't know where to start. It probably ends with Mak-Thar being bitten on the butt."

"I don't find that very funny," said Twilight.

"It *would* be funny if we didn't have to watch our language," said Helen. " 'Our *mule* was kicking *butt* when he got bitten on the *hindquarters.*' That's just not as funny as it could be."

"Vulgarity is not equivalent to humor," said Twilight.

"I don't think Fred was *trying* to be funny," said Mak-Thar. "I think he was suggesting a story that makes me sound heroic."

That absolutely was not the direction Fred had been going. But he said, "That's right."

"Yet even though I am sure to get an experience bonus from my extraordinary contributions to our victory," said Mak-Thar, "I must admit that I am somewhat tempted to concur with Twilight. These random encounters are preferable to side quests, of course, but they do not advance us toward our goal. And, what is worse, the experience points I am earning might all be wasted when I return to my true form."

"I can't think of anything worse than wasted experience points," said Twilight.

"Indeed," said Mak-Thar.

"Except maybe trying to dress a wound on a mule's rump. There's nothing for me to wrap a bandage around."

"Maybe if you had a really long bandage?" suggested Fred.

"It's no use," said Twilight. "I'm trained as a doctor, not a veterinarian. Mak-Thar, I've sewn it shut, and that's all I can do. Until it heals, I need you to promise me you won't roll on the ground."

"But my back gets so *itchy*!"

"If you roll on the ground, there's a twenty percent chance of infection."

Mak-Thar's head drooped. "Oh. Okay. ... Wait, how do you know the exact percentage?"

Twilight grinned.

"Oh, now you're just making a fool of me."

"Well," said Helen, "he's already made a mule of you."

"That rhymes!"

"Mak-Thar was made a mule by the grace of Selene," said

Twilight. "It had nothing to do with me."

Mak-Thar said, "It had a lot to do with you, my friend. And I am grateful. Selene was certainly not going to help me without your intervention. But as for my muleness, well, I know that was not your fault."

"It's not a fault," said Twilight. "Your body is a divine gift."

"My divine gift's back itches."

CHAPTER ELEVEN: IN WHICH— WOMBATS!

THE NEXT MORNING, Fred was awakened by a strange conversation:

"My elf yawns and stretches and says, 'How long have I been sleeping?'"

"Elves don't sleep!"

"Who else is asleep? I try to pick Fred's pockets."

"What? Why would you pick Fred's pockets?"

"Just for practice."

Stiff back. Chilling armor. Leaves in his hair. Fred was not dreaming. This was another morning of camping. Twilight and Nightshade were arguing.

"Nightshade!" Fred sat up.

"Hi," she said. "Sorry I missed the last session."

"Session?" asked Fred.

"You know. Adventure-thingy. Battle. Whatever it was I missed. But I'm here now."

"You weren't missing," said Fred. "You were asleep."

"Yes," said Twilight. "And elves don't sleep. I think you owe us an explanation."

"Look, I just had more important stuff to do, that's all."

"You weren't *doing* anything," said Mak-Thar. "You were *sleeping.*"

"Yeah. I get it. That's why I did the whole 'Yawn, how long have I been sleeping' thing."

"Three days," said Helen. "You've been flaking out for three days."

"Well excuse me for having a *life*."

"What 'life'?" asked Twilight. "You were *sleeping*."

Nightshade said, "Okay. Right. Let me try to explain this in a way you can understand. You see, I've got this soul thing that can fly to other worlds and do other stuff. So, like, you might see my body sleeping, but my soul is, like, totally doing important stuff."

"Are you speaking of astral projection?" asked Mak-Thar.

"Yep. Totally. I just projected my astral right out of here."

(Helen turned to Twilight. "Are you going to let her get away with that one?"

"I think so."

"So I'm allowed to laugh with an unladylike snort?"

"I don't think I can stop you.")

"Astral Projection is a ninth-level spell!"

"Relax," said Nightshade.

"It's not even in *The Adventurer's Guide*!" said Mak-Thar. "It's so powerful that the only people who can cast it are the ones who wrote the book!"

"Yeah. Okay. I said I was sorry, and it won't happen again. Can we just, like, start playing now?"

"Sorry," said Helen. "I left my dice in my other pants."

Nightshade looked Helen up and down. "You aren't wearing pants."

"And I don't own dice," said Helen. "Do you want some breakfast, or are you a vegetarian this morning?"

"Okay, sure. Go ahead and give me another chunk of bloody deer."

"This is last night's pork," said Helen. "We finished the venison yesterday morning."

Helen passed out bits of reheated boar meat. They ate some breakfast. Then Twilight and Nightshade started loading all of Mak-Thar's stuff onto his back.

Mak-Thar asked, "Nightshade, do you need to memorize any

spells this morning?"

"I don't think so. Did my elf cast any while I was gone?"

"You cast two cantrips before you went to sleep," said Mak-Thar.

"I did?"

"Yes," said Mak-Thar. "You should keep a list of your spells. When you use one, you can check it off. And when you re-memorize it, you can erase the check mark."

"I'm confused," said Twilight. "If she has the cantrips memorized, why does she need to *re*memorize them?"

"Because she doesn't have them memorized anymore," said Mak-Thar.

"She forgot them while she was asleep?"

"No, no. She forgot them as soon as she used them."

"That makes no sense."

Fred had to agree. When he used his sword, that made his arm stronger. He didn't have to relearn all his sword strikes every morning.

"Look," said Mak-Thar. "Let's say I still had fingers and could cast my Fireball spell. What do you think would happen if casting a fireball did not cause me to forget the spell?"

"You would cast it all the time," said Nightshade.

"I would cast it all the time," said Mak-Thar.

"That would be cool!" said Nightshade.

"Yes it would," agreed Mak-Thar. "But it would also upset the game balance. We would no longer need fighters and clerics and thieves, because every problem could be solved by a fifth-level mage."

"Not every problem can be solved by a fireball," said Twilight.

Helen said, "Okay. *Now* I believe that this is only your second adventure."

"Will you teach me Fireball?" asked Nightshade.

"No," said Mak-Thar. "You're too low-level. Now listen, because here is the point. If I could cast fireballs all the time, I could win every combat. And that would be ...?"

"Cool!" said Nightshade.

"Perhaps," said Mak-Thar. "But soon it would be *boring*. When one strategy is obviously better than all the others, there is no point in playing the game."

Twilight said, "I'm still sure there are many situations that cannot be resolved by a fireball. Well, okay, they can be *resolved* by a fireball, but sometimes 'everything is charred to a crisp' is not a good resolution."

"If *I* could cast fireballs," said Helen, "I'd go hunting and barbecuing at the same time."

Mak-Thar snorted. "My point is: limits on spells lead to interesting decisions. And that's what keeps the game interesting."

Twilight said, "So because the Mages' Guild believes that life is just a game, they artificially limit your spells to keep you interested in the services the guild has to offer."

"It's not an artificial limitation imposed by the Mages' Guild," said Mak-Thar. "It's a natural feature of how magic works in this world."

"Really?"

"Yes."

"Then how do dragons breathe fire?" Twilight asked. "Do you think they say, 'Oh, sorry, I already fried a knight this morning—come back tomorrow, after I've memorized a new spell'?"

"In the first place," said Mak-Thar, "not all dragons breathe fire. Some breathe frost, and some even breathe acid."

"Yuk!" said Twilight and Nightshade.

"In the second place, a dragon's breath weapon is a natural ability, not a magical spell. In the third place, dragons *do* have a limitation—they can use their breath weapon only three times per day."

"See?" said Twilight. "Now if wizard magic worked like that, I'd buy it. If you told me that wizards have magical energy and they need to sleep to regain that energy—that's a system that makes sense. But the idea that you can forget something you 'memorized'—and the idea that remembering it actually causes you to forget it—well, that doesn't sound like magic at all. That sounds like something out of *The Adventurer's Guide.*"

"Okay, so while you guys argue, my elf memorizes her cantrips."

"I think that would be best," said Mak-Thar. "This may take some time."

* * *

An hour later, they were again wandering through the forest. Yellin' Helen was striding through the ferns with a faint smile on her lips. Nightshade was bounding from tree to tree, claiming she was being stealthy. Mak-Thar was clomping along, complaining about his itchy back. And Twilight was bending low branches, trying to keep them from tangling in the mess of stuff attached to Mak-Thar's pack saddle.

"I'm going to scout ahead!" said Nightshade.

"Good luck," said Helen.

"Um," said Fred.

He had a lot of faith in Helen's ability to lead them through the wilderness. And he admired Nightshade's enthusiasm. But something about the tone of Helen's voice had suggested to Fred that Nightshade's enthusiasm might not have Helen's sense of direction.

Fred decided to try diplomacy. "Actually, I'm a little worried about Mak-Thar's packs and bags and pouches. The forest is thicker here, and I think the boys could really use some help keeping the equipment from getting caught in the branches."

"Okay. My elf casts Grease on Mak-Thar."

"No!" shouted Mak-Thar.

"No?"

"I resist! And I protest. It's hard enough to coordinate four legs without being greased."

Nightshade made a pouty face. "Well, fine then. I guess I'll guard the front with Helen so Fred can help with the branches."

The faint smile on Helen's lips was replaced by a faint frown.

Fred dropped back to help Twilight bend branches. This was

where he had wanted *Nightshade* to be. How had *he* ended up here instead? Fred realized he might not be very good at diplomacy.

"I'll break trail," said Nightshade. She took out a slender knife with a four-inch blade and started stabbing individual leaves.

After a few minutes, Helen said, "Nightshade, you're drifting."

"No, I'm scouting."

"Fred asked you not to scout."

Had Fred done that? He thought he'd been more diplomatic than that.

"Okay, I'm going to forage for mushrooms."

"Well," said Twilight, "I'm sure we could use some variety in our diet."

"Not me," said Mak-Thar. "I'm happy to eat grass all day long. Grass, grass, grass. The only problem is, it's becoming more sparse as we go deeper into the— WOMBATS!"

His last word came out as more of a loud bray.

Fred drew his sword and looked up at the sky. A deep, guttural growl reached his ears in a rapid crescendo:

VrrrrRRRRRRR ...

Fred threw himself flat on the ground as a terrifying black shape swooped down upon them.

... OOOOMMMMMMMMmmmm!

"He stole some rations!" shouted Mak-Thar.

"Here comes another!" shouted Twilight.

VrrrrRRRRRRR ...

Fred rolled on his back and looked up to see two rows of razor-sharp claws fly at Mak-Thar's back.

... OOOOMMMMMMMMmmmm!

Sacks ripped, and individually wrapped packets of iron rations flew into the air. Panicked, Fred rolled through the ferns as ration packets thudded into the ground, cratering the spot where he had just been.

Vrrrrrrrrrrrrr ...

"There are three of them," said Helen grimly.

... rrrrRRRRR ...

Mak-Thar asked, "Does anyone have a net?"

... OOOOMMMMMMMMmmmm!

Nightshade screamed. The beast had seized her spunky little backpack in its claws and was carrying her toward the tree canopy.

Fred got to his feet, but there was nothing he could do.

Nightshade cried, "I can't reach my sword!"

"Slide out of the straps!" called Twilight.

"I can't afford to lose my stuff!"

Twilight got a determined look in his eye. He unslung his bow, nocked an arrow, and in one fluid motion shot an intervening tree.

"Called shots have at least a minus-four to-hit penalty!" Mak-Thar shouted. "They're almost always suboptimal!"

VrrrrRRRRRRR ...

Fred whirled around and pointed the tip of his sword at the wombat. He knew that armored animals are often vulnerable in the mouth, but this wombat had five mouths, and he wasn't sure which one to aim at.

The beast banked away from him.

... OOOOMMMMMMMMmmmm!

"They're too high!" Mak-Thar shouted. "I can't kick them!"

"Your packs are like armor!" Twilight shouted as he shot an arrow that disappeared among the branches overhead. "Keep your head low, and you will be protected like a turtle in its shell!"

VrrrrRRRRRRR ...

The wombat carrying Nightshade was diving at them.

"EeeeeeEEEEE ..." screamed Nightshade.

"AaaaarrrrRRR ..." shouted Helen, charging in from the other side.

... OOOO ...

"... EEK!"

"... RRRRGGGH!"

Helen stepped on a fallen log, jumped into the air, raised her sword above her head, and swung it with both hands into the wombat's armored wing.

Crunch!

In the sudden shock of pain, the wombat released Nightshade, who went tumbling through the ferns.

... OOOOMMMMMMMMmmmm!

Nightshade rose to her feet and drew her sword. "Right. Now my elf is mad."

"Use your bow," shouted Twilight, as he shot another arrow into the trees. "They're staying out of sword reach."

Fred didn't have a bow. All he had were his hours of adventuring experience, his sword, and his wits.

VrrrrRRRRRRR ...

As the wombat dove toward his head, Fred really wished he had a bow.

Fred raised his sword to fend off the wombat's claws. Rows of razors struck his blade, spitting sparks and sending shivers through Fred's wrists.

... OOOOMMMMMMMMmmmm!

Fred felt a sharp pain in his face, just below his left eye. He reached up and pulled a severed claw out of his cheek.

Nightshade read some magic words off a scroll and jumped into the air.

Nightshade didn't come down. She was flying.

"Well now I don't have a safe shot anywhere," said Twilight.

Nightshade caught up to the wombat that had attacked Fred. She drew back her sword to strike.

"Beware the tail club!" yelled Mak-Thar.

With a thump, the tail caught her in the chest and sent her spinning backwards.

VrrrrRRRRRRR ...

Mak-Thar yelled, "Helen! Six o' clock!"

"I'm a barbarian! I can't tell time!"

"Behind you!" said Fred.

Helen ducked.

... OOOO ...

Helen stabbed upward.

"Skreeeech!" *... OOOOMMMMMMMMmmmm!*

Droplets of blood and downy feathers drifted down from above.

Hovering in midair, Nightshade yelled, "Fireball them, Mak-Thar! Fireball them!"

"I'm a mule!" shouted Mak-Thar. "And besides, there's no way we could get all three within a sphere of diameter forty feet."

VrrrrRRRRRRR ...

Twilight turned and loosed an arrow. The diving wombat snatched the arrow out of the air with its tentacle.

"I'll save you!" Nightshade yelled. She pointed her sword at Twilight and flew down toward him, head first.

Twilight's eyes grew wide, and he dove away from Nightshade, into the bushes.

... OOOO ...

Nightshade's sword met the wombat's back directly above the place where Twilight had been standing. Quills shot up into Nightshade's face.

... OOOOMMMMMMMMMmmmm!

Nightshade hit the ground with a thump, clutching her face in pain.

"Don't just lie there!" Mak-Thar shouted. "Your Fly spell has a duration of at least twenty minutes!"

VrrrrRRRRRRR ...

The one with the wounded wing was diving at them again.

Twilight nocked an arrow. "Let's gang up on it!"

Fred and Helen took up positions between Twilight and the diving wombat. His arrows whizzed over their heads, striking the beast's underbelly.

"You know," said Fred, "the Wounded Wombat would be a good name for a tavern."

... OOOO ...

Fred sidestepped the razor-claws and raked his sword along the leathery membrane of the wombat's wing, his swordpoint bouncing off the bones.

On the other side, Helen's sword pierced the wing, and the force of the wombat's swoop yanked the weapon from her grip.

... OOOOMMMMMMMMmmmm!

Helen's sword fell from the wombat's wing and landed in a briar patch.

Nightshade was still lying on the ground, her face full of quills. "Elf down!" she shouted. "Elf down! Heal me, Twilight!"

"Make the wombats stop diving at us, and we'll talk about it!" Twilight yelled.

Helen picked up a stick and gingerly poked at the briars that concealed her sword.

VrrrrRRRRRRR ...

Nightshade reached into her backpack and pulled out a scroll. She read some magic words and pointed at the diving wombat. A web spread through the trees.

... OOOO— "Squawwwk!"

"We've got one! We've got one!" shouted Mak-Thar. "Fred, jump on my back so you can reach it."

Fred jumped on Mak-Thar's back and thrust upward.

Twilight shot an arrow into the struggling mass of fur and feathers and quills and wings. "Careful! We don't want to cut it loose."

Fred kept jabbing. The wombat was already trying to cut itself loose with its razor claws. Any moment now, the beast might fall and give Fred a really close shave.

"Oh," said Mak-Thar. "I just realized that, in allowing for sixteen hundred coins of additional weight, I was only ensuring that I am able to carry your equipment. Because Fred himself weighs more than one hundred sixty pounds, having him on my back has immobilized me."

Fred found a weak spot between two of the wombat's scales and thrust his sword into it.

"But this should work in our favor," said Mak-Thar. "Because I am completely immobilized, Fred should not suffer a penalty for standing on an unstable surface."

VrrrrRRRRRRR ...

"Here comes another one!" shouted Helen. Grimacing, she

shoved her bare arm into the briar patch and yanked out her sword.

"See?" said Mak-Thar. "Right now, for instance, a normal mule would fail its morale check and run away. But because I am immobilized, you can have complete confidence in your footing."

Fred wrenched open a hole between the wombat's scales. This was not much like swordfighting and a lot like opening doors—except for the shrieks of pain.

Actually, some doors did sound like that when you opened them. Fred asked, "Should we oil the wombat?"

"What?" asked Mak-Thar.

… *OOOOMMMMMMMMmmmm!*

The other wombat flew away with two arrows sticking out of its belly.

Above Fred's head, the entangled wombat gave a final shudder and went still.

VrrrrRRRRRRR …

Nightshade was back on her feet again. "My elf leaps into the air to meet it."

Helen said, "I'm not sure that's such a—"

But Nightshade had already left the ground. The petite elf met the diving wombat head on and buried her arm up to the shoulder inside the wombat's upper left mouth.

… *OOOOMMSH!*

Elf and beast crashed to the ground. When the noise of their impact had died away, the battlefield was still.

A dead wombat lay on the forest floor, Nightshade's sword-point sticking out the back of its head. Of Nightshade could be seen only her boots with the funny rollover cuff things that Fred didn't know the name of.

Helen shook her head and said, "What some people do for attention."

Twilight held a hand to his pointy ear. They heard nothing.

After a moment, Fred asked, "Do you think the third one flew away?"

"I could calculate the odds," said Mak-Thar. "Fred, as long as you're up there, pull out my copy of *The Adventurer's Guide* and look up a wombat's morale statistic."

Fred jumped down from Mak-Thar's back and sheathed his sword. "Nightshade could smother under there. Help me roll the wombat off her face."

Helen and Twilight exchanged worried glances. They came to help. Together, the three of them rolled the dead beast over to reveal an elf with a face full of wombat quills.

Nightshade opened her eyes. "That was great! We really kicked some Mak-Thar!"

The mule said, "Oh, don't *you* start."

Twilight said, "Do not move, my brave comrade. Lie still and tell me if you have any broken bones."

Mak-Thar said, "I hope not. I haven't read the *Expanded Damage* supplement."

"I think my bones are fine," said Nightshade. "But what will these wombat quills do to my comeliness stat?"

CHAPTER TWELVE: IN WHICH WE DISCOVER SOMETHING NEW ABOUT MAK-THAR.

ONCE TWILIGHT WAS DONE pulling all the quills, Nightshade had two dozen tiny holes in her face. But Fred doubted she would have to worry about her comeliness stat. Twilight was an expert surgeon, and the wounds would certainly heal in time.

Helen had wrenched her shoulder when her sword had been torn from her hands. Twilight showed her how to brew a tea that would reduce inflammation.

Fred had forgotten he was hurt until Twilight offered to sew up the cut on his cheek. Then he knew he was hurt because Twilight was poking a needle into him.

"I'm going to take a nap so I can rememorize my spells," said Nightshade.

"It doesn't work that way," said Mak-Thar. "You need a full eight hours' sleep."

"Elves don't sleep," said Twilight, tying a knot on Fred's face.

"The bottom line," said Mak-Thar, "is that a first-level mage can use only one spell slot per day. Although you seem to have used two."

"I have three," said Nightshade.

"Yes, you mentioned this before," said Mak-Thar. "I assumed you were confused, but now you have proven me wrong." He glanced slyly at Twilight. "However, it would not be the first time that an experienced adventurer has claimed to be first level."

"Oh, I'm totally experienced!" said Nightshade.

"I thought so," said Mak-Thar. "To cast Fly, one must be at least fifth level."

"No, I'm first level. Just, you know, really experienced. It's part of my back story."

"What?"

"That's why I get three spell slots."

"But how do you cast higher-level spells?"

"Scrolls!" said Nightshade. "I memorize Read Magic, which is a first-level spell, and then I use it to cast whatever I want off a scroll. Cool, huh?"

Mak-Thar's ears perked up. "That's brilliant! Of course, it only works for as long as you have magical scrolls, which are very difficult to find."

"Oh, I have lots. It's part of my back story."

Mak-Thar put his ears back. "That's cheating!"

Twilight dabbed some moss on Fred's face to disinfect it. "Try to keep these stitches out of the dirt. If you need to sleep on a cape, you can borrow mine when we camp for the night."

"I suppose I could try sleeping on my back," said Fred.

"It might be easier if you take off your armor," suggested Twilight.

"I didn't bring—"

"Well, maybe you *should* have brought your pajamas and bunny slippers," said Twilight. "Regardless, you can borrow my cape."

Fred didn't want to borrow Twilight's cape. The elf barely had any meat on his bones. The nighttime breeze would blow right through him.

Twilight stopped working on Fred's face and went to look at Mak-Thar's rump.

"And poor Mak-Thar has also been clawed." He started dabbing at Mak-Thar's newest wounds with some elf-moss. "Honestly, we're fortunate we survived."

Mak-Thar flapped his ears. "Well, when Sage said we'd have to fight wombats, I knew it wouldn't be easy."

Twilight said, "I was imagining something different."

"Like what?" asked Fred.

Twilight shook his head. "I don't know. I always thought that wombats were medium-sized burrowing animals. Sort of like a fat woodchuck. Are you sure these were wombats?"

"Well, we can look it up," said Mak-Thar. "Nightshade, would you fetch my *Adventurer's Guide?*"

"My elf is still mad at you because you said her back story was cheating."

"I didn't say your back story is cheating. I said that starting a first-level character with numerous magic scrolls is cheating."

Twilight threaded his surgery needle. "Perhaps if you told us your story, we would understand your situation better."

"Oh, well, my back story has, like, all these adventure hooks in it. So it's kind of a secret. But trust me, it's really cool."

"See, now that didn't help," said Twilight. To Mak-Thar he said, "This may sting."

"It stings," said Mak-Thar. "Fred, to take my mind off my pain, it would be nice if someone could help me look up 'Wombat' in *The Adventurer's Guide.*"

Fred went to Mak-Thar's packs and pulled out *The Adventurer's Guide.* Mak-Thar asked for it about twenty times a day. By now, they all knew where it was kept.

"Monsters start on page 29," said Mak-Thar. "But 'Wombat' will be at the end of that section."

Fred leafed through it. "Before or after 'Wolf'?"

"Immediately after," said Mak-Thar.

"I can't find it," said Fred.

"Show me."

Fred showed him.

"You're right. It goes straight from 'Wolf' to 'Wraith'. I wish I had a copy of *The Bestiary*."

"I brought *The Bestiary*," said Nightshade.

"*Revised and Expanded Edition*?" asked Mak-Thar.

"I think so." She fished it out of her tiny, little backpack.

Twilight asked, "How do you fit a tome that large inside your tiny, little backpack?"

"It's a Backpack of Holding," said Nightshade.

Mak-Thar flashed the whites of his eyes. "A first-level character has a Bag of Holding?"

"*Backpack* of Holding," said Nightshade. "That's why I couldn't let the wombat steal it."

"I've been searching *years* for a Bag of Holding!"

Nightshade shrugged. "You should have written yourself a better back story."

Twilight said, "We do not choose our back stories. They choose us."

"Yeah, whatevs."

"You should listen to him," said Mak-Thar. "Twilight has a very sensible back story with a solid adventure hook. Show her your amulet, Twilight."

"Right now I'm busy sewing your, um, hip."

"Yes, well," said Mak-Thar. "Anyway, on our last adventure, we found the sacred Amulet of Spring. ... Wait. Twilight, didn't you say your religion has no holy symbols?"

"The amulet is not a symbol," said Twilight. "It's, um, a sacred artifact of my people."

"An artifact?" asked Mak-Thar. "You mean like an ultra-powerful magic item of the sort that even career-long adventurers may never find?"

"Sort of," said Twilight. "Except, I'm not sure it's ultra-powerful ..."

"But it *is* magical?" Mak-Thar insisted.

"Well, you know, you heard my legend."

"Yes," said Mak-Thar. "And as I recall, when you got to the part about what the amulet actually does, the legend was rather vague."

"He doesn't know," said Nightshade, leafing through *The Bestiary*. "Mister World's-Expert-on-Back-Stories doesn't know what his amulet does."

"I was sent to find it," said Twilight. "My people didn't tell me what it does. They just said they wanted it back."

Mak-Thar twitched his ears. "We should get it identified."

Twilight got defensive. "I recognize it, okay? My parents showed me pictures."

"No, no. *Magically* identified. So we know what it does."

"We could visit Sage again," said Fred.

"One of my colleagues at the Mages' Guild can identify it," said Mak-Thar. "There shall be no need to visit Sage the Sage. Ever again."

Twilight had stopped stitching and was staring at Mak-Thar's back end. Something about Mak-Thar's tail had surprised him.

"There's no wombats in *The Bestiary*, either," said Nightshade.

"May I see the index, please?"

Nightshade found *W* in the index and held it up for Mak-Thar's inspection.

"You're right," Mak-Thar admitted. "No wombats."

"How about wallabies?" asked Twilight.

"No," said Mak-Thar. "There are no wallabies."

"Check *K*," said Twilight. "I have a theory."

Nightshade turned the pages to *K*.

"What are we looking for?" asked Mak-Thar.

Twilight started dabbing at his finished stitches. " 'Kangaroo'. Or 'Koala'."

"Not appearing in this index," said Mak-Thar. "Not even 'Koala comma Giant'."

Twilight said, "The Bestiary seems completely devoid of marsupials."

Mak-Thar asked, "Are you suggesting that marsupials don't exist?"

"What's a marsupial?" asked Fred.

"An animal with a pouch," said Mak-Thar.

"You have pouches," said Fred. "You exist."

Twilight said, "I'm not saying marsupials don't exist. I'm just saying they aren't listed in your rulebooks. So you don't know what real wombats look like."

Fred looked at the dead wombats—the one lying in the dirt, and the one hanging from the web in the trees. They looked pretty real to him.

"These have to be wombats," said Mak-Thar. "Are you done sewing? I want to see if they have pouches."

"Only female marsupials have pouches," said Twilight.

"Oh," said Fred. "So Mak-Thar's not a marsupial because he's male?"

"How can we tell if these wombats are male or female?" asked Mak-Thar.

Helen burst out laughing.

"What's so funny?" asked Mak-Thar.

"Nothing," said Helen.

"Um ..." said Twilight.

"Yes?" asked Mak-Thar.

"Well, this is a little embarrassing, since I'm supposed to be a physician ... but as I said, I'm not a veterinarian ... well, anyway, as I was closing your wound just now, I um ..."

Mak-Thar's ear twitched. "You just now realized that my back end is female?"

"Um ..." said Twilight, "... yes."

"Well," said Mak-Thar, "you're not nearly as intelligent as I gave you credit for."

"So you knew?" asked Twilight.

"Of course I knew," said Mak-Thar. "How could I not know that my body is female?"

"Wait," said Fred. "You mean Mak-Thar is a girl?"

Mak-Thar said, "Evenstar the mule is a girl, yes."

"So that makes you … a marsupial?"

Helen fell over laughing. "Oh. My ribs!"

"Honestly," said Mak-Thar, "how could it take you this long to notice? It's not like I can cover up anything back there."

Twilight said, "I guess I've just been so attached to Evenstar's face that I never bothered to think about the other end."

Helen said, "Fred's the worst, though. Fred, I thought you grew up on a farm!"

"I grew up on a chicken farm," said Fred. "We tell boy chickens from girl chickens by looking at their combs."

"Their combs! Oh, my ribs!"

"Why didn't you say anything?" asked Fred.

"What's to say?" asked Helen.

Nightshade said, "So you used to be a boy, but now you're a girl. Isn't that weird?"

"I assure you," said Mak-Thar, "it's not nearly as weird as being a mule. Look, you are all making too big a deal of this. Evenstar is and always has been female. She knows how the back end works, and I leave all that up to her. I'm in charge of the front end. So when you are talking to me, you are talking to someone who remembers being male. But none of this matters. As was so delicately pointed out by Sage the Sage, mules cannot reproduce. Even if we could, we certainly would not be reproducing with any of *you*, and therefore this issue of male or female is irrelevant."

Helen said, "Hey, Fred, can I borrow your *comb*?"

"I didn't bring a comb," said Fred.

"Oh, my ribs!"

CHAPTER THIRTEEN: IN WHICH WE SEE THE END OF THE WOMBAT WILDERNESS.

WHEN TWILIGHT HAD FINISHED taking care of everyone, he turned his attention to the lifeless body of the wombat that had nearly crushed Nightshade. After walking all the way around it, he drew his knife and stood staring at its head.

"It's a good thing I am so well versed in all the arts of woodcraft," he said. "Otherwise I would have no idea how to skin an animal that has fur, feathers, scales, and barbed quills."

After a while, he walked around the wombat in the opposite direction. Then he stared at it some more.

"I have a conundrum," said Mak-Thar.

"That sounds bad," said Helen. "Ask Twilight to make sure it's not infected."

Mak-Thar put his ears back. "You're very amusing, I'm sure. But this is serious. We all need to heal for at least twenty-four hours. However, for every eight hours we spend here, there is a one-in-three chance we shall be attacked, giving us an expected value of one attack per day."

"You're right," said Helen. "That *is* a conundrum."

"Ah, so you see what I mean."

"Yes. You mean number, number, number. At least, I assume that's what you mean, because that's all I heard."

"Honestly! Barbarism is no excuse for innumeracy. Regardless, I shall explain the crux of the matter."

"Oh, do!" said Helen. "Do explain the crux!"

Nightshade said, "You don't have to be mean just because he's smarter than you."

"What? I wasn't being mean."

Nightshade said, "You think you're better than us just because you're an underwear model with the Hunting proficiency."

"I do what now?"

Fred said, "I think what Mak-Thar is trying to say is that he's sorry you hurt your shoulder."

"No, no," said Mak-Thar. "Well, yes, of course I *am* sorry. But more importantly, I want to draw your attention to the conundrum."

Helen opened her mouth to say something, looked at Nightshade, and decided to say, "I'm going for a walk."

"But you can't heal without complete bed rest!" said Mak-Thar.

"Fine. I'll go forage for a bed." She disappeared among the trees.

"Honestly, where did you find her?" asked Nightshade. "She's such a sour puss."

Twilight said, "She's also the only one of us who might know how to skin a wombat. I really could have used her help."

"Well, her attitude certainly throws off my calculations," said Mak-Thar. "I was going to say that if each random encounter can be expected to deal us less than a point-and-a-half of damage, then we should stay here and camp. But if Helen won't sit still, then I can't assume an expected healing rate of one-and-a-half hit points per day, so now I'm not sure what to think."

"I can heal as I walk," said Nightshade.

"No you can't," said Mak-Thar. "Healing requires complete bed rest. *The Adventurer's Guide* is quite explicit."

Fred said, "Helen started this adventure with rat bites on her legs. They got better as she walked."

"Sometimes movement can help the healing process," said Twilight, "as long as the wounds are properly cared for."

"Aha!" said Mak-Thar. "You admit it!"

"Admit what?" asked Twilight.

"You've been healing us! I suspected as much when I awoke this morning. I was at full hit points, despite the damage from yesterday's random fire beetles."

Twilight threw up his hands. "All right, Mak-Thar. You caught me. All that time when I pretended to be disinfecting your wound and stitching it closed, I was actually trying to heal you."

Mak-Thar's lower lip quivered in satisfaction. "I knew it!"

"Oh, cool!" said Nightshade. "Does that mean I'm back to full hit points, too?"

"You need to take it easy," said Twilight. "Only your armor saved you from cracked ribs and internal organ damage. I'm worried you may have a concussion, but in your case I'm not sure how I would tell."

"Be that as it may," said Mak-Thar, "I believe the conundrum is solved. Twilight—despite the thematic window-dressing provided by his back story and nonstandard rules supplement—is functionally equivalent to a cleric. Therefore, we need not rely exclusively on bed rest. Which is fortunate, because the aforementioned probability of random encounters is not in our favor."

"So you're saying we can keep going," said Twilight.

"Yes."

"Just as soon as I have skinned two wombats, cured their hides, cut them to precise dimensions, and sewn them together to make parkas," said Twilight.

"Yes," said Mak-Thar. "Approximately how long will that take?"

Twilight turned and walked away into the forest calling for Helen.

* * *

Skinning the wombats took the remainder of the day. In fact, they had to finish by the light of the glowing beetle glands on Mak-Thar's pack.

Helen and Twilight decided that they should not, in fact, wait around for the hides to cure. They would cure them on the way. And so, at first light on the very next morning, our heroes once again set out through the forest.

That evening, they had to stop early because of some woodsy thing that Helen and Twilight had to do to cure the hides. The process involved making an exceptionally smoky fire and then griping for two hours about how difficult the hides were to work with.

Mak-Thar was surprised that curing hides was so compli-cated. "The leather was flexible enough when the wombat was wearing it, so why should it stiffen up now?"

Mak-Thar offered several other helpful comments, with the end result that he was sent into the forest to help Fred collect firewood. They found a lot of firewood and took a long time doing so.

Nightshade said that, since Helen was busy, she would help by hunting for their evening meal. She brought back one squirrel, which she didn't know how to cook.

They didn't run into any random encounters until two days later (seven hobgoblins who ran away when they saw that the party was tough enough to skin wombats). And no one got wounded again until the next afternoon, when a wild boar charged Fred and nearly took off his leg.

* * *

That evening, as they sat around their campfire under the trees, eating roasted pork, Mak-Thar said, "If we'd known our random encounters would be so light, we could have stayed in one place until the hides were cured. We would be back to full hit points now—except for Fred, of course."

Twilight asked Mak-Thar, "Do your wounds still pain you?"

"They're just itchy. Mind you, that is not an invitation to scratch my backside, even though that is exactly what Evenstar wants from you right now."

"If your wounds are healed, you can roll on the ground again."

"Thank you," said Mak-Thar. "That might help."

"I'm *almost* back to full hit points," said Nightshade. "Can I climb trees again?"

"No," said Twilight. "Tree climbing is still forbidden."

"You know," said Nightshade, "I looked it up, and there's no 'concussion protocol' in *The Adventurer's Guide*."

"I'm your doctor, and you'll do as I say."

"Hmf. I go carve a wooden flute and learn to play it."

Twilight smiled serenely. "I am glad you will have something to occupy your time."

"Fred," said Helen, "tell us a story."

Fred shrugged. "Maybe Twilight would like to tell a story. Have you heard the legend of the Amulet of Spring?"

"Evenstar and I have heard it multiple times," said Mak-Thar.

Twilight shifted like he had a bug in his pants. "To tell the truth, I'm not as excited about the Amulet of Spring as I used to be."

"Adventurer's remorse," said Helen. "You always want the treasure until you get it."

"Yes," said Twilight. "Perhaps that's it."

Nightshade said, "My back story is so cool, you'd all be jealous if I told you. But, of course, it's a secret until we reveal my cool plot hooks."

"That's very exciting," said Fred. "What about you, Mak-Thar? Do you have any stories?"

"Why yes, I have a back story," said Mak-Thar. "Most characters do. Although, now that I'm an NPM, I probably don't need one anymore."

"Oh, please tell us," said Twilight. "I'd love to learn more about your past."

"Very well," said Mak-Thar. "When I was a youth, I realized that I liked to read and I liked math. So I thought I should be a mage. Then I went to a wizard and became his apprentice. When my apprenticeship was done, I joined the Mages' Guild and became a first-level mage."

The fire crackled. Fred finished chewing his pork. Helen shifted position to keep the smoke out of her eyes.

"That's it?" asked Twilight.

"Perhaps it's not particularly imaginative," said Mak-Thar. "But it's more realistic than assuming an untrained youth would be sent out all alone to recover a sacred amulet."

Twilight stared glumly into the fire. "See, I didn't have any trouble believing that. Stories are always about untrained youths.

Competent people are boring."

Fred didn't think Yellin' Helen was boring, but he chose not to interrupt.

Twilight continued, "But now I've started to realize that adventures are boring. I wanted to do something heroic. Instead, we crawled through a dungeon at a pace of two steps per minute. When we finally got the amulet, one of my friends got stabbed by a person I didn't like very much. To keep him from stabbing more people, I killed him. That wasn't heroic. It wasn't like I had vanquished a great evil. I just killed a guy whose indifference to life had gotten out of hand.

"And now we're walking through the forest day after day, with the monotony broken only by random terrifying brushes with death. Honestly, sometimes I lose sight of the fact that our quest has a noble purpose."

"If you don't like walking through the forest," said Helen, "you should rent a room in Basetown and just do town adventures. And if you don't like random terrifying brushes with death, you should go back to your people and tell them you want to be a horticulturalist."

"Are you kidding?" asked Twilight. "Do you know how many elves want to be a horticulturalist? There's a three-century waiting list just for unpaid apprenticeships."

"Oh, um, I meant ... uh ... fishmonger."

"Well *I* don't want to be a horticulturalist," said Nightshade. "I think this is fun. And it would have been more fun if you guys had let me kill those hobgoblins yesterday."

"They were running away," said Twilight.

"Hobgoblins and elves are racial enemies," said Nightshade. "I read it in *The Adventurer's Guide.*"

Twilight said, "If you have to read about your deep-seated racial hatred in a rulebook, then it's not really a deep-seated racial hatred. Besides, I'm opposed to deep-seated racial hatreds on principle."

"Twilight is good," explained Mak-Thar. "I'm neutral, so I don't care about racial hatreds."

Twilight said, "If you were truly neutral, you would be opposed to racial hatreds because they are so polarizing."

"Ah," said Mak-Thar, "but what you fail to consider is that ... Hm. No, actually, on second thought, you may be right. I suppose I *should* be opposed to deep-seated racial hatreds."

"Well, I'm glad we let the hobgoblins run away," said Fred.

"You are?" asked Helen. She gave him a look that said, *You're supposed to be a fighter.*

Now it was Fred who was shifting like he had a bug in his pants. It wasn't a real bug. He was just uncomfortable admitting this to Helen. "Sometimes I see Twilight's point. I can see why he doesn't want to fight when the fight doesn't mean anything."

"And that passive attitude is why our dinner nearly gutted you today," said Helen.

"The boar wasn't tall enough to gut me," said Fred. "Or, wait. Do I have guts in my knee?"

"You're lucky you still have cartilage in your knee," said Twilight. "You are walking only through the grace of Selene."

"And the grace of your walking stick," said Helen.

* * *

The next morning, Fred's knee felt much worse, and he really *did* need his walking stick to keep up with Helen. Helen's shoulder was still bothering her, and she would swing her arm around from time to time to keep it loose. Nightshade was back to climbing up trees, even though she had never once seen anything from a tree top that they had not noticed from the ground.

"I don't like the way Fred is limping," said Mak-Thar. "*The Adventurer's Guide* does not mention any penalties for being at low hit points, but I'm afraid Fred may be experiencing penalties anyway."

"Oh, I'm fine," said Fred. Twilight—and Selene—had done what they could for him. Now he just had to walk it off.

"I could try to bandage it," said Twilight. "But my bandages are more for hygiene than joint support."

From a nearby tree, Nightshade called, "My elf reaches into her backpack and pulls out a knee brace."

"Really?" asked Twilight.

Mak-Thar called, "You can't have it if it isn't written down."

"I don't have anything written down."

"Then you don't have anything," said Mak-Thar.

"Well, like, what if my backpack already had stuff in it when I got it?"

Twilight said, "Unless you got it from a physical therapist, it probably doesn't have a knee brace."

"You can check my inventory list to see if I am carrying a knee brace," said Mak-Thar. "Sorry it's not alphabetized."

Twilight asked, "Are you likely to have something that's not in *The Adventurer's Guide*?"

"Aren't knee braces listed under Clerics' Equipment?"

Nightshade came down the tree carrying her *Adventurer's Guide.*

"Page twelve," said Mak-Thar.

"There's nothing labeled Clerics' Equipment," said Nightshade. "There are Thieves' Tools and Holy Symbols."

Helen said, "Too bad Twilight isn't a cleric of the Sacred Order of the Knee Brace."

Mak-Thar said, "Well, if knee braces aren't in the Equipment List, then they aren't necessary for adventures."

"Right," said Twilight. "Because when you are hiking several leagues through the wilderness, what you really need are holy symbols and lock picks."

"Precisely," said Mak-Thar, completely missing the sarcasm. "Well, I guess that settles it. Fred should have no penalties for a sore knee."

Fred was glad that was settled. He didn't want penalties for a sore knee.

He hobbled on through the day, and sometimes the knee seemed to be better and sometimes worse. He never asked for a break, but he was always grateful when Helen suggested they take one.

Helen and Mak-Thar said they had gone around the Impass-able Mountain Range and were now heading south. Fred didn't really notice any difference, but he assumed Helen was right about these things.

Shortly after noon, Nightshade climbed down from a tree to report, "I think we're almost out of the woods."

Half a minute later, they were standing at the edge of the forest. On their left was a dismal, murky swamp. On their right was a vast desert, with sand stretching as far as the eye could see.

CHAPTER FOURTEEN: IN WHICH OUR HEROES LIVE ON THE EDGE.

TWILIGHT WOULDN'T BELIEVE IT until he had climbed a tree and seen it for himself. When he came down, he reported what the rest of them already knew.

"It's like three entirely different landscapes meet at this point. The trees at the edge of the forest form two perfect lines that meet at an angle."

"A 120-degree angle," said Mak-Thar.

"Yes," said Twilight. "And ahead of us, the line between the swamp and the desert is perfectly straight. Cattails and rushes on the left, dry sand on the right."

"So we must be here," said Nightshade pointing to a place on Mak-Thar's map.

"Yes," said Mak-Thar. "We seem to have gone off course."

"We seem to have gone due south and found the desert," said Helen. "I'm pretty sure that was the plan."

Mak-Thar swished his tail. "We seem to have veered some-what southeast. Due south would have put us on the hexagon's southern edge, but you can see for yourself that we are on the hexagon's corner."

Twilight was exasperated. "Why is the forest growing in hexagons?!"

"Because the *map* is in hexagons," said Mak-Thar. "And it's a good thing, too. Maps on squares get tricky if you try to move diagonally."

"This is ridiculous," said Twilight. "How can this place even exist? A desert right next to a forest and a swamp? It's like the landscape isn't even *trying* to make a smooth transition."

"My elf will scout the desert. One of you guys should scout the swamp and report back."

"The whole desert?" asked Twilight. "Your elf—I mean, *you*—are going to scout the entire, treeless, waterless desert?"

"No, just this hex." She pointed to a hexagon on the map.

"You should be aware," said Mak-Thar, "that each hexagon is six miles across."

"Okay. I'll just scout ahead for an hour then."

"It's a flat, treeless plain of sand," observed Twilight.

"Okay. I'll scout the swamp, then. But now my elf is mad at you guys because she doesn't want to get her leggings muddy." Nightshade flounced away with the map.

"Wait," said Mak-Thar. "I'm not done looking at that."

"I think we should stick together," said Fred.

"We should definitely stick together," said Helen.

Nightshade flounced back. "You guys haven't let me have any fun since I killed those wombats."

She held up the map for Mak-Thar again.

"We now have a decision to make," said Mak-Thar. "On the one hand—to be precise, on the *right* hand—we have a desert. Deserts have standard travel times, but they have no water. On the *left* hand, we have a swamp. That has water, but the travel times are slower and the encounter probabilities are higher."

"That's a conundrum," said Helen.

"It is," agreed Mak-Thar.

"Don't we have to go into the desert to visit the hermit?" asked Fred.

"We do," agreed Mak-Thar. "But we don't have to enter the desert immediately. As you can see, if we wade through the swamp, we will eventually be in the region of Herman's local map. The swamp path would minimize our desert travel, making it more manageable. However, the swamp is much more dangerous. We need to find the optimal balance between the desert's lesser encounter probabilities and the danger of running out of water."

"Why don't we just walk along the edge of the desert?" asked Fred. "Then we can travel fast, but we'll be right next to water if we get thirsty."

"Walk along the edge?" asked Mak-Thar. "Can we do that?"

Helen said, "I don't see a sign that says 'Keep Off the Sand.' Of course, if I *did* see a sign, I couldn't read it anyway."

"Walk along the edge," said Mak-Thar. "Oh, that's brilliant!"

"It's absurd," said Twilight. "How can this be a desert if it has water right beside it? Water has to come from *rain*."

Fred said, "We found water in the forest, and it never rained."

"Yes," said Twilight. "Isn't it odd that we went so many days without rain? Especially this time of year."

"The weather tables are optional," said Mak-Thar.

Twilight said, "I'm just going to pretend you didn't say that."

"Good idea," said Fred.

"Yeah, okay," said Nightshade. "So my elf just kind of goes along with you and scouts, like, *everything*. Okay?"

Nightshade fell asleep.

"Oh dear," said Twilight.

"Oh bother!" said Mak-Thar.

Helen looked down at the fallen elf and said, "That's excellent, Nightshade. I don't know what we would do without your keen scouting abilities. Guys, don't bother looking around, okay? Nightshade has us covered."

Mak-Thar pointed his ears at Nightshade's sleeping form. "You don't suppose she meant she was going to scout ahead astrally?"

"Yeah," said Helen. "I'm sure that's what she meant. If she sees anything, I'm sure she'll tell us right away."

"Unless she has more important stuff to do," said Twilight.

Mak-Thar stuck out his tongue. "Oooooooh!"

"What is it?" asked Twilight.

"More Important Stuff To Do. M-I-S-T-D. Oh, that's awful."

Fred asked, "Is this why she shouldn't climb trees?"

"Hmm," said Twilight. "Yes, I suppose this fainting episode could be a symptom of a concussion. Although that doesn't really explain why she passed out the first time. Unless she hit her head on a branch while climbing her tree."

Helen said, "Well, if you're saying something is wrong with her head, I won't argue with the doctor."

"I suppose we shall have to continue without her," said Mak-Thar. "Or, rather, *with* her on my back but *without* her help in combat. I just hope the encounters adjust to compensate for our smaller party size."

* * *

And so they discarded the beetle glands—which had already lost most of their glow anyway—and loaded Nightshade onto Mak-Thar's back. Then they set out through the desert.

Or rather, they set out along the edge of the desert. Under their feet was sand. Ahead was more sand. About fifty yards away was a swamp full of rushes and croaking frogs. Every so often, a brightly colored bird would swoop through the air and land in a moss-laden tree. But on their side of the line, it was nothing but sand.

"You know," said Twilight, "generally speaking, even deserts have *some* vegetation."

This one didn't.

Behind them, the line of the forest gradually shrank to a dark smudge on the horizon. As the afternoon made its way into evening, a dark splotch ahead of them gradually resolved itself into a continuation of the swamp. Distant trees became larger trees. Sparkling patches of light became ponds of open water. And blobs of green became a wall of tall cattails growing directly in their path.

"We have reached the corner," said Mak-Thar. "We're half-way through our first desert hex."

The boundary between the swamp and the desert turned abruptly to the right. Twilight said, "And I suppose the angle is precisely 120 degrees."

"Of course," said Mak-Thar.

"Never in my journeys have I felt so far from my beloved Silverleaf Forest."

"This isn't much like where I grew up, either," said Helen. "This desert has no fuel whatsoever. At least on the steppe we can burn dung."

"Yak dung or buffalo dung?" asked Twilight.

"Ogre dung. Well, I guess we should stop and set up camp. We can find wood in the swamp. We might have to dry it on the sand a while before it will burn."

"Yes, I've been thinking about that," said Mak-Thar.

"Oh good," said Helen.

"The party can only move as fast as its slowest member. Since I am at maximum encumbrance, and since Fred is in plate mail, that means he and I have already reached our movement limit of two hexes per day. You and Twilight, however, have a movement rate of four hexes per day. That means each of you can make one trip into the swamp *and back*."

Twilight looked at the swamp, which was only fifty yards away. "You mean I can walk all the way there *and back*? That's great!"

"Well, it is fortunate we have differing movement rates," said Mak-Thar. "Otherwise, none of us would be able to gather water and wood at all. Now I want you both to pay attention, because this next bit is important."

Mak-Thar drew some lines in the sand that looked kind of like a sideways *Y*. "Because we are on the corner of the desert hexagon, that means we are at the north-south boundary between two swamp hexagons. Two *different* swamp hexagons. Do you follow me so far?"

"Pretend that we do," said Helen. "What's your point?"

"Well, we have established that you each have two more hexagons of free movement today. But only two! If you cross this north-south line, you won't be able to leave the swamp without doing a forced march."

"A forced march," echoed Twilight.

"A forced march is a heroic daily movement tactic which allows you to move fifty percent farther, but at the cost of forcing you to rest for all of the following day. It's really only useful when your movement allowance runs out within sight of town."

Twilight pointed at the swamp. "So what you're saying is that if I go in there and then walk around the corner, I'll cross some imaginary line that will prevent me from coming back."

"Unless you do a forced march, yes."

"Even if the total distance walked is less than three hundred yards."

Mak-Thar swished his tail. "Hmm … I suppose it depends on whether movement limits are measured in distance traveled or in hexes. Could you hand me my copy of *The Adventurer's Guide*?"

Twilight said, "Look, Mak-Thar, even if the world's biomes do grow in hexagons—and I am forced to acknowledge that perhaps they do—even so, don't you think it's more reasonable to assume that people get tired from walking long distances, and *not* from moving to a new hexagon?"

"At this point in the adventure, I'm not sure we can risk it," said Mak-Thar. "Not unless the language in *The Adventurer's Guide* is unequivocally in support of your interpretation."

Twilight sighed. "Okay, Mak-Thar. Because I realize you are feeling anxious, I promise that I won't cross your imaginary line between two arbitrarily differentiated parts of the swamp."

"Yeah, me too," said Helen. "Can we get wood now?"

Chapter Fifteen: In which scorpions pose a problem.

So they did it Mak-Thar's way for the next couple of days. They tramped through the sand, going mostly straight until the border zigzagged. Then they'd follow the new line of travel until they reached the next zigzag. Mak-Thar let them do two zigs and two zags each day. In the evenings, Twilight and Helen would go into the swamp for water and firewood, being careful that Mak-Thar saw them crossing the border at the same place both ways. (If Helen crossed over any imaginary lines while she was out of sight, Fred figured that was her business.)

Fred felt kind of bad about not helping with the foraging. On the other hand, he was glad that Mak-Thar's rulebook gave him an excuse to avoid the swamp. His injured knee was not getting any better, and he suspected that the uneven footing in the swamp would only make it worse.

The knee injury lasted longer than the roasted pork. When the meat ran out, Helen caught them snakes and frogs. Fred was not fond of the frogs, but he didn't complain. (The snakes were pretty good. They tasted kind of like cockatrice.)

Twilight foraged armloads of cattail shoots. They tasted okay, but Fred was glad that Mak-Thar ate most of them.

It didn't take long for them to realize that Mak-Thar would eat all the cattails Helen and Twilight could bring him. Mak-Thar was hungry. Helen started making unauthorized trips to the swamp to bring him forage while he slept.

Fred was surprised that Mak-Thar never noticed that a few scraps of cattails had turned into a large heap by morning. On the other hand, Mak-Thar never could keep track of anything that wasn't written down.

"I really shouldn't need to eat these," Mak-Thar would insist whenever he browsed on his cattail snack. "*The Adventurer's Guide* doesn't say you need forage for your pack animals."

"Eat the cattails anyway," said Twilight. "I'm sure they will give you a morale bonus."

So Mak-Thar ate the cattails ... and he did get the bonus.

* * *

One evening after fighting a band of kobolds, Twilight observed, "This adventure is much quieter when Nightshade is asleep."

Helen said, "I'm not sure what she'd do with herself out here. The desert has no trees to climb and no bushes to hide behind."

"I miss her," said Mak-Thar. "Mages are useful. I believe we can all tolerate a little exuberance in exchange for tactical options."

"She sure made a mess of those wombats," said Fred.

"She was showing off, and it nearly got her killed," said Mak-Thar. "But if she learns a little caution, I think she can be a fine mage. I keep trying to teach her, but she doesn't take instruction well."

"I'm not missing her," said Helen. "Girls like that wear me out."

Mak-Thar said, "I'm a little worried about meeting a challenge we can't handle with swords and hooves. How much longer do we think she'll be asleep?"

"Who knows?" asked Helen.

"Elves don't sleep," said Twilight. "We have more important stuff to do. ... Actually, I wonder if that's not part of the mystery."

"What mystery?" asked Fred.

"What if she's not an elf?" asked Twilight.

"Her ears are pointy," said Fred.

Twilight went over to the sleeping Nightshade and knelt by her head. He tugged on her ear. It did not come off. Nightshade did not wake up.

"Are her ears an illusion?" asked Mak-Thar.

"They feel like real ears," said Twilight. "But they're the only part of her that seems real."

The thief that had killed Mak-Thar hadn't seemed real. He'd asked questions like *Are we there yet?* when it was obvious they were not there yet. And he'd said he was doing things as he did them, like *I light a torch.*

No, actually, it was Mak-Thar who had lit a torch that way. And Mak-Thar wasn't a bad guy. Nor a bad mule.

"If she wakes up, we can ask about her religion," said Fred.

"As a mage, she doesn't need one," said Mak-Thar. "Although I do wonder about her alignment. I hope she's not part of that new-fangled 'chaotic' alignment the strange woman was propagating at the Temple Square."

"Before you can have a religion," said Twilight, "you have to be able to commit to something for more than five minutes. That's another thing that makes me think she's not an elf. When you've been alive for a century and a half, you develop a certain amount of patience."

Fred thought that if Twilight really had patience, he wouldn't complain so often. In fact, the real difference between Twilight and Nightshade was that when Twilight got bored, he complained, but Nightshade tried to *do* something about it.

Nightshade was impulsive, incautious, and flighty. The fact that she would spontaneously fall unconscious for days at a time made her unreliable. But she was also *active.* Nightshade wanted to make things happen. Fred realized that was something they should admire.

But as Nightshade continued to sleep—all through the following day—their criticisms continued to pile up. Whatever redeeming qualities she had, she was not demonstrating them now. In the hot desert sun, Nightshade was just a dead weight.

* * *

As Fred hobbled through the sand, he was glad that his treasure sack was still empty. His injured knee ached so much that he was just dragging that leg along.

How long had it been since the last break? Helen had called

a lot of breaks today. She said it was because of the heat, but Fred knew she was trying to baby him.

He wasn't sure how he felt about that. Maybe he should resent being babied, but right now he was hoping that he would be babied very soon. His knee was going to kill him.

Helen could tell he was having trouble. Only a minute later, she said, "Let's stop here."

Fred stopped. Immediately. He sat down on his empty treasure sack and stretched out his leg.

Helen stretched her arms and then sat on the sand.

"How can you sit on the sand?" asked Twilight. "Doesn't your armor turn into an oven?"

Helen shook her head. "Nycadaemon Knickers: Say goodbye to hot, cross buns."

Mak-Thar asked, "Isn't this rest stop premature?"

"It's just a short break," said Helen.

"I was hoping we could rest in the shade of those dunes."

"What dunes?" asked Helen. She stood up so she could see better.

Twilight shaded his eyes. "I don't think those are dunes. They're moving."

Wincing, Fred rose to his feet. Three sand-colored creatures were creeping toward them.

Mak-Thar said, "Oh, you're right. Those aren't dunes. They're giant scorpions."

Fred drew his sword. As the insects drew closer, he could tell they were scorpions because they had those freaky tails with the nasty, bulbous stingers on the end. He could tell they were giant because they were as big as Mak-Thar.

"This isn't good," said Mak-Thar. "Their tails are poisonous."

Twilight loosed an arrow that flew into the distance and bounced off a scorpion's claw. The claws were impressive. They looked like the sort of claws that could just grab a man and rip him in half.

"He's right about the tails," said Helen. "One hit and you're dead." She had her sword drawn, but she wasn't charging. If Helen was being cautious, Fred was scared.

Twilight loosed another arrow. The three scorpions ignored him and casually closed the distance. Two more emerged from the sand.

"We need more long-range attacks," Mak-Thar said. "Helen, can you use Nightshade's bow?"

Helen rushed to Mak-Thar's side and removed the bow from the body of the sleeping elf.

"The difficulty levels of these encounters are quite uneven," said Mak-Thar. "Yesterday we fought kobolds. Kobolds will die if you sneeze on them. Today we have to fight four-hit-die monstrosities with poison attacks and an armor class as good as plate mail."

Helen raised the bow and shot an arrow into a scorpion's head. The scorpion didn't seem to notice.

"Maybe we should run," Twilight suggested. He managed to shoot an arrow into the joint of a scorpion's leg, but the monster continued to advance.

"Perhaps," said Mak-Thar. "Oh, if only I could cast Edwin's Weird Dweomer!"

Two more scorpions emerged from the sand and crept toward them. Everyone started backing away.

"How good are you at neutralizing poison?" Mak-Thar asked Twilight.

"I guess we'll find out," said Twilight. "Unless I get hit. Then we'll find out how good *you* are at neutralizing poison."

"Normally, I'd try some sneaky trick like throwing sand in their eyes," said Helen. "But considering they live here, I think they know how to deal with sand." She loosed another arrow.

Mak-Thar said, "See, this is why every party needs a mage."

"The scrolls!" said Twilight. "Nightshade's scrolls!"

Twilight ran to Mak-Thar's side and reached into Nightshade's backpack. He pulled out a scroll and unfurled it before Mak-Thar's doleful eyes.

"Mak-Thar, you can still read!"

"I can read normal writing," said Mak-Thar. "This is magical writing."

"But you're a *mage*."

Fred thought the scorpions were awfully close now.

"I'm a mule."

"A mule who *reads*."

"To read a magic scroll, I have to cast a spell on it. To cast the spell, I have to move my fingers. No fingers. Q.E.D."

The scorpions were now almost close enough to attack. Fred was thinking maybe he should lunge at them. But then he'd probably get poisoned and die.

"So do we let them eat us?" asked Twilight. "Or do we run?"

"Let's run!" said Mak-Thar. He turned and started galloping through the sand, parallel to the swamp border.

Twilight turned and ran after Mak-Thar.

Helen shot an arrow at point-blank range. She gave Fred a look that said, *I really hope you run now, because if you don't, I'll have to die here with you.*

Fred turned and ran after Twilight. Helen turned and ran with him. They covered quite a bit of ground before Fred's knee gave out. He fell to the sand.

Helen helped Fred to his feet. The scorpions were still coming after them, but the sprint had bought them a little time.

Mak-Thar and Twilight came back, looking worried.

"Can't you fix his knee?" Mak-Thar asked Twilight. "I think he's giving us a penalty on the Evasion and Pursuit Table."

"I don't have as much control over Selene's miracles as you think I do."

Helen shrugged. "Fred can still stand. If he can't run, we can just stay here and fight."

Twilight loosed an arrow.

"Poison is the great equalizer," said Mak-Thar. "It doesn't matter that you are both high-level fighters with heavily-gendered-yet-surprisingly-effective armor. The bottom line is: you have to hit them multiple times; they only have to hit you once. You won't win."

Helen said, "But if I go down, Twilight will pick me back up. We can do this."

Mak-Thar snorted and laid his ears flat. "If we weren't being attacked by scorpions, I would do the math and prove to you that we *can't!*"

"Look," said Fred. "Maybe we're making too big a deal of this. Let's try running away some more."

They turned and ran away until Fred collapsed again.

Now even Helen was looking worried. Fred didn't like to see her worried.

Twilight loosed another arrow. "I wonder if Selene would send giant eagles to help adventurers dying in a random wilderness encounter."

"I'm beginning to hate random wilderness encounters," said Helen.

"It *is* a terrible way to die," said Mak-Thar. "I'm afraid all we can do is run. Or maybe we can wait until they kill Fred and *then* run."

"Do you think they'd follow us into the swamp?" asked Twilight.

"The swamp!" said Mak-Thar. "Twilight, you're a genius! Fred, can you run into the swamp?"

"Sure," said Fred. "Honestly, my only problem is that sometimes my knee collapses because of excruciating pain."

"Then into the swamp!" yelled Mak-Thar. "But don't forget that Fred and I have used up our movement allowance. This counts as a forced march!"

CHAPTER SIXTEEN: IN WHICH OUR HEROES MARCH THROUGH THE MARSH.

THIS WAS FRED'S FIRST TRIP into the swamp. And what he noticed about the swamp was that it sure was wet. The water was up to mid-calf, and as he sloshed through the cattails, it soaked into his clothing and started climbing. "My pants haven't been this wet since we ran into that blue dragon."

"See, that's one reason I don't wear pants," said Helen. "I don't like wicking water to my knickers."

Well, Fred was glad that one of them was staying dry and comfy.

"Where did all the fog come from?" Fred asked.

"It's a swamp," said Helen. "You get fog in swamps."

"Do you think we can stop running away yet?"

"Is your knee hurting you?"

"Yes."

"We can stop."

In truth, they had stopped *running* as soon as they had reached the swamp. After that, they had merely been wallowing away. Helen had her arm under Fred's arm, trying to give him something to lean on. Fred had his arm on Helen's shoulder, and in that hand, he also had his treasure sack and his walking stick. His other hand held his sword. The arrangement was rather awkward.

Helen held him upright while he sheathed his sword. Once his hand was free, Fred rearranged his things and put his weight on his walking stick.

Splooooooosh! Fred fell face first into the swamp.

Helen grabbed him by the collar of his armor and hauled him up again.

"My walking stick!"

"The bottom is kind of soft here," she said.

"My lucky walking stick!" Fred got down on his knees and scrabbled around in the water.

Helen gave him a look that said, *The things I do for my friends.* She drew her humongous sword and probed the water.

"I think that's it."

Fred followed the line of Helen's sword and seized the stick at the sword's point. He pulled it out of the water.

It had a tree branch attached to it.

"That's not it," said Fred.

"Twiliiight!" yelled Mak-Thar.

"Mak-Thar?" yelled Twilight.

The fog made it seem like they were both a long ways away.

"It's got to be here somewhere," said Fred.

"Yeah, um ..." Helen wiped off her sword on her forearm and returned it to her scabbard. "You've, ah, got something on your face ..."

Fred could feel it. Something was stuck to his cheek just below his wombat-claw scar. He reached to brush it off and felt something cold and squishy, like a boneless finger.

Helen drew her knife. "It's a leech. Let me ... ah ... there."

"Thanks," said Fred.

"Sure. What are friends for?"

"Twiliiight!"

"Mak-Thar?"

Helen shook her head. "Poor Twilight couldn't find his mule with both hands."

Fred looked around. All he could see in the fog were some cattails and a few gnarled trees. "I'm sure glad we picked the desert. This place is terrible." He looked down at his feet. "My stick is gone, isn't it?"

"I think it's gone, Fred."

"I was so proud of it when I left home. I remember finding it and thinking it was the perfect way to begin my life of adventure."

"Well, I'm glad you didn't end your life of adventure playing scorpion pat-a-cake."

"Yeah." Fred was glad to be alive, but he was gonna miss that stick.

In the distance—somewhere—they could hear Mak-Thar saying, "You didn't have to run so far. Because the scorpions came from the Wilderness Encounter Table, they were unable to follow us once we changed terrain type."

"Gee," said Twilight, "and here I thought it was just because scorpions don't like being up to their carapace in water."

"Well, I assume the ankle-deep water is the reason they don't appear in the Swamp column of the encounter table."

To Helen, Fred said, "Let's try to get to Mak-Thar. He says the water there is only ankle deep."

They sloshed in the direction of the voices. There was some comfort in hearing the familiar sound of two friends bickering.

"What's all this fog doing here?" asked Twilight. "I thought weather was supposed to be optional."

Mak-Thar said, "And I thought that *you* of all people would appreciate the atmosphere."

"I appreciate atmosphere when it makes sense," said Twilight. "But when I go from a scorching desert afternoon to a foggy swampy evening, I have difficulty suspending my disbelief."

"We're in a new hex," said Mak-Thar. "Of *course* the weather and time of day will be different."

"This is stupid."

"You know, considering all the elven mumbo jumbo you claim to believe—"

"The sacred path of Selene is *not* mumbo jumbo!"

"—it amazes me that you have such difficulty accepting basic facts of reality."

Fred's knee collapsed. Helen caught him and guided him to a sitting position on a nearby log.

Nightshade asked, "Hey guys, what did I miss?"

"You! Get off my back right now so I can lecture you in the face!"

"Ew! Are we in a swamp?"

"Why yes," said Twilight. "Didn't you want to be in a swamp?"

"Not really. My elf climbs a tree to see if she can get above the fog."

"We should try to find Fred and Helen," said Twilight. "I thought they were right behind us."

"If you hadn't run away so far, I'm sure they would have been."

"You guys abandoned Fred and Helen? O. M. G.!"

"We didn't abandon them," said Mak-Thar. "We simply outran them."

"I always assume Fred can take care of himself," said Twilight. "But with that knee ..." Twilight called, "Fred!"

Fred opened his mouth to shout back, but Helen put her hand on his arm.

"Wait a bit," she said. "This is good stuff."

"Abandoning the fighters," said Nightshade. Her voice sounded like she was, perhaps, in a tree now. "That's cold. And Fred's so sweet. Real dumb. But sweet."

Fred cocked an eyebrow at Helen.

Helen smiled and shrugged.

Nightshade continued, "I mean, I can understand abandoning Helen. She's a—"

"I hope you are going to say she's a barbarian," said Twilight.

"Yes," agreed Nightshade. "That's exactly what I was going to say."

Helen's shoulders shook with laughter.

"Because she may have just given up her life to help us escape," said Twilight. "She may be the bravest human I've ever known."

Helen called, "I didn't know you cared!"

"You fiend!" yelled Twilight. "Where are you? Why didn't you answer me?"

"You asked for Fred, not me."

"I'm here, too," said Fred. "Just a second, and we'll catch up."

Fred braced himself to stand, but Helen put a restraining hand on his knee. "Forget that! You guys need to come to us. Fred's done walking for the day."

"Okay," said Twilight. "We're coming."

Their voices came closer. Nightshade wanted to know why they were in the swamp. Mak-Thar wanted to reprimand her for not being awake. Twilight was just in a bad mood, sniping at both of them.

Because of an intervening pond, it was some time before the five of them were reunited. But finally, they were close enough to see each others' faces—or at least the grey, foggy silhouettes of each others' faces—and Twilight said, "Helen, please tell us you know the way out of this accursed swamp."

Helen shrugged. "I'm sure any direction leads out if you walk far enough."

"You're a big help," said Nightshade.

"I'm afraid we can go no farther today," said Mak-Thar. "Fred and I have been forced to make a forced march. Entering a new hexagon is now impossible."

"That, and Fred's knee hurts like a barbarian," said Helen. "We're camping here, kiddos."

"Well, my elf didn't have to walk today, so she finds the way out and makes a nice camp for you all in a dry, grassy meadow."

"Yeah, okay," said Helen. "I've been trying to be nice to you, but I'm getting real sick of you telling us about your elf. Furthermore, if you pass out one more time, I'm just going to leave you there, even if we're fording a river."

Nightshade sniffed. "Yes, well, I may not be able to walk into the woods and bring back a big chunk of bloody meat, but I'm also not going to take orders from a half-naked chick who's dumber than the party's mule."

"Ah, in point of fact," said Mak-Thar, "my intelligence score has remained unchanged by my reincarnation, so there is actually no shame in—"

"I may be dumb, but I'm reliable," said Helen. "You think being cute and perky gives you a license to be useless."

"Useless?" asked Nightshade. "You think I'm useless?"

"I'm sure she didn't mean—" said Mak-Thar.

Nightshade said, "Those wombats would have eaten you for

breakfast if I hadn't been there to save your fat, armored butt!"

"You weren't trying to save us," said Helen. "You were just trying to save your stylish little backpack!"

"I've got more power in my stylish little backpack than you have in your entire barbarian body!"

"You want to cross me, little sprite? You want to draw that blade and show me what your petite little arms can do?"

Desperation in his voice, Mak-Thar said, "Actually, sprites are—"

"You know," said Fred. And everyone stopped arguing and looked at him. "It's been a while since I've told anyone a story."

CHAPTER SEVENTEEN: IN WHICH FRED TELLS A STORY.

I WAS OUT ON THIS ADVENTURE one time with an elf and a thief and a mage. We were in a dungeon, and I thought things were going pretty good.

Things hadn't started out so good. The thief was one of those types that just wants to get things done, and the mage was one of those types that wants to sit and plan. But they were both professionals, and they knew how to work together.

The elf was on his first adventure, and I guess it wasn't as grandiose as adventures in his imagination. It was a dungeon crawl—a pretty good dungeon crawl—goblin king, pit traps, secret doors, treasure chests—the whole bit. But it wasn't exactly what you would call a heroic quest, and he was disappointed. At least for a while. By the time we got to the big treasure room, he'd kind of calmed down. So I guess that's why I thought things were going good.

Everybody was still arguing, but I thought they'd all kind of accepted each other, you know? The elf knew the mage was going to be magey and quote rulebooks all the time. The mage knew that no one was going to care as much about planning as he did. The thief had long since realized that things were going to happen only as fast as they happened, and I can't say he was particularly happy about that, but I thought he'd *accepted* it.

I dunno. When I think about it now, I wonder, where does Fighter Fred fit into all this? Did the thief see me as a guy who kept things moving, or was I slowing him down? Did the mage need my help making plans, or was it enough for me to do whatever wacky thing he thought up next? Was the elf just a whiner, or was there something I could have done to make the adventure more adventurous for him?

I guess what I'm getting at is that I often ask myself whether I did enough. And now that I'm sitting here telling you the story, I have to admit that I didn't. To tell the truth, I didn't do much at all. You know me. I don't think; I react.

So I didn't worry about what my friends might need. I didn't try to plan ahead. I just tried to get along with everyone. I made sure I wasn't the problem. But now I can see they needed more than that.

They needed more, and I let them down. Here's what happened in the end:

We got into a big battle—a lot like the one we just ran away from. It was giant spiders instead of scorpions, and we had a treasure we wanted to escape with, but otherwise it was the same kind of battle—too many bugs for the four of us to fight.

The difference was, we had a mage who could cast fireballs. I dunno, maybe we should have run away. Or maybe running wouldn't have worked. It wasn't like we had a nice swamp to hide in. We had long corridors of dungeon between us and the exit and no reason to believe the spiders would ever stop chasing us.

So the elf and the thief and I made a stand. Not a final stand—we just had to buy the mage a little bit of time. So we hacked at the spiders and held them off while the mage worked up enough magic to cast his fireball.

The spiders were jamming the corridor so tight that the ones in back were climbing over the ones in front. It was like a wall of spiders, and I thought for sure it was going to collapse on us.

Well, right as the wall starts to tumble, this flaming ball roars past my ear and disappears up the corridor. Behind the wall of spiders, I see this flash, and then there was this tremendous roar, and the roar was made of pure, red heat.

I swear it was so hot that my eyebrows came off.

When the flames cleared, the battle was over. All the spiders were husks of ash. They didn't even twitch.

I looked at my friends, and we were also in pretty bad shape. Our clothes were smoking. Our faces were blistered. Our hair was charred. But we were all still alive. We had done it.

I felt so proud of everyone. Even though we'd had our differences, we'd all pulled together when it mattered most. We'd made a stand and bought the mage the time he needed. We had won.

And there in that soot-blackened corridor, as we were all congratulating the mage for the fireball that had saved the day, the thief stabbed the mage right in the gut.

It happened that quick. The mage went from hero to corpse. The thief went from comrade to traitor.

And me? ... I couldn't react.

One of my friends had killed another, and I couldn't believe it had happened. I froze. I completely froze. In that moment, the thief could have killed me, too, and I wouldn't have been able to stop him. I couldn't even move.

The only thing that saved me was that the elf was between me and the thief. He couldn't kill me without going through the elf first.

Those two were evenly matched. And they'd both been evenly cooked by the fireball. Whoever got the first strike would win, and this time it was the elf who was quicker.

Good thing for me, because, like I say, I wasn't moving. I was still staring at the corpse of the mage when the thief's corpse was added to the floor.

I'm telling you this story because it's the only adventure I've been able to think about since then. I can't remember my other stories because this is the one that keeps haunting me. I keep thinking about what happened. I keep wondering where I went wrong. And I think the answer is that I didn't realize it was my job to make things go right.

My friends murdered each other. And I was the one who could have stopped it.

CHAPTER EIGHTEEN: IN WHICH OUR HEROES STAND AROUND IN A SWAMP.

THE FOGGY SILHOUETTES were silent for a moment. A duck flew overhead and landed somewhere with a gentle splash.

Mak-Thar shifted his hind legs and said, "That's not precisely the way it happened. Fred has left out certain facts."

"We know how it happened," said Twilight. "Fred's story isn't about facts. He's trying to explain how he feels."

"Fred feels gloomy," said Nightshade. She sounded surprised.

"He feels responsible for a lot of bad stuff that wasn't his fault," said Helen. She shook her head. "I thought you were getting over this."

"I don't think I *should* get over it," said Fred. "I think it's happening again, and I have to be the one to stop it."

"What's happening again?" asked Mak-Thar.

Twilight said, "Helen and Nightshade were threatening to kill each other."

"But I ..." Helen didn't finish her excuse. There was guilt in her voice.

"We have to get along," said Fred. "Because our party is the only thing we've got. Our treasure does us no good until we get to a place where we can spend it. A sword in your hand does you no good unless you have a friend at your back. Everything we do, we have to do together."

Helen said, "I'm sorry I threatened Nightshade. It won't happen again."

Nightshade said, "Well, I don't want to fight with party members." She remembered Mak-Thar. "Or NPMs."

Mak-Thar nodded.

Nightshade said, "It just seems like every time I try to help, you guys say I'm doing it wrong."

"You really did do a great job of fighting the wombats," said Fred. "Everyone's grateful we survived that."

"Yeah," Helen admitted.

Fred said, "I think, maybe, you're a little bit young for an elf, and the rest of us are a little bit jaded."

Twilight said, "I, too, was once a young elf excited about his first adventure. That was only a few weeks ago! I should be more understanding, but sometimes your enthusiasm just reminds me of how cynical I have become. I think, like Fred, I am having trouble dealing with how much I have changed because of our previous adventure."

"Well, if anyone was changed by the adventure, it was me," said Mak-Thar. "And I don't understand what any of you are talking about. Fred, what happened in the Dungeon of Doom was not your fault. The thief who was sometimes known as 'Paul' was simply evil. He told me he was neutral, but it was foolish of me to take his word for it. I was the one who invited him into the party, so I must bear the full blame. I should have taken him to the Temple of Good and asked them to cast Detect Evil on him."

Twilight said, "I'm not sure evil works that way."

"It most certainly does. At present, it is too dark to read, but in the morning I will be able to show you the exact page of *The Adventurer's Guide*."

Helen said, "Fred, you should listen to the mule. He knows what he's talking about."

Mak-Thar lifted his head and flipped his ears with satisfaction.

It was weird to see Helen and Mak-Thar agreeing on something. Obviously, they were just being nice, but that was weird, too. Helen and Mak-Thar were both quite willing to tell truths that weren't nice.

"So ... are people starting to reconsider my pact idea?" asked Nightshade. "I mean, I know Helen just apologized, and that was ... nice, I guess. But if we have a no-kill pact, I think I'd sleep a lot easier."

"Elves don't—" said Twilight. "Oh, never mind. Nightshade, if it makes you feel any better, I solemnly promise not to kill my fellow party members."

"Or NPMs," said Nightshade.

"Or Mak-Thar, whom I also count as a party member."

"Yeah, okay," said Helen. "This *should* go without saying, but I also promise not to kill any of you guys, and if I threaten you, it just means I think you need your butt kicked."

"I promise not to initiate violence against any party members," said Mak-Thar. "And if I fail my NPM loyalty check, I will attempt to run away rather than betray the party."

"That's sweet," said Helen.

"Okay, I'll go next," said Nightshade. "I promise not to kill any of you guys, not even if it's the only way I can hide a dark secret from my back story."

Another duck flew in and joined the previous duck. They quacked at each other for a bit and agreed to share the pond.

"Fred?" asked Nightshade. "It's your turn."

They expected him to take a turn? After the story he had just told them, how could they not know his heart?

"Nightshade," he asked, "do you trust me?"

"Yeah."

She was the one who didn't know him. Helen was an old friend who didn't need to hear his promise. Mak-Thar and Twilight were new friends, but the three of them had been through so much together that they didn't need to hear his promise, either.

But Nightshade was new. And she was here only because Fred had invited her along. Helen was here only because she wanted to help him. If the two of them couldn't get along, it was Fred's fault for putting them together.

Mak-Thar had claimed responsibility for Paul. Fred was

responsible for Nightshade and Helen ... and all of them, really. He was at the center, and he had asked Helen to lead.

Fred now realized that had been unfair.

"Does everybody trust me?" he asked. They all did, but he wanted to make them say it.

They said it.

"Okay," said Fred. "Then I promise to be in charge. If someone else in this party is causing you problems, I promise to be the one you can talk to. If something needs to be said to someone, then I promise to be the one who says it. I know you all think I'm kind of dumb, so I won't do any thinking. But I promise to listen to what you all think and then be in charge of picking the thing we do."

Helen said, "That won't stop us from arguing."

Twilight said, "*Nothing* can stop Mak-Thar and me from arguing. That's not really the point."

"Well, as an NPM," said Mak-Thar, "I can't have any input on whom we choose for party leader. But if Yellin' Helen is comfortable stepping down into the role of guide—"

"I'm not your guide."

"Helen's still in charge of telling us what we need to do to stay alive," said Fred. "I'm just in charge of making sure you listen to her."

"Oh," said Mak-Thar. "Can I be in charge of combat tactics?"

"No," said Twilight.

"Sometimes," said Fred. "But sometimes other people have good ideas, too."

"Why are people suddenly in charge of stuff?" asked Nightshade. "I thought we were adventurers, not a military unit."

"I want Helen in charge of telling us how to stay alive so that we can all stay alive," said Fred. "And I think I should be in charge of asking you to do what she says because it seems better than letting her kick your butt."

"You should trust him," said Twilight. "He has your best interests at heart."

"I trust him," said Nightshade. "I said I trust him. But you guys all know each other, and now I feel like you're all ganging up on me."

Nightshade was going to be his biggest problem. It certainly didn't help that she'd missed out on several battles.

"Well, we all have things to prove to each other," said Fred. "To tell you the truth, Nightshade, I'm not sure how this will work out. I've never tried to be in charge before, so I probably won't be very good at it. But I think I should try. If it doesn't work out ... well, you can leave the party as soon as we find a safe place. What do you say? Will you give it a try?"

"Yeah, sure. Whatever. My elf— I'm going to look for some mushrooms."

CHAPTER NINETEEN: IN WHICH OUR HEROES SIT AROUND AND SMELL.

FRED DIDN'T KNOW HOW TO BUILD A FIRE in a swamp, but that was okay. Fred didn't know how to build a fire in a forest, either. Fire was one of those things that just sort of happened in the world. Mages could cast spells. Thieves could pick locks. Adventurers who were not Fred could start fires.

Because they had all just promised not to kill each other, the evening was a moment of solemn camaraderie. Helen and Twilight worked together to build the fire. While searching for wood, they found a grassy tussock big enough for everyone to stand on. Mak-Thar made them beds on the tussock by grazing and trampling the marsh grass. Nightshade helped by not falling unconscious in the fog. Also, she brought some mushrooms.

So they camped in the swamp, and it was almost like camping in the forest except that they had to eat snakes and then listen all night long to the croaks of frogs.

In the morning, they were still in the swamp and the swamp was still in the fog. As Helen restarted the campfire, she sighed.

Mak-Thar and Nightshade were taking advantage of the morning light to read *The Adventurer's Guide* together. Twilight was out in the swamp somewhere.

Helen looked pointedly at Fred and sighed again. She was trying to tell him something, but Fred wasn't getting it. Maybe she wanted to talk to him in private, but that was impossible because the tussock was so small.

"Hellooooo," called Twilight.

"Hellooooo," shouted Helen.

"Oh, thank goodness! Say 'hello' again?"

"Hellooooo," called Helen.

After a bit more helloing, Twilight sloshed into view. "This fog is terrible! I was completely turned around."

"I guess maybe we should stay together while we're in the swamp," said Fred. "At least until the fog lifts."

"I liked the forest better," said Nightshade. "How long are we going to be in the swamp?"

"We can't move!" said Mak-Thar.

"We *can* move," said Twilight. "But I'm not sure which way we should *go*. I was scouting around, and I confess that I couldn't find the desert anywhere."

Helen sighed again. Fred realized the sigh meant, *Yeah, Fred. That's what I've been trying to tell you. We're stuck in this swamp, and I'm afraid to admit that I don't know the way out.*

Nightshade said, "My— Um … my, oh my. I think I'll climb a tree and look for the desert."

"We can't *go* to the desert," insisted Mak-Thar.

"Oh, right," said Nightshade.

"Why not?" asked Fred.

Mak-Thar said, "Show Fred the book."

"… Okay." Doubtfully, Nightshade handed Fred the *Adventurer's Guide* that she and Mak-Thar had been reading.

"Read the bit about 'Forced March'," said Mak-Thar.

Aloud, Fred read, " 'If a party continues beyond one hundred percent of its movement allowance, the additional movement is considered to be a forced march.' "

"Fred can read!" said Nightshade.

"Of course he can read," said Helen. "Did you think he was a barbarian?"

"Well, yeah!"

Helen shook her head. "If you can't see his navel, he's not a barbarian."

"Yes, yes," said Mak-Thar. "Fred's literacy is an amazing accomplishment. But he didn't read the important bit. Fred, read what happens to parties who fail to rest after a forced march."

There were a lot of sentences about Forced March. Why was—? Oh. Mak-Thar was probably worried about this bit: " 'For each ten percent increment by which the party moves, beasts of burden have a ten percent chance of dropping dead.' "

"Dropping dead!" said Mak-Thar. "Did everyone hear that?"

"Considering we're all standing on a tussock only seven feet wide," said Twilight, "I think it is safe to say that we all heard that."

"Well, that should settle it," said Mak-Thar. "We aren't going anywhere today."

Fred looked to Helen. "Can we rest here for a day?"

Helen looked around at the brackish water, the dense fog, and the curious eyeballs of the nearby frogs. "Sure. This is a great place to camp."

So they rested. All day. And they were careful not to talk much, because they were miserable. The only thing worse than spending all day within seven feet of a wet mule is spending all day within seven feet of a wet mule and a wet barbarian.

During that long, wet day, only one good thing happened: Twilight had time to work on the wombat hides. He laid them out on the tussock and cut them according to Sage's pattern. He offered to teach everyone how to sew, but only Nightshade was interested. The only thing worse than spending all day within seven feet of a wet mule and a wet barbarian is sitting right next to a wet mule and a wet barbarian because the elves are taking up too much space with stinky wombat hides.

Well ... actually, lots of things are worse.

That evening, as they were eating their barbecued frogs, Fred said, "You know, this reminds me of the time that I was guarding a caravan with the half-pint Stinky La Foote. We were only seven days out of Basetown, and already we'd been attacked by a tribe of orcs and two gangs of bandits. We'd lost a few guards, and some others were wounded. The merchants were getting nervous. But then Stinky came up with a plan.

"He said that the next time we were attacked, we should just offer up a treasure chest. If the bandits were reasonable, they'd realize that getting one chest with no fight is better than tangling with a caravan that had already won three battles.

"Well, the merchants thought that was a terrible plan, especially when Stinky said they should give up their largest chest. But when he told them *why* he wanted to use their largest chest, they all agreed."

Fred waited.

Mak-Thar asked, "Can we assume that you will tell us why your colleague wanted to use their largest chest?"

"I'm glad you asked," said Fred. "You see, I didn't tell you right away because Stinky didn't tell *me* right away. I didn't find out about the plan until the caravan leader spotted bandits riding over the hill.

"As soon as the warning cry rang out, all the other caravan guards got in position to defend the wagons. But Stinky grabs my arm and says, 'Come on. We've got to do our part of the plan.'

"I say, 'What plan?'

"He says, 'I got a plan.' And he takes me into one of the covered wagons.

"Well, their biggest chest was there, and it was a pretty big chest. Whatever it held, I sure didn't want to carry it. Stinky opens the chest and ... it was empty!

"Before I can ask what happened to the stuff in the chest, Stinky says, 'Get in!'

"You know me. I like to get along with people. So I got in. And Stinky got in with me. Then he closed the lid.

"You ever close a self-latching chest? That's a real satisfying sound, isn't it? You just close the chest, and there's a tiny little *snick!* And then the chest is latched.

"Yeah, well, it doesn't sound so pretty when you're inside the chest. I was about to ask Stinky what he'd gotten me into, but that would have been dumb because he would have just said, 'The chest!' I realized I had to keep quiet and see how the whole thing played out.

"And you know, at first, it wasn't so bad? There was a tiny bit of light that slipped in through the crack around the lid, and I said to myself, if there's light, there must be air. So I didn't panic.

"And the chest was made of this real nice wood that smelled kind of earthy and kind of pungent and kind of sweet. So for a while, I convinced myself that being trapped inside a chest with a half-pint on top of me wasn't so bad. Not so bad.

"Merchants are good talkers, so the first part of Stinky's plan went off without a hitch. The bandits were convinced to accept the chest as ransom, and Stinky and I were hauled off the wagon.

"But a problem came up right away. I was too heavy to lift. That got them all excited, of course, because they figured that Stinky and me must be a real nice heap of treasure. They had ropes and poles and things, and as the caravan rolled away, the bandits figured out how to hook us up to a pair of horses and drag us along the ground.

"I don't know if you've ever been dragged along the ground, but the funny thing about the ground is that it's not as smooth as it looks. In fact, it's bumpy. So Stinky and I were bumping our plate mail together, and it was a good thing we both had armor, because otherwise we would have bludgeoned ourselves to death. In fact, even with the armor, we got a little tenderized. But you know, that was not the worst part.

"Do you know how Stinky La Foote got his name?"

"I assume," said Mak-Thar, "that his father's name was 'La Foote' and his mother named him 'Stinky'."

Fred considered this. "Well, maybe. But I want to be clear

that this was a good name. It wasn't meant ironically. It wasn't a case like, say, you have a friend who's half hill giant and you call him 'Tiny'. Stinky's name is somewhat accurate. And when you're trapped inside a wooden box with him, it becomes especially accurate.

"Now, I didn't have a sundial, but we must have bumped along the ground for three or four hours, and over that time, the sweet smell of the wood faded beyond distant memory, and Stinky's name just got more and more accurate. Did I mention it was summer? There was no sun inside the chest, of course, but half-pints can put out a lot of heat. They may eat two breakfasts, but they burn it all off by lunchtime. Sharing a box with a half-pint is like sharing a box with a campfire, except that campfires don't have luxurious mats of hair on their feet.

"In fact," Fred admitted, "it was so warm inside that box that I may have started to sweat. And after four hours, I may not have smelled so good, either.

"Well, all this would have been awful if the bandits had left us in the chest for four hours before opening it. But it was awfuller than that. Can you believe they left us there overnight?

"In the middle of the night, when I think all the bandits are asleep, I'm telling Stinky, 'Let's get out. I think I can break this chest apart with my bare hands.'

"But Stinky says, 'No. Gotta wait till morning. Stick with the plan.'

"So I stuck with the plan, which apparently was to jump out and surprise the bandits. Of course, Stinky was cutting off circulation to my legs, so I wasn't sure I could jump anymore.

"But I needn't have worried. Long about noon the next day, the bandit chief comes riding into camp and wants to know what the boys have brought for him. Stinky and I can hear him walking all around the chest, and I'm so excited to get out that the only way I can keep from screaming is to gnaw on Stinky's helmet.

"When you meet him, ask him to show you the teeth marks.

"Anyway, the bandit walks all around the chest two, maybe

twenty times, and finally he stops and puts his hand on the latch. "*Snick!*

"The top came off that chest so hard that it broke his jaw. Yep. It knocked him out cold. And the bandit chief was the lucky one. Because the next thing to come out of that chest was our smell.

"The bandits tried to run, but it was too late. Our smell chased them all around their campsite and beat up every one of them. In the confusion, Stinky and I got away. We never even had to draw our swords.

"As an added bonus, there was no place for us to bathe before we reached the market town. The caravan leaders put Stinky a quarter mile in front of the caravan and me a quarter mile behind. All the goods were delivered safely, because not even orcs would attack a caravan that smelled that bad."

CHAPTER TWENTY: IN WHICH OUR HEROES FIND A SIDE QUEST.

THE NEXT MORNING, the fog still had not lifted. Mak-Thar, however, no longer believed that he had a ten percent chance of death, so he was ready to go. Fred's knee felt better, so he was ready to go. The elves and Helen had spent most of the previous day stuck on the tussock with Fred and Mak-Thar, so they were very ready to go. Clearly, it was time to go. The only problem was, they didn't know how to pick a direction.

Both Helen and Twilight insisted that there was no way the party could have wandered very far from the desert, but neither had been able to find it again. Not even Nightshade claimed to know where the desert was, although she did climb several trees to look for it. Finally Mak-Thar, after taking a look at the map, proposed a solution:

"Let us simply start walking in one direction. The swamp is only one hex wide. As long as we maintain the direction, we are likely to hit the desert or the Impassable Mountains. Of course, the swamp is several hexes *long*. If we accidentally choose north or south, we will still be in the swamp at nightfall. In that case, however, we will be able to eliminate not only the direction of travel, but also its opposite, thus guaranteeing that we shall escape the swamp on the following day."

Helen approved, so Fred said, "Great. Let's go this way," and they began wading through the swamp.

The fog did not lift.

After a few hours of sloshing through the fog, Twilight asked, "When you say that weather is optional … what does that mean?"

Mak-Thar lifted his chin and assumed the pose of a mule lecturer. "Most of *The Adventurer's Guide* discusses principles that apply universally. For example, the experience points you gain on one adventure are not taken away if you journey to a new town. Some of these principles are only *mostly* universal—for example, the fact that goblins carry two to twelve electrum pieces. It might be possible to run into some goblins that carry silver or gold, but those will be setting-specific goblins. Randomly encountered goblins will have electrum.

"But there are also *optional* rules, and these are true only some of the time. To be precise, they are true 25 to 75 percent of the time, so if you like, you can think of optional rules as being in the interquartile range."

Twilight asked, "Are there people who like to think of things as being in the interquartile range?"

"I've been to the Interquartile Range," said Helen. "The water flows west on the other side."

Mak-Thar put his ears back. "The point is that, although *The Adventurer's Guide* is quite clear about how the weather works, in fact it only works that way in some places. Other places, like the Wombat Wilderness, apparently don't have weather."

"So you think this fog is just following the rules?" asked Twilight.

"I am not certain," admitted Mak-Thar. "Fog counts as

special weather, so it has only a one-in-thirty-six chance of occurring, according to the Weather Change Table. However, once we *have* fog, there is a one-in-six chance that it will persist each day. So three days of fog *is* unusual, but the chances of it being foggy again tomorrow are still one in six."

"What are the chances that the fog is made by someone who hates us and wants us to stay lost in this swamp forever?" asked Nightshade.

"Actually," said Mak-Thar, "there is a group of scholars who believe that some weather simply comes into being because it is dramatically appropriate. Divine intervention or psionic feedback are hypothesized as possible causes of such a phenomenon. Personally, I think it's rubbish."

"Rubbish?" asked Twilight. "I've been feeling *exactly* like this fog rolled in just so we would become lost."

"Yeah!" said Nightshade. "We elves are sensitive to this sort of thing."

"Elves are emotional and easy prey for confirmation bias," said Mak-Thar. "When we got lost in the Wombat Wilderness, there was no fog. No one felt that being lost was dramatically appropriate."

"We didn't get lost," said Helen.

"Well, one could argue that we are not truly lost now," said Mak-Thar. "Or one could argue that this episode of being lost is not, in fact, dramatically appropriate. Twilight and Nightshade are simply seeing situations which confirm their hypothesis and ignoring situations which contradict."

"Yeah, well, now I'm perceiving lizard men," said Nightshade. "Are they *really* slithering through the water to ambush us, or is that just elven confirmation bias?"

"Lizard men?" asked Mak-Thar. "Where—"

Six scaly humanoid figures rose from the murk of the swamp—one of them so close that it was able to throw a sack over Twilight's head. Fred and Helen tried to put themselves between the lizard men and the rest of the party, but the footing was treacherous, and the lizard men were agile. As two of them hoisted Twilight onto their shoulders, the other four drew flashing blades.

"Don't attack us!" yelled Mak-Thar. "I'm neutral just like you!"

The lizard men hesitated, staring at the talking mule.

Helen drew her sword and struck a lizard man down. Fred protected her flank and called, "Nightshade! Don't let them steal Twilight!"

Blades clashed. Fred had to block attacks from all directions as the lizard men danced around him. His own feet could barely move.

"Sleep spell, Sleep spell," murmured Nightshade, rummaging in her pack. "Where'd I put my Sleep spell?"

"HEE-HAW!" yelled Mak-Thar, and he went charging after Twilight.

Helen cut another lizard man off at the knees. Fred got lucky and poked one in the arm. The wounded creature fled, leaving one unwounded lizard man all alone.

The unwounded one looked from Fred to Helen ... then he turned and ran away.

Meanwhile, Mak-Thar had managed to catch up to Twilight's abductors. He grabbed the sack in his teeth, saying, "Lert herm ger! Thert's *mer* erlf."

The lizard men let go, and Twilight fell into the swamp with a splash. Mak-Thar stopped, and the lizard men kept running. The sound of splashing feet and swishing tails diminished into the fog.

Twilight sat up and removed the sack from his head. "What was that all about?"

"Another random encounter," said Mak-Thar.

"They were after me!" said Twilight. "Why?"

"Probably because you were closest," said Helen.

"I don't really understand lizard men," admitted Mak-Thar. "*The Adventurer's Guide* says they are neutral, but it also says they like to abduct people and eat them. That sounds evil to me."

"All those frogs and snakes we ate probably think that *we* are evil," said Nightshade.

"Hm. Good point."

"Oh," said Twilight. "Do you think the lizard men are the sacred guardians of the swamp's amphibians and reptiles?"

"No," said Mak-Thar. "I think they are just another entry in the Swamp column of the Wilderness Encounter Table."

"We'll see," said Twilight. "What treasure are they supposed to have?"

Nightshade already had *The Adventurer's Guide* out and was looking them up. "Lizard men. Treasure type D."

"That's in their lair," said Mak-Thar. "Is there an individual treasure type listed?"

"No," said Nightshade.

"Then they have no treasure," said Mak-Thar.

Twilight said, "So if we search them and find treasure, you will have to admit that this was not a random encounter."

Mak-Thar bit off a cattail and chewed on it. "Well … that would be evidence supporting your hypothesis."

Helen said, "They aren't carrying any treasure."

"Ah," said Mak-Thar. "That is consistent with *my* hypothesis. Put the swords in one of my saddle bags, and we can continue on."

"These random encounters are really low on treasure," said Nightshade.

"Don't worry," said Mak-Thar. "We'll at least get the experience points—even for the ones who ran away."

"I think talking mules frighten them," said Fred.

"Really?" asked Mak-Thar.

"It makes sense," said Twilight. "*I* was frightened by two giant lizards throwing a sack over my head, so why wouldn't they find us equally strange?"

"I certainly find you guys equally strange," said Helen.

Twilight fingered the muddy sack that had been thrown over his head. "I wonder where they got this material."

"Maybe they took the sack from the last adventurers who came through this swamp," said Fred.

"Were they wearing clothes?" asked Twilight.

Helen looked at the bodies lying in the water. "They are wearing clothes."

"Serapes," said Nightshade.

"What are serapes?" asked Mak-Thar.

"It's like a blanket with a hole in the middle."

"Oh," said Mak-Thar. "What's the difference between a serape and a poncho?"

Nightshade frowned. "I thought a poncho was a rain coat."

Twilight lifted the edge of the cloth worn by a fallen lizard man. "I think it's called a tabard. But you humans have a lot of words that mean the same thing."

"I'm not a human," said Nightshade. "I'm an elf."

"Oh, right."

Helen asked, "Why would you wear clothes if you like to ambush people by slithering through the mud?"

"Are they uniforms?" asked Fred.

"I don't think it matters," said Mak-Thar. "*The Adventurer's Guide* is very vague on clothing. In fact, it's not even on the Equipment List, despite the fact that you are all wearing some. I assume that means that clothing should not be construed to be significant."

"It's not significant for *mules*," said Helen. "But for the rest of us, clothing is important. Haven't you noticed that Basetown has tailor shops?"

Mak-Thar frowned thoughtfully. "I thought they were just there to give out adventure hooks."

Helen looked at the footprints in the mud. "We could backtrack them."

"And find their lair," said Nightshade. "Treasure type D has lots of gold pieces."

"I don't think we should," said Mak-Thar. "That sounds like a side quest. And if we need to retreat, there is no place nearby where we can safely regain hit points."

"Fred?" asked Helen.

Fred thought that getting some treasure might make people happy. But getting a chance to really dry out their socks would make them even more happy. "Let's stick with the plan of walking in one direction."

So they continued walking. But that was not their last encounter with the uniformed lizard men. Less than an hour later, they came upon a path through the swamp.

"How can you tell it's a path?" Nightshade asked. "All the dirt here is underwater."

"It's a path because the vegetation has been knocked down, and because I see footprints and tail marks in the mud," said Helen.

"So maybe that just means a lot of lizard men have walked by here," said Nightshade.

"Yes," said Helen, patiently. "That's what a path is."

Mak-Thar came forward to inspect the path. "Oh, this is bad. We shouldn't be getting terrain details like this for a random encounter. This is some sort of side quest."

"Perhaps it's a way out of the swamp," suggested Twilight. "We should see where the path leads."

Fred asked Helen, "What do *you* think?"

"I think this trail was made by a lot of lizard men," said Helen. "If we just go barging into them, we'll get our mule whupped."

"I do not wish to be whupped," said Mak-Thar.

"I want you to let me scout," said Helen.

"I'll scout with her," said Nightshade. "My elf— Uh. My *elven* boots make me sneaky."

"Your boots are sneaky in the forest," said Helen. "In the swamp, you slosh."

"I don't slosh."

"You slosh. You need elven hip waders."

"Take her with you anyway," said Fred. "I don't think any of us should wander off alone."

Helen scowled, but she didn't argue.

To Nightshade, Fred said, "Please do what Helen says and stay out of trouble. If you run into any lizard men, I want you both to come back and warn us."

And so Helen and Nightshade sloshed away into the fog. Fred, Mak-Thar, and Twilight stood in the water beside the path and waited.

After a while, Fred began to wonder if they would come back. Maybe he should have specified how *far* they were allowed to follow the trail.

"Was that wise to send them off together?" Mak-Thar asked. "I don't think they like each other."

"It was brilliant," said Twilight. "Remember how you and I faced the band of goblins together and then became fast friends?"

"That's not precisely how it happened," said Mak-Thar. "In fact, we were not *facing* the goblins; we were running away. And we had to become fast friends, because slow friends would have perished."

Twilight raised his eyebrows. "Why, Mak-Thar! Was that a joke?"

"Yes it was," said Mak-Thar. "And do not act so surprised. Although I am a mule, I have retained my original sense of humor."

Fred hadn't known Mak-Thar had a sense of humor, but maybe he just wasn't educated enough to get any of Mak-Thar's jokes.

"I'm not expecting them to become friends," said Fred. "I just thought that if she had someone else along, she wouldn't be tempted to charge into the lair and take them all on herself."

"Good point," said Twilight. "Although, in that case, you could have just sent Helen."

Twilight thought Fred had been talking about Nightshade? Oh well. Fred didn't bother to correct him.

"She's not as foolish as you think," said Mak-Thar. "Using scrolls to overcome the limitations of first-level spellcasting is quite a clever stratagem. I don't approve, of course. I believe the power of higher levels should be earned. But if she had the opportunity, she was quite wise to take advantage of it."

"How *did* she get all those scrolls, anyway?" asked Twilight.

"It's a puzzle," said Mak-Thar. "No doubt the answer is in her 'really cool' yet mysteriously vague back story."

"Does it bother you that she refers to her own past life experiences as a 'back story'?" asked Twilight.

"Of course not," said Mak-Thar.

"I guess I was asking Fred."

Fred didn't answer. He thought he heard sloshing.

Twilight cupped a hand to his ear. A minute later, Nightshade and Helen had returned. Neither was dead. They weren't even maimed.

"You tell *me* to stay out of trouble," complained Nightshade. "I practically had to *drag* her out of harm's way."

"I'm very quiet, and I think I could have gotten closer," said Helen.

"We were close enough," said Nightshade. "If you had wanted us to get closer, you should have let me turn invisible."

"Yeah," said Helen. "Funny thing: Invisibility doesn't mean as much when you're sloshing through half a foot of water."

"Are either of you going to tell us what you saw?" asked Mak-Thar.

"It was a temple," said Nightshade.

"An *evil* temple," said Helen. "Fred, let me go overthrow it. I'll be back in an hour."

Mak-Thar and Twilight exchanged questions with a glance.

Fred asked, "Can you get us close enough that we can *all* take a look?"

CHAPTER TWENTY–ONE: IN WHICH OUR HEROES SPY ON AN EVIL TEMPLE.

IN THE CENTER of a small, shallow lake sat an impressively huge slab of black granite. The granite formed the foundation underneath a circle of white marble pillars, which supported a red granite dome.

"See?" said Nightshade. "It's like a scoop of Neapolitan ice cream."

"What's Neapolitan ice cream?" asked Fred.

"It's an elven thing," said Nightshade.

"Neapolitan ice cream is not an elven thing," hissed Twilight.

Twilight was hissing not because he was turning into a snake, but because the five of them were hiding on the lake's edge, and Twilight didn't want to attract anyone's attention. The temple in the middle of the lake was approachable only by a wooden walkway. As they watched, a group of humans in gray tabards walked along the walkway, heading toward a group of bedraggled lizard men.

Fred realized the lizard men were looking bedraggled because they wore mud-soaked clothing. Had they been naked, they would have looked scary.

The humans met the lizard men, and a woman with a staff started speaking.

Fred couldn't understand what she was saying. Her voice was muffled by the fog, but not so much that he would be unable to make out words. Fred guessed that she was speaking in the language of the lizard men.

Whatever she was saying did not take very long. The lizard men bowed their heads and disappeared among the trees.

"See?" said Helen. "It's an evil temple. Let's go overthrow it."

"Evil temples are often run by a powerful cleric," said Mak-Thar. "Or even an undead being that has forced the locals into servitude."

"Okay, Mak-Thar's in favor. Who else wants to come?"

"That was *not* an endorsement," said Mak-Thar. "You think the scorpions were bad? Poison is nothing compared with Power Word Kill."

"Oo!" said Nightshade. "I wonder if they have the power word written down anywhere."

"Nightshade's in," said Helen. "What do you say, Twilight?"

"Whatever I say," hissed Twilight, "I'd like to say it a little farther away from the temple."

"You know," said Fred, "I think that sounds reasonable. Let's pull back about, oh I don't know, maybe two hundred yards. Or a quarter mile."

Helen asked, "We're not backing out, are we, Fred?"

"All I know," said Twilight, "is that whenever we tried to have a discussion in the Dungeon of Doom, we were inconveniently interrupted by goblin attacks."

"Confirmation bias again," said Mak-Thar. "We had plenty of conversations that did not lead to goblin attacks."

"Yes, well, given our close proximity to—"

"I think we might be backing out," said Fred.

"But Fred!"

"Get us out of earshot," said Fred. "Then we can talk."

* * *

It takes a while to move four people and a mule a quarter mile through a swamp—especially when you are trying to do it quietly while avoiding any well-traveled paths. But Helen was a pro, and Fred knew he could count on her to focus on that goal no matter how long it took to find a safe place to discuss the situation. After a long and somewhat intense period of slogging through the swamp, Helen finally declared that they could talk without being heard by the people at the temple. And more importantly, she had calmed down a little.

"Okay," said Fred, still talking in a low voice because he wanted everyone to continue being calm and careful, "I think you all should know that barbarians have a certain primal need to destroy evil temples."

Helen nodded. "I once skipped *breakfast* just so I could destroy an evil temple."

"However," said Fred, "Helen is an experienced adventurer and a high-level member of the Fighters' Guild, so she knows she can't just leave us standing here while she attacks an entire evil temple by herself."

Helen looked confused. "Would that be against the code?"

"It would be against the code," said Fred.

"Oh." Helen frowned. "You're sure?"

"So what I would like," said Fred, "is for us to explain to Helen why she should not attack the evil temple at this time. I think it will help her control her cravings."

"Oh!" said Nightshade. "Is this like an intervention?"

"Is an intervention that thing where you hold someone down while her head spins all the way around?" asked Fred.

"No," said Nightshade.

"Oh," said Fred. "Then maybe this isn't like an intervention."

"Point of information," said Mak-Thar. "I believe *The Adventurer's Guide* suggests that barbarians should be of neutral alignment. This is inconsistent with the idea that they would be driven to destroy evil temples."

Helen said, "When we destroy good temples, people get mad."

"Ah," said Mak-Thar. "Thank you. All is now clear."

Twilight said, "We're all just *assuming* the temple is evil because it's allied with the lizard men and it's in the middle of a swamp."

"And because the clerics wore serapes with green skulls on them," said Nightshade.

"Were those skulls?" asked Twilight. "I thought they might be smiley faces."

Between the fog and the mud, Fred hadn't seen more than vague smudges. Somehow, he doubted that the clerics had been wearing smiley faces.

"Regardless," said Twilight, "their choice of clothing does not necessarily make them evil. Perhaps they wear skulls to acknowledge that death is an integral part of life. Perhaps at other times of the year they adorn their robes with flowers or seeds."

"They're really bad at painting skulls," said Nightshade. "If they tried to paint seeds, they would just look like blobs."

"They all looked evil to me," said Helen. "And they're buddies with the lizard men."

"Lizard men are neutral," said Mak-Thar. "Usually."

"Is that one of those 'mostly universal' rules?" asked Twilight.

"Anyone can become evil when they are recruited by an evil temple," admitted Mak-Thar.

"That settles it," said Helen. "Let's get 'em."

"Please, no," said Mak-Thar. "Regardless of the temple's alignment, it is not our problem. Sage was very specific about the steps needed for our present quest. This temple is for an entirely different adventure."

"Sometimes you find adventure," said Helen. "Sometimes adventure finds you."

"Is that another slogan for Nycadaemon Knickers?" asked Nightshade.

"No," said Helen. "But it should be."

Twilight murmured, "Sometimes adventure finds your knickers; sometimes your knickers … You know, I'd really rather not contemplate what that means."

"The temple is a side quest," said Mak-Thar. "But we don't *need* a side quest. We're having a terrible time with the main quest."

"We've already finished three of the wombat parkas," said Twilight. "And if we can get out of the swamp soon, maybe they won't mold."

"I'm not disparaging your efforts," said Mak-Thar. "I'm just asking us not to spend hit points on a temple that is not our problem."

"They've already attacked us once," said Helen.

"That was an adventure hook," said Mak-Thar. "Don't take the bait."

Helen asked, "What do you think, Fred?"

Fred met her eyes. "You know what I think."

Helen shook her head. "I'm not sure I like this serious side of you. What happened to the fighter who was up for anything?"

Ouch. Did being a leader mean he would no longer be any fun? Fred didn't want that.

He looked at all their faces. Being a leader meant he would

be responsible if the elves got captured and eaten. It meant he would be responsible if the party's mule became the property of the temple. Fred didn't want that, either.

Fred didn't want to have to worry about bad things when he was on a fun adventure. Fred liked to focus on the fun things. Being a leader was not fun.

Hadn't Fred brought Helen along to make the adventure fun?

Fred sighed. His sigh meant, *I'm beginning to regret that I promised to be the party leader,* but he hoped no one realized that.

He said, "Helen, I'll be up for anything again. Just as soon as we get Mak-Thar turned back into a mage. If you want me to overthrow a Neapolitan temple, I'll ask, 'How high?' But on *this* adventure, we've all agreed that we're going to find a magic spring. So I think we should just try to get out of this swamp and leave the temple for another day."

Helen gave him a measuring stare. "You're just saying that because your socks are wet."

"Yeah," said Fred. "You're probably right."

CHAPTER TWENTY-TWO: IN WHICH OUR HEROES DRY THEIR SOCKS AND CONSIDER LIONS.

FIGHTER FRED WAS A BIG STRONG GUY with a sword. The thing about big strong guys with swords is that people tend to listen to them.

And yet, adventuring parties are frequently led by scrawny guys with books. Scrawny guys with books *need* people to listen to them.

Fred had always let the mages be in charge. He sensed that they needed it more. Mages have wacky ideas, but sometimes those ideas work. So Fred had *listened* to Mak-Thar's plan for escaping the swamp.

Mak-Thar wasn't a scrawny guy with books anymore. Now

he was a roundish, muddy, and apparently female mule with a pack saddle. But he was still a mage. Fred didn't care what the Mages' Guild said. Casting spells didn't have anything to do with it. A mage was someone who walked into a combat zone with no armor and no combat training and assumed that his knowledge of the rulebook would get him out alive. That was Mak-Thar.

So Fred was not surprised that Mak-Thar's plan actually worked. Fred had been counting on it.

Fred had picked the wrong direction on the first day. Mak-Thar assured him that it was just bad luck. The next day, they walked in a different direction and they found the desert by noon.

As soon as their feet hit the sand, they stopped and took off their boots and socks. Nightshade made them all turn their backs so she could take off her leggings.

"I'm glad I don't wear underwear," said Mak-Thar.

"I guess there are some advantages to being a mule," said Twilight.

"Erm … yes," said Mak-Thar. "Yes. That's what I meant."

Helen snickered.

"Don't you want to change, too?" Nightshade asked Helen.

Helen shook her head. "Nope. I'm good. 'Nycadaemon Knickers: Patented fibers wick water away to another dimension.' "

They just stood around for a while watching their clothes dry. Fred dried his trousers by sitting in the sand. After a while, Mak-Thar got Nightshade to pull out their map.

"I'm certain we went into the swamp at that hex there. Then we traveled for one day. We know we traveled *south*, because we found the desert by veering right. Therefore, we must now be on that hex there."

"This one?" asked Nightshade.

"No. That one."

"It's really hard to tell where your nose is pointing. That one?"

"No. That one. I'm looking right at it."

"Your eyes are on the sides of your head. That one?"

"Yes."

Nightshade made a tick mark on the map.

By now, the map had a lot of tick marks. And yet, all the tick marks were near the Impassable Mountain Range. Most of the map's hexagons were still unexplored. Fred was amazed. "It's like there's a whole world out there."

"That's what I thought when I left the Silverleaf Forest," said Twilight. "But I'm beginning to have my doubts."

"Reality is an illusion," said Nightshade. "Come to the astral plane. We have cookies."

"Yes," said Mak-Thar. "And I'm sure you keep them in a Magic Jar. Regardless, it looks like we are now quite close to Herman the Hermit. Let's take a look at the local map."

Nightshade dutifully unfolded the map that was supposed to lead them to Herman. It had a bunch of little mounds drawn on it.

"It's all sand dunes," said Twilight. "Your map doesn't have any landmarks."

"Well," said Mak-Thar, "we shouldn't need any landmarks as long as we start on the correct hex. I'm pretty sure it's this one. So this is where we must turn away from the swamp and head out into the desert."

"What if you're wrong?"

Mak-Thar gazed at Twilight seriously. "If we discover I am wrong, we should turn back. Our waterskins will last only seven days. I suppose this is our last chance to fill them."

"We might not find anything to eat, either," said Helen. "I'm tempted to catch a bunch of frogs and dry them for when times are tough."

"Times are really tough if we're eating dried frogs," said Twilight.

"I still have the iron rations," said Mak-Thar.

Helen made a face.

"How bad can they be?" asked Twilight. "I mean, when compared with dried frogs?"

"You know," said Fred, "that's a really tough question."

"You might be able to find protein in the desert," said Mak-Thar. "Nightshade, check the Desert column of the encounter table. Is there anything to eat besides giant scorpions?"

Nightshade consulted *The Adventurer's Guide*. "There's lions."

"I'd have to be really desperate to eat a lion," said Twilight.

"There are camels," said Nightshade.

"Yum. Lion."

"Giant rattlesnakes."

"Well," said Twilight, "I have to admit that snakes taste better than frogs. I hope we don't meet any giant ones, though."

"Everything in the desert is ferocious," said Mak-Thar. "I can see why *The Adventurer's Guide* recommends that first-level adventurers stay close to town."

"I don't see how anything can live out here at all," said Twilight. "Lions, for example—how can lions live here with nothing to eat?"

"The encounter table also lists antelope," said Nightshade.

"Really?" asked Twilight. "And these antelope eat sand?"

"Maybe the antelope do like we do," said Fred. "Maybe they go to the swamp when they are hungry or thirsty, and the rest of the time they just wander around and get eaten by lions."

"Or adventurers," said Twilight.

"Well, if we don't find any antelope," said Helen, "we can always eat iron rations."

"Right," said Fred. "Show us how to dry frogs."

* * *

Helen came back an hour later with a mess of frogs. They didn't take too long to dry in the hot sun. She also fetched as many cattails as she thought Mak-Thar could carry.

Twilight filled the waterskins. He had some special elf-sense that showed him how to find pure water in the swamp. Helen said that anyone who could get sick from drinking a few little swimming things probably wasn't tough enough to be an adventurer. Fred figured it would all end up tasting like the inside of the waterskin anyway.

Once the waterskins were full and the frogs were dry, the five brave heroes set out into the desert.

"And you're sure you know where we're going?" Twilight asked.

"Reasonably confident," said Mak-Thar. "We need to head toward the sand dunes and away from the Impassable Mountain Range."

"But we can't see the Impassable Mountain Range," said Twilight.

"Duh," said Nightshade. "That's why it's called *impassable*."

"*Impassable* doesn't mean *invisible*," said Twilight.

"Oh. Right. Sorry."

"So why can't we see it?" asked Twilight.

"Because we're not adjacent to it," said Mak-Thar. "We can only see mountains in adjacent hexes."

"So we can't see a mountain seven miles away?" asked Twilight. "That doesn't sound right."

"It must have something to do with the curvature of the earth," said Mak-Thar.

They tromped through more sand. After a few minutes, Twilight asked, "What makes you so sure the earth has curvature?"

Mak-Thar rolled his eyes. "Because we can't see the mountains. Look." He stopped and drew a circle in the sand with his hoof. "That's the earth." He drew a short line standing on top of the circle. "That's you. Your line of sight is cut off by the earth's curvature." He drew a line from the top of Twilight's imaginary head to a point on the circle. "See?"

"No," said Twilight.

"Of course you don't," said Mak-Thar. "That's because your line of sight is cut off. Now, the interesting thing is that we can actually calculate the earth's circumference. This is a right triangle. This leg is six miles. This is radius r. The hypotenuse is r plus your height … Let's call that one thousandth of a mile … So r squared plus thirty-six equals r squared plus two thousandths of r plus something too small to worry about … "

Mak-Thar scribbled some letters in the sand. Fred couldn't read them. It was just a lot of Rs.

"The earth is thirty-six thousand pi miles around," said Mak-Thar.

"What are pie miles?" asked Fred.

"It's how you measure cake walks," said Helen.

"Look," said Twilight, "I don't speak scribble, but aren't you forgetting that mountains might be a mile tall? If they are impassable, probably more like two miles tall."

"Hm," said Mak-Thar.

He drew more things in the sand. He muttered. After a while, Fred stopped watching him and just stood there being hot.

"I wish I could write on paper," said Mak-Thar. "It's much easier to catch my mistakes on paper."

"What if you haven't made a mistake?" asked Twilight.

"If I haven't made a mistake," said Mak-Thar, "and if you assume the Impassable Mountain Range is a mile higher than this desert, then the earth must be about one hundred miles around."

"A hundred miles is a long ways," said Fred.

"It's less than twenty hexes," said Mak-Thar. "If my calculations were correct, we would be able to walk all the way around the globe in ten days."

"What globe?" asked Helen.

"It's just an expression," said Mak-Thar.

When they stopped for the evening, Mak-Thar got Nightshade to write out his calculations in a little notebook, but even in the notebook, they gave him the same answer. Fred expected that Twilight would offer the mule a reassuring word, but Twilight was busy sewing another wombat parka.

* * *

They really didn't like eating dried frogs. Twilight even ate half an iron ration. Nightshade sort of went on a hunger strike.

Mak-Thar did not complain about his cattails on the first day. But by the third day, the cattails were just dry husks.

Fortunately, the sun was so hot that no one felt like eating much.

As they trudged through the sand, Mak-Thar said, "I thought you said that even deserts have bushes."

"They do, okay?" said Nightshade. "Usually. I didn't know you were leading us into the Great Wasteland of Nothingness."

"What about oases?" asked Twilight. "Is there a way to find oases?"

"I think that swamp was our last oasis," said Helen.

"I climb a dune to look for trees," said Nightshade.

"If there were any trees nearby, I think we would see them," said Twilight.

"We *should* be seeing Herman the Hermit somewhere around here," said Mak-Thar. "But I'm not sure what we can see anymore."

"I see something gross on the other side of this sand dune," said Nightshade.

The rest of them climbed up the dune to investigate.

Fred's first impression was that an adventurer had dropped a sack on the ground, because the thing was about the size of a small treasure sack, stuffed full. But the outside of the bundle had fur on it. And bones poked out at odd places.

"This," said Helen, "is an owlbear pellet."

"What's an owlbear?" asked Twilight.

"Half owl, half bear," said Helen.

"Bears and owls cannot interbreed," said Twilight.

"Bears and owls *should* not interbreed," said Fred. "But sometimes mages figure out ways to make it work."

"Mages have too much time on their hands," said Twilight. "Is that why the Mages' Guild encourages its members to go on adventures?"

Helen knelt by the owlbear pellet and fingered a tuft of hair that looked like the tip of something's tail. "I would now like to get very far away from here."

"Because owlbears are nasty?" asked Twilight.

Helen nodded. "This pellet used to be a lion."

154 JASON A. HOLT

"Check the map," said Mak-Thar. "How close are we to Herman?"

"Hopefully, closer than we are to the thing that ate that lion," said Twilight.

"Maybe the owlbear is full," said Fred. "Maybe it's having a nap."

Nightshade spread out the map. "I think we're pretty close to Herman, if I've been making the tick marks right. But it's hard to tell. According to the map, Herman is just an X in the middle of nowhere."

Twilight said, "If we get there and he is literally standing on the letter X ..."

"Relax," said Mak-Thar. "The key to using maps is to always travel at a constant rate."

"But we don't travel at a constant rate," said Twilight. "We take breaks to rest and drink water and chew on dried frogs."

"The breaks are factored into our constant rate," said Mak-Thar. "It's all according to the rules in *The Adventurer's Guide*. Follow the movement rules to the letter, and we'll find the hermit."

"Follow them to the letter X," said Fred, to show he was paying attention.

"Although ..." said Mak-Thar, "... according to this map, we should be there already."

"I climb a dune to look for the hermit," said Nightshade.

"You already climbed a dune," Twilight reminded her. "We are now standing on it."

"Oh. Are there any bigger dunes?"

"There's an owlbear," said Fred. He pointed at a shambling figure in the distance.

"Oh no," said Helen.

"Should we run away?" asked Twilight.

"No," said Mak-Thar. "We should run toward Herman's X."

"Won't he be upset if we lead an owlbear to his X?" asked Nightshade.

"That's not an owlbear," said Helen.

"Then what is it?" asked Fred.

"It's *two* owlbears."

"Oh yeah." Now that she mentioned it, Fred could see a second figure shambling behind the first.

"They're a long ways from water," said Helen.

"Desert creatures can go many months without water," said Mak-Thar.

"Months?" asked Twilight. "That's ridiculous."

"Owlbears are forest creatures," said Helen.

"Are they?" asked Mak-Thar. "Let me see *The Adventurer's Guide*."

"I think they've spotted us," said Fred. "They're turning this way."

"Look," said Mak-Thar, "Herman is supposed to be a sage. Sages are supposed to be wise. He'll know how to deal with owlbears. And if he doesn't want to get hugged to death, he'll have to give us the information for free."

"Hugged to death and then puked up in the desert," said Helen. "What a way to go."

"Nightshade," said Mak-Thar, "use your Fly spell. Go up high and look for the hermit."

"I already used my Fly spell," said Nightshade. "My spells are on scrolls, remember? Once I use them, they're gone."

"Oh, look!" said Twilight. "A third owlbear."

They were coming closer. Each creature had the height of an ogre and the build of a giant bear. They walked upright on stocky legs, dragging even stockier tails. Their ferociously huge arms swung as they lumbered over the dunes. Yet despite their bear-like bodies, there was something owlish about their faces. Their eyes were large—no wonder Fred and his friends had been seen!—and their snouts were cruel beaks.

"Well, I suppose we can attempt to fight the owlbears," said Mak-Thar doubtfully. "Nightshade, do you know Edwin's Weird Dweomer?"

"I don't know anyone named 'Edwin'."

"Too bad," said Mak-Thar. "It would be very useful in this situation."

"So that's the plan?" asked Helen. "Fight owlbears?"

"You scared?" asked Nightshade.

"I can take one," said Helen. "Fred can probably take another. And then the two elves and their sprightly little bows will have to keep our mule from becoming pellets."

"Oh, look!" said Twilight. "There's a fourth owlbear."

"Maybe they don't see us," said Nightshade. "Maybe they are just walking in this direction by coincidence."

The owlbears crested the adjacent dune and lumbered down the near side. Fred wasn't sure he could outrun them.

Helen drew her humongous sword. Fred drew his regular sword.

Twilight unslung his bow. "I'm worried that shooting at them will make them angry."

"Yeah," said Helen. "It's not wise to anger an owlbear. But here we go!"

Chapter Twenty-Three: In which our heroes are stupid enough to fight owlbears.

With a mighty war cry, Yellin' Helen charged down the side of the dune. Fred tried to keep up with her, but she was too fast. She was going to put herself right in the middle of all the owlbears. Fred hoped she was too big to swallow in one gulp.

Fred veered off to the side, hoping to draw one of the owlbears away, but they fixed their owlish eyes on Helen and broke into a run, charging straight up the hill.

As the crazy barbarian sprinted into the wall of fur and feathers, the owlbears opened their arms to receive her with ferocious hugs. Helen ducked, slid between their legs, sliced at their tails, and kept on running.

The owlbears stopped, confused.

Twilight loosed an arrow and hit an owlbear. There were four owlbears, each six feet wide and eight feet tall—it would have been very difficult to miss.

Nightshade scampered partway down the hill, unfurled a scroll, and read something.

Now the owlbears were *really* confused. Fred figured no one had ever read to them before.

Flames shot out of Nightshade's fingers, catching her scroll on fire.

"Ow, ow, ow!" She dropped it in the sand and ran back up the dune to Mak-Thar.

"Burning Hands is *not* a good spell to cast from a scroll," said Mak-Thar. "Also, the range is only three feet. Given the fact that an owlbear's reach is *more* than three feet—"

"Okay, okay! You don't have to rub it in!"

Twilight hit another owlbear with an arrow. The owlbear did not seem to notice.

"Whoooo's ready for a fight?" yelled Helen.

The owlbears decided to ignore her. They charged up the hill, away from Helen, toward Mak-Thar and the elves.

"Oh come on," said Helen. "That was a really bad one-liner! I can't believe they want to attack someone else."

"Maybe they didn't get it," said Fred.

Fred's attempt to draw the owlbears away had also failed, but now he had a good angle of attack. Fred charged their flank.

An owlbear turned to meet him, squawking and sweeping its massive paws through the air. Fred needed a way to fight it without getting too close.

Maybe the trick was to keep moving. Fred sidestepped, jabbed at a knee, stepped behind the beast, sliced some fur off its tail. He worked around the owlbear in a circle, wounding it with tiny jabs.

An arrow flew into the owlbear's shoulder, but it didn't care.

"Don't make me run back up the hill!" Helen yelled. "Hey! Your smell is un-*bear*-able. Get it? Because you guys are like *bears*? And you have a smell?"

"I think they're immune to puns!" yelled Twilight.

"But are they immune to this?" asked Nightshade. She read some words off her scroll and pointed at the owlbears.

The owlbears kept charging.

"A Sleep spell?" asked Mak-Thar. "Yes. They are in fact immune to that. Sleep spells never work on five-hit-die monsters."

"If they have five hit dice," asked Nightshade, "why are we fighting them?"

Fred had hoped that by circling and jabbing, he could wear his owlbear down. But really, when you dance in circles around an owlbear who has taken up a stationary position on a steep slope of very loose sand, the owlbear is not the one who gets worn down. Fred got tired pretty quick. And his knee started to ache. After about three-and-a-half circles, he was thinking he should have chosen a different tactic. Then the owlbear swept Fred's legs with its tail, and Fred went tumbling down the side of the dune.

So far, Fred hadn't done a very good job of slowing the owlbears down. He hoped Mak-Thar and the elves were good at dodging. Fred got to his feet, took a deep breath, and started slogging back up the hill.

In the meantime, Helen had caught up to the owlbears, powered solely by her indignation. "You think you can ignore me, bird brain? Well this ought to make you *owl*!"

She thrust her blade into an owlbear's hip, and the owlbear did indeed make a loud noise.

"See? It's like 'make you howl', but I said 'owl' instead."

Fred didn't think the owlbear got it. But he didn't say so, because he needed all his breath for slogging up the hill.

Helen's owlbear turned on her and swung its massive arms. But it was eight feet tall, and Helen was on the downhill side. She ducked easily. Then she stepped in close and drove her sword into the owlbear's leg. The creature fell—right on Helen.

Nightshade pulled another scroll out of her backpack. "Am I close enough for Magic Missile?"

"Yes," said Mak-Thar.

Nightshade read some words, and a dainty little green ball

darted from her hands and flew into an owlbear's shoulder, resulting in a cute puff of smoke.

"Hah!" said Nightshade. "Got him!"

The owlbear grabbed her with both hands, lifted her into the air, tipped its head back, and opened its beak.

"Stop! Stop!" said a scratchy old voice.

The owlbears turned and looked across the dunes.

The distant voice called, "Put that down, Bigby! Armor isn't good for you."

The owlbear roared and shook Nightshade above its head. Miscellaneous equipment fell from her backpack and disappeared into the owlbear's mouth.

"I said no! Put it down."

The owlbear squawked and dropped Nightshade headfirst into the sand.

"Good owlbear," said the scratchy voice. "You can eat the unarmored one."

"Ah," called Twilight, "can we talk about this?"

"Talk?" the scratchy voice shouted. "If you wanted to talk, you shouldn't have attacked my owlbears. How come I only see three of them? Where's Tenser? I hope you haven't hurt Tenser."

Twilight looked down the slope. "I think he's lying on top of our barbarian."

"Tenser's a she!"

"Do we have to shout at each other?" Twilight asked. "Maybe we could meet in the middle and talk like reasonable people."

"Oh no. You look like an adventuring party. You stay out of Fireball range or my owlbears will eat you all."

By this time, Fred had managed to make it to the top of the dune. The owlbears were standing around looking confused again, casting nervous glances at Twilight, then at a figure on a distant dune.

The scratchy-voiced man seemed to be coming from the same direction as the owlbears. He was hard to see because he wore a dune-colored robe. He leaned on a gnarled staff that might have been magical and might have been just a walking stick.

"But your owlbears are already threatening to eat us all," said Twilight. "Call them off, and we can talk."

"If I liked talking, I wouldn't have become a hermit."

"Are you Herman the Hermit?" asked Mak-Thar.

"Egad! Is that a talking mule?"

"Allow me to introduce myself," said Mak-Thar.

But Twilight didn't want Mak-Thar to introduce himself. "Yes, he's a talking mule. If you want to know more about him, you'll have to call off your owlbears."

"Bigby, come! Nystul, Tenser, come! Mordenkainen, come!"

Sheepishly, the three owlbears at the top of the hill turned toward the hermit and began shambling down the slope. The one lying on top of Helen squawked, but it didn't move. Helen didn't move, either.

"Fred," she gasped. "Get this thing off me."

Fred clambered down the sand dune, with Mak-Thar and the elves close behind him. Most of Helen's body was pinned to the slope by the great weight of the owlbear.

Fred surveyed the situation. "I think we can roll it off you."

"Good. Do it."

"We have to roll it downhill over your face."

Helen grimaced. "All right. Be quick. I'll hold my breath."

The owlbear was so heavy that Fred couldn't budge it by himself. ("And Fred has a ten percent chance of being able to lift an iron portcullis," commented Mak-Thar.) Fred needed help from the elves, and it took a few tries to find the positions where they would be most effective. It didn't help that the owlbear kept taking lazy swipes at their heads.

But eventually, Fred got everyone pushing in the right places at the same time, and the owlbear started to roll. Helen's feet appeared, pressed into the sand.

"Don't stop!" yelled Fred. "Don't stop!"

They didn't stop. By the time they could see Helen's face, the owlbear was rolling down the hill.

They stopped, then, but the owlbear kept rolling. Its body was basically round, and it rolled all the way to the bottom and partway up the other side.

Unseen, the hermit called, "Tenser, come! Tenser?"

Twilight bit his lip. "Run to the top of the next dune and try to stall the hermit. I'll see if I can save Tenser."

Helen sat up and shook her head. "I'm sorry. I must have sand in my ears. I thought you said you would try to heal the owlbear."

Fred held out a hand, and Helen pulled herself up onto her feet.

"Do you want *me* to talk to the hermit?" asked Nightshade. "I have really high charisma."

"Maybe Fred should do the talking," said Twilight. "But hurry. We don't want him to come over the hill and see this." Twilight gestured to the trail of blood that led downhill to the squawking owlbear.

"I can cover that up." Helen grabbed the sack of party treasure from Mak-Thar's saddle. "I'll drag this over the tracks. You guys go stall."

"Mak-Thar should stay with me," said Twilight. "He's our best bargaining chip."

"Yes," said Mak-Thar, "but after you've sold your mule in exchange for your freedom, you won't have much reason to complete your heroic quest, will you?"

"Actually," said Helen, "I've always wondered if this is my true form, or if I might really be even tougher and more gorgeous."

"Gorgeous and half-naked are *not* the same thing," said Nightshade.

Fred touched Nightshade's shoulder. "Come with me. We have to buy Twilight some time."

CHAPTER TWENTY-FOUR: IN WHICH OUR HEROES NEGOTIATE WITH HERMAN THE HERMIT.

FRED STOOD NEXT TO NIGHTSHADE and waited nervously at the top of a sand dune. Behind them, at the bottom of the slope, Twilight was trying to heal the wounded owlbear. As the hermit appeared atop a nearby dune, Fred had to remind himself that Twilight and the owlbear were hidden from the hermit's view.

The hermit had the other three owlbears with him. They shuffled their feet and swung their shoulders, like they weren't comfortable standing still. Fred asked, "Why don't they eat you?"

"Well, there's two ways to make owlbears," said the hermit. "You can either make an owlbear that eats you or one that doesn't. I like to make the second kind. You only get to make the first kind once."

"Cool!" said Nightshade.

"How did you make a talking mule?" asked the hermit.

Twilight had warned them not to explain Mak-Thar's quest. Twilight's theory was that as long as the hermit thought he had a chance of getting a talking mule, he would be willing to negotiate. So when talking about the mule, they were supposed to be vague.

"Oh, you know," said Nightshade. "The usual way."

That was pretty vague.

"We're looking for Herman the Hermit," said Fred. "He knows something about a bridge."

"You must be looking for some other Herman the Hermit. I got no bridges here. No water, see?"

"The bridge is on the way to a magic spring," said Nightshade. "And it's guarded by a white dragon."

"Oh, *that* bridge. Did Sage the Sage send you?"

"That's right," said Fred.

"Well, knowledge has its price," said the hermit.

"What's your price?" asked Fred.

"One elf," said the hermit.

"We aren't for sale," said Nightshade.

"You want information; I want to feed my owlbears."

"My armor makes them sick, remember?"

"So take it off. Or give me the other elf. Where is it?"

Fred looked over his shoulder. "He's, uh, coming. Soon. He's just a little slow."

"He's butchering my owlbear," said the hermit. "It seems only fair that I should butcher one of your elves."

"He's not *butchering* anyone," said Nightshade. "He's a healer, and he's trying to heal Tenser."

"That's funny," said the hermit in a voice that was very menacing and not at all funny. "Tenser looked just fine when I saw her last."

"I think Tenser hurt her paw when she mauled our barbarian," said Nightshade.

"You know," said the hermit, "adventuring parties aren't the only ones who know Fireball."

Fred said, "The other elf is kind of a cleric. If he heals Tenser, I expect you to let us all leave here alive."

Nightshade put her hands on her hips and gave Fred an indignant look. "And if Twilight fails, you'll hand over a few elves to be eaten?"

Oh. Fred hadn't meant that. He wasn't very good at negotiation.

On the other hand, he was great at fighting. If he failed at negotiation, he could still come out a winner. Especially considering that Helen had finished covering Tenser's blood trail and was now coming up the slope behind him.

"I know quite a bit about owlbear anatomy," said the hermit. "If you don't want your elves eaten, you should let me come over there and help."

"Okay," said Fred.

"What?" asked Nightshade. "No, that's terrible! He'll just

sneak attack when his owlbears are in melee range."

Fred called, "But no sneak attacking when your owlbears are in melee range. Okay? That's our deal."

Nightshade shook her head. "You really should have let *me* negotiate."

* * *

Owlbear surgery was kind of a complicated thing. Herman the Hermit knew a spell powerful enough to make Tenser hold still, which made Fred suspect that he hadn't been kidding about knowing Fireball. Twilight was grateful for Herman's spell, because the owlbear was grumpy and didn't seem to like having its tendon stitched.

None of the other three owlbears liked the surgery either, and all they had to do was watch. Herman commanded them to stand off to one side, but Fred kept wishing they were farther away. Mak-Thar insisted he was keeping an eye on them, but how useful would 360-degree vision be against a creature big enough to swallow an elf whole?

Even with one owlbear immobilized and lying on the sand, Fred still felt that his party was overmatched.

Once Twilight had the tendon sewn back together, he started stitching the wound closed. That's when the owlbear started twitching.

"I think he's coming out of it," said Twilight. He tried to stitch faster.

"Tenser's a *she*," said Herman.

"I think she's coming out of it," said Twilight. "If you know anything about surgery …"

Herman grabbed a needle and started stitching from the other end.

They met in the middle. Twilight barely had time to tie his final knot when the owlbear roared and rolled onto her feet.

Herman raised a hand. "Steady, Tenser. Steady."

The owlbear squawked.

"It's not as bad as all that," said Herman.

The owlbear growled, suggesting that perhaps it was as bad as all that.

"Go stand with the others," said Herman. "Go."

The owlbear shook her head and squawked again. But she lumbered across the sand to stand with the other three owlbears.

"Are they intelligent?" Mak-Thar asked.

"No," said Herman. "In fact, they're barely obedient. I have Charm Monster spells handy at all times. Honestly, I wouldn't bother with them at all, but they eat lions."

"What do the lions eat?" asked Twilight.

"They eat hermits. That's why I need the owlbears."

"How did you make them?" asked Mak-Thar.

"You know. Secret wizard stuff. How did you learn to talk?"

"Secret wizard stuff," said Twilight, giving Mak-Thar a look that reminded him to say no more. "Honorable Herman, wise resident of the shifting sands, on behalf of myself and my friends, I apologize for the wounds we have inflicted on your hungry and aggressive creations. I hope that my efforts to mend these wounds have also helped to mend the bonds of friendship which ought to unite us. We were sent hither by the sage of Basetown, a half-pint known to us as Sage, who said you may be able to help us on our quest."

"Yes, and I'm sure she's angling for an affiliate commission," said Herman. "But my asking price is one whole elf, and I doubt she'll be pleased with her ten percent."

"Ew," said Nightshade. "Is he being gross? Because it sounds to me like he's being gross."

"Really!" said Twilight. "I had hoped that our shared experience would move us beyond petty threats."

"Not a threat. I have something you want. You got to offer me something I want. Unfortunately for you, I don't want much. The thing I want most is for people to leave me alone. The thing I want second most is to feed my owlbears."

"Ah," said Twilight, "so if we agreed to leave in peace—"

"Not a chance," said Herman. "If you wanted to leave in peace, you should never have come. My owlbears are hungry.

And when they're hungry, they can outrun a lion."

"I find your hostility surprising," said Twilight, "considering that I just aided your owlbear as a sign of good faith."

"You wounded my owlbear then healed her to play on my emotions. It won't work. I'm neutral."

"As it happens," said Mak-Thar, "I am neutral, too. Perhaps we can work out an arrangement in which no sentient beings are eaten on either side."

"On either side, eh? I don't think you are going to eat *me*, mule. But if you want a fight, I'm ready to see who eats who."

"Was that an owlbear pun?" asked Helen.

"No," said Herman.

"Oh, okay."

"I think he's bluffing," said Mak-Thar. "Since he is at a high enough level to cast Hold Monster—and since he has four owlbears on his side—he must know that he could easily turn us all into owlbear food. Because he has not attacked, we can conclude he is not truly after our lives."

"Maybe I'm not attacking because I don't want to risk more injury to my owlbears."

Mak-Thar flipped his ears. "I don't think so. If you're neutral, you don't care about your owlbears. They are simply a tool."

"They're a tool that keeps lions from eating me in my sleep. I don't want to risk losing one."

"Ah," said Mak-Thar. "But you have already revealed to us that you can cast Hold Monster. Therefore, you have access to fifth-level spells. Therefore, you must also have access to Animate Dead."

"I tried guarding my bed with skeletons. The lions thought they were kitty toys."

"I'm not talking about human skeletons," said Mak-Thar. "I'm talking about owlbear zombies. An owlbear zombie would be just as effective as an owlbear at guarding your bed."

"Wait, really? Would that work? I thought Animate Dead only works on humanoids."

"Nightshade, show him the rulebook."

Nightshade fished her *Adventurer's Guide* out of her backpack, found the relevant page, and handed it to Herman.

The hermit read it. "Well, I'll be darned. You're right. I can make owlbear zombies."

"And zombies gain one more hit die than the original creature," said Mak-Thar, "so an owlbear zombie would actually be harder to kill than a regular owlbear."

"Eh," said Herman, "but look at the armor class. Owlbears have AC 5; zombies have AC 8. That's not a good trade."

"Do the math," said Mak-Thar. "The chance of getting hit goes up only fifteen percent. That's an average of one more hit every seven rounds. That hit is completely canceled out by the extra hit die, so in any fight that goes fewer than seven rounds, the owlbear zombie is superior."

"Hmm. I guess you're right. Not many lions can go more than seven rounds with an owlbear." Herman scratched his chin. "Okay, you've convinced me. Since I can turn any of my dead owlbears into owlbear zombies, I guess it's in my best interests to kill you all."

"Wait!" said Twilight.

"Gee," said Fred. "Mak-Thar's even worse at negotiation than me."

"I must admit," said Mak-Thar, "that was not the result I had been anticipating."

Herman raised his hands to cast some dreadful spell. Fred and Helen drew their swords.

Twilight shouted, "Affiliate commission!"

Herman froze. For a second, Fred thought that Twilight had said the magic words for a hermit-freezing spell.

But Herman was not *literally* frozen. He was simply forced to reconsider.

"Sage is expecting her affiliate commission," said Twilight. "That's how the sage business works, right? You trade favors for favors. If Sage doesn't get her commission, she'll want to know what happened to us. Our trail leads directly to you. Sage lives by her reputation. She needs repeat business. She can't have you killing her customers. There will be repercussions."

Herman lowered his hands. "Say, that's a good point."

"So I would like you to agree that our lives must not be on the negotiating table," said Twilight.

"If my owlbears can't eat you, I'm not sure what use you are to me."

"We can trade favors for favors."

"Not a side quest!" said Mak-Thar.

"Information for information," said Twilight. "We want to know the secret of the Cursed Bridge. You want to know how we got a talking mule."

"Ah, you're very clever," said Herman. "Yes, I *did* want to know how you got a talking mule. But now that I know your mule has memorized large sections of *The Adventurer's Guide*, I figure she pretty much has to be a mage. Probably a male mage, because that doesn't sound like a mule's natural voice. So it's pretty obvious which of you needs to return to his, her, or its true form. The mystery is solved. Reincarnation spell, am I right?"

"I'm not saying," said Mak-Thar.

"I'm right."

"You're a jerk," said Nightshade. "Why can't you just tell us so we can help our friend? All this time, I thought you were going to be some kooky old coot who says crazy stuff that turns out to be really helpful in the end. But it turns out you're just a homicidal maniac."

"No," said Mak-Thar. "He's not a maniac. He's just … neutral. He can't help us unless we give him something equivalent in return."

"He sent owlbears to attack us," said Nightshade. "And he was willing to make owlbear zombies. That's not neutral. That's evil!"

"Wait," said Herman. "Have the evil wizards acquired exclusivity on animating dead?"

"Not yet," said Mak-Thar. "But they're working on it."

"These are troubling political times," said Herman.

"He's not evil," said Mak-Thar. "He's just a really, really selfish kind of neutral, largely indifferent to the suffering of others."

"Like Paul," said Fred.

"Somewhat like Paul," agreed Mak-Thar.

"You said Paul killed you because he was evil," said Fred.

"I said— Hm."

"I just want to get my owlbears fed," said Herman.

"How desperate are you?" asked Twilight.

"Desperate enough to let them eat a few elves before I call them off," Herman admitted.

"We have iron rations," said Twilight.

"You do?"

"Three months' worth," said Twilight.

"Oh. ... Can owlbears *eat* iron rations?"

"Anyone can eat iron rations," said Fred. "They just have to be desperate enough."

"But—" said Mak-Thar. He had bought all those rations so that the party would not eat him.

"Relax," said Helen. "You'll be fine as long as we don't find mustard."

"At some point you have to trust us," said Fred.

"Even if Helen's jokes are in poor taste," said Twilight.

"I like the taste of mustard," said Helen.

"That's not helping," said Nightshade.

"Oh, very well," said Mak-Thar. "We can offer you three months of rations."

"For four people," said Twilight. "So that comes out to ..."

"Lots of rations," said Herman. "Very well. I accept."

"But," said Mak-Thar, "this information had better be good. If it's some useless riddle, then no deal."

"Well, it *is* sort of a riddle," admitted Herman. "I guess I could tell it to you, and then you could decide whether or not it's useless."

"That sounds fair," said Mak-Thar.

Of course, if Mak-Thar didn't like the trade, the alternative was that they would all be killed by a powerful wizard and eaten by his owlbears, but as long as Herman and Mak-Thar were getting along, Fred didn't need to mention this.

"Okay," said Herman. "So when I tell people the secret of the Cursed Bridge, I have to use a very specific wording, and I'm not allowed to answer any questions about what I say."

"Yeah, that sounds like a riddle," Twilight agreed.

"Okay. Here goes: Any man who sets foot on the Cursed Bridge shall fall to his doom unless his heart is pure."

"Any man …" echoed Nightshade. Her words trailed off as she fell into contemplation.

There was silence for a moment as all of Fred's friends thought about the riddle.

"So …" said Nightshade, "… we're good, right?"

Helen nodded. "Yeah. I think we're good."

"Yes," agreed Mak-Thar. "Apparently, we're expected to misinterpret the words broadly, when in fact our only limitation is the strict literal meaning."

"So since elves aren't men …" said Twilight.

"And women aren't men …" said Helen.

"And mules aren't men …" said Mak-Thar.

"Then the only one we have to worry about is Fred," said Nightshade. "And I think his heart is pure, isn't it?"

"Could be pure," agreed Helen.

"There's no need to risk it," said Mak-Thar. "The riddle specifically says 'sets foot'. I can carry Fred on my back, and he will never set foot on the bridge."

"That might work," said Nightshade. "Don't you think?"

Helen shrugged. "We'll cross that bridge when we come to it."

"Very well," said Mak-Thar. "I concede that this is, in fact, valuable information. I will yield up ninety percent of the rations."

"Why only ninety percent?" asked Nightshade.

"We must deliver ten percent to Sage as her affiliate commission."

CHAPTER TWENTY-FIVE: IN WHICH OUR HEROES ENCOUNTER EVIL ACOLYTES.

AS SOON AS MAK-THAR was unloaded, Fred and his friends were once more walking across the dunes. And they weren't exactly hurrying, but they were walking faster than usual because they wanted to get some distance away from the owlbears.

"I admit that traveling through the desert without rations makes me quite fearful," said Mak-Thar.

"Relax," said Helen. "We still have plenty of dried frogs."

"I think I'm going to fast," said Nightshade.

"No, this is a good pace," said Fred. He wanted to keep moving in case Herman changed his mind.

"*Fast*," said Nightshade. "As in 'not eat'. When elves fast, they attain enlightenment."

"When elves fast, they get lightheaded and become a burden to their traveling companions," said Twilight. "You'll eat your frogs."

"We still have a few iron rations," said Helen.

"Okay. I'll eat my frogs."

Mak-Thar looked a lot smaller now that he was carrying only ten percent of the rations.

"You must be feeling more comfortable," suggested Fred.

"I feel like I'm floating away," said Mak-Thar. "It's somewhat unsettling. I hadn't realized I was carrying so much weight."

"I thought it foolish of you to carry so much," said Twilight. "But as it turned out, we were fortunate to have a way to pay for the hermit's information."

"That was some good negotiating," said Helen. "There were two or three times where I would have said, 'Done talking; fight now,' but he probably wouldn't have given us as much information without his head."

"Unless Selene has given Twilight the ability to Speak With Dead," said Mak-Thar.

"Speak With Head," said Helen.

"Speaking with heads is much easier when the heads aren't dead," said Twilight.

"I can't believe that guy was such a jerk," said Nightshade. "I was thinking I would have to backstab him."

"It was so tempting to stab first and ask questions later," agreed Helen.

"I don't know," said Fred. "The owlbears were tough. I'm not sure we would have won."

"Aw, come on," said Helen. "We've been in worse situations."

"Worse than being pinned under a hamstrung owlbear?" asked Twilight.

"There was the time the giant sat on me," said Helen.

"Oh yeah!" said Fred. "That was a good one!"

Helen said, "The point is that no matter how bad the situation seems, there's always a way to get out of it."

"That sounds like survivorship bias," said Mak-Thar. "Adventuring parties always think there's a way out because the ones who get trapped in an unwinnable situation do not show up in the tavern to tell stories about how they died."

"But if they do," said Fred, "you should consider finding a different place to drink."

Helen said, "I'm sure we could have found a way to handle those owlbears."

"I think we *did* find a way to handle the owlbears," said Fred. "We let Twilight negotiate."

Mak-Thar said, "It disturbs me to realize that we staked our lives on the negotiation talents of an elf who once offered to pay extra for a mule because she had a star on her forehead."

"But now you're glad we got Evenstar," said Twilight.

"Of course," said Mak-Thar. "And I'm glad that I convinced you to pay standard price. Really, the problem here is the outdated conventions of the Sages' Guild. They should establish standard exchange rates and list them in *The Adventurer's Guide*."

"Hey," said Nightshade. "It looks like there are people out there." She pointed ahead, across the desert plain. They were too far away to see details, but six people were tramping through the sand.

"Who would be crazy enough to travel through the desert on foot?" asked Twilight. "Present company excepted."

"Could be zombies," said Helen. "Or ghouls. Ghouls like deserts."

"Those people don't walk like monsters," said Fred.

"True," said Helen.

Twilight said, "Mak-Thar thinks that anyone not in the party is a monster."

"They're monsters if we have to fight them," said Mak-Thar. "But they may simply be NPMs."

"So you're saying we could talk to them," said Twilight.

"Perhaps."

"Talking?" asked Helen. "Again? Is this going to be a habit?"

"I don't think you have to worry," said Mak-Thar. "Twilight wanted to talk to the monsters on our last adventure, but no one wanted to talk back."

"Hey," said Fred. "Tell them the story about impersonating the minocow."

"I shall not tell that story," said Mak-Thar, "and if you value my friendship, neither shall you."

"Is this story likely to embarrass our mule?" asked Helen.

"It is," said Twilight.

"I'll get Fred to tell me later," said Helen.

"But—" said Mak-Thar.

"It's no use," said Helen. "Fighters always talk."

"Well, *I* don't need to embarrass Mak-Thar," said Nightshade. "It looks like we don't have time, anyway."

Indeed, the people walking through the desert had spotted Fred and his friends and had changed direction to meet with them.

Nightshade asked, "Can I have a turn negotiating? I'm really good-looking, and I get the same racial reaction bonuses as Twilight."

"Well ..." said Fred.

"Hail!" cried the woman leading the travelers.

"Hail!" cried Twilight.

"It's *my* turn," insisted Nightshade. "Hail! Hail! I shout louder than Twilight so they'll know that they should use my reaction bonuses."

"This is going to go so well," muttered Twilight.

"I promise not to draw my sword until it looks like it might be fun," said Helen.

"Shut up, you guys," said Nightshade.

"Are you lost?" called the travelers. "Would you like us to show you the way?" They were now close enough that Fred could see they were wearing gray tabards with green blotches on them.

"It's the evil priests!" said Helen.

Fred did not recognize any of them personally, but their uniforms did look an awful lot like those worn by the clerics from that temple in the swamp. In full daylight, the green blotch on the chest looked like neither a skull nor a happy face. Maybe it was a beetle?

Helen reached for her humongous sword. "Oh, this will be fun!"

"Wait a minute, please," said Fred.

"We still do not know for certain they are evil," said Twilight. "They may be guardians of the swamp."

"In the desert?" asked Helen.

"We're not lost!" shouted Nightshade. "We just want to know more about your religion."

"Certainly," said the woman in front. "What would you like to know?"

A flash of sunlight glinted off the armor underneath her tabard. She carried a mace on her hip.

In a quieter voice, Nightshade asked, "What do we want to know, guys?"

"Ask them their alignment," suggested Mak-Thar.

"Ask which deity they serve," said Twilight.

"What deity do you guys serve?" called Nightshade.

"We worship Toxia, goddess of the insinuating venom."

Twilight squinted at the insignia on the clerics' tabards. "Oh. I guess it's supposed to be a snake's head."

Fred wasn't seeing it. "Are you sure it's not a venomous beetle?"

"So is that some sort of snake goddess?" called Nightshade.

"Yes." The stranger did not seem pleased to be answering the question.

"So definitely evil, right?" asked Helen. "I can draw my sword?"

"Snakes are neutral," said Mak-Thar.

"So was Herman," said Nightshade. "But he was still nasty."

"Even so," said Twilight, "I think we should avoid a quarrel if we can."

"Okay," said Nightshade, "I'll bargain for our freedom."

"What?" said Helen. "We can take these guys."

Now only about thirty yards away, the clerics-who-couldn't-paint-snake-heads were also huddled in discussion.

"It can't be that hard to paint a snake," said Fred. "You just do a wiggly green line and add some fangs."

"I agree," said Twilight. "All beings must stretch if they are to grow, of course, but it looks like the snake's head stretched their artistic talents a bit too far."

"Can we fight them now and do art criticism later?" asked Helen.

The woman on the opposite side called, "My people want to know if any of you are aligned with good."

"Should we lie?" asked Nightshade.

"If you're good, you can't lie," said Mak-Thar.

"Then I suppose no one is truly good," said Twilight.

"Gold dragons are," said Mak-Thar.

"And you've never met a gold dragon who lied?" asked Twilight.

"I've never met a gold dragon," said Mak-Thar. "Do you know one?"

Helen said, "Fred's good, and he doesn't mind stretching the truth if it makes a good story. I think we're allowed to lie."

"Okay," called Nightshade. "We've talked it over, and we've decided to tell you that we're all neutral."

After a brief conversation, the clerics broke huddle and arrayed themselves in a line. "If you're all neutral," said the spokescleric, "then you won't mind if Bradly casts Detect Good on you."

One of the clerics started mumbling and waving his arms.

"Now we're in for it," said Mak-Thar. "Twilight, see if you can detect evil before he detects good."

"If they detect good and then attack us," said Nightshade, "I think that makes them evil."

"Good point," said Mak-Thar.

"They're good," said Bradly.

Everyone looked at the spokescleric. She thought a moment, then she smiled and said, "Great! We're glad you're good. Since you're good, you won't mind if I cast, um, Bless. Yes, I'm casting Bless, okay? Because you're so good."

Helen drew her sword and said, "And you won't mind if I draw my sword, right? It's eight o' clock, and I always draw my sword at eight o' clock to check for rust spots."

"It's not eight o' clock," said Bradly.

Helen said, "I can't tell time."

The spokescleric raised her arms.

"Shoot her, shoot her!" said Mak-Thar. "Don't let her cast!"

Fred didn't think the spokescleric was *really* planning to bless them. He was glad that his friends agreed with him.

"Wait!" called Twilight. "Before we fight ..."

Green fog spread from the spokescleric's fingers. Helen dove to the sand and rolled. Fred dove the other way, because when a spell hits, you want your party spread out as much as possible.

"... I'd just like to know ..." said Twilight.

The green fog passed over Fred's head.

"Attack!" cried the spokescleric.

"... if this is about the animals we ate in your swamp," said Twilight.

"I shoot an arrow," said Nightshade, "okay, guys?"

The green-blob clerics drew their weapons and charged. Fred and Helen rolled to their feet and charged from the flanks.

"Oh, that's interesting," said Mak-Thar. "I was expecting some sort of poison attack, but it seems to be just a special effect."

"Your mule is wrong," said the spokescleric as she raised her mace and charged at Nightshade. "You've all been blighted!"

"Is that bad?" asked Nightshade. "That sounds bad."

Fred swung his sword at the cleric named Bradly. Bradly caught the blow on his shield and swung his war hammer at Fred's knee. Fred pivoted, and the blow bounced off his knee plate with a loud clang. It did not feel pleasant.

Fred was feeling sensitive about his knees, and he kind of took that personally. Fred sidestepped around Bradly's shield and drove his sword through the cleric's backplate. Bradly was the first to die.

"Blight is actually not that bad," said Mak-Thar. "We're all at minus-one on to-hits and damage, but the minus-one morale penalty should only apply to me." Mak-Thar pivoted and kicked an attacker in the chest. "Really, if Blight is her best spell, we should win this battle easily."

Helen had killed her first opponent, so the clerics were already outnumbered. Nightshade had been too indecisive with her bow, and now she was forced to draw her sword. The spokescleric's mace struck her in the shoulder and Nightshade stumbled back.

Twilight was by her side, sword in hand. His thrust slid off the spokescleric's armor—a harmless blow, but enough to prevent the spokescleric from pressing her attack.

Fred found himself fighting a woman with a quarterstaff. Really, a quarterstaff is just a spear without the sharp bit, so it shouldn't have been so scary, but when she jabbed him in the eye and everything turned blurry, it suddenly became a little scary.

Fred moved to a defensive stance, blocking blurred attacks

with his sword. He was pretty sure his friends were winning, and he just needed to hold out a few moments longer.

"We surrender!" yelled the spokescleric.

The woman with the quarterstaff stopped swinging it at Fred. After a few blinks, his vision had cleared enough that he could see three clerics on their knees. The other three were lying dead in the sand.

"Ha!" said the spokescleric. "You're good, so you can't kill us after we've surrendered."

"*I'm* not good," said Helen, raising her blade.

"Just a minute please," said Fred.

Helen scowled and lowered her blade.

"Oh, cool," said Nightshade. "Now I get to negotiate terms of surrender. I'm going to make them cast Cure Light Wounds because my shoulder hurts like a barbarian."

"Evil clerics don't cast Cure Light Wounds," said Mak-Thar. "They cast Cause Light Wounds."

"That's not a real thing," said Nightshade.

"It's a real thing," said Helen. She turned so that everyone could see the bruise-colored handprint on her ribs.

"Cause Light Wounds has to be the most useless attack ever," said Mak-Thar. "You have to get close enough to slap the target with your bare hand, and it doesn't do much more damage than a war hammer."

After getting whacked in the knee, Fred was of the opinion that war hammers hurt quite a bit.

"We offer cash for our freedom," said the spokescleric.

"Cool!" said Nightshade. "How much cash?"

"Four hundred gold pieces."

"That's not bad," said Nightshade.

"And we get experience points for defeating all of them," said Mak-Thar. "Even though we only killed three. I think Helen can stop threatening them now."

"I'm not threatening," said Helen. "I'm just standing guard in case negotiations break down."

Nightshade said, "But four hundred gold pieces is good, right?"

"I don't know," said Twilight. "Shouldn't we take them prisoner?"

"Then we'd have to feed them and find them water," said Mak-Thar.

"And we'd have to watch them to be sure they don't murder us in our sleep," said Helen.

"Elves don't sleep," said Twilight.

"I guess they can all be *your* prisoners, then," said Helen.

"Please have mercy," begged the spokescleric. "See? I begged for mercy. Because you are good, you now have to do whatever I say. Let us go. We need to take the dead bodies back to our temple so our superiors can cast Raise Dead before they spoil."

"That's gross," said Nightshade.

"This whole situation is morally ambiguous," said Twilight. "I wish I understood *why* you were attacking us."

"Because they're *evil*," said Helen. "It's not morally amphibious at all!"

"I have to say," said Mak-Thar, "that I agree with Helen. Note that they did not choose to attack us until they were certain that some members of our party are good. This is consistent with the evil hypothesis and not consistent with your ecosystem-manager hypothesis."

"I guess you're right," said Twilight. "So if they're evil, then perhaps we have to kill them so they don't spread their evil further."

"Yes, that would be the logical thing to do," agreed the spokescleric. "But you can't. Ha! Because good characters can't kill prisoners!"

"That *is* what it says in *The Adventurer's Guide*," agreed Mak-Thar.

"I think we have to let them go," said Fred.

"We do?" asked Helen.

"We can't really waste time dragging them along," said Fred. "And I don't like killing people who aren't fighting. That doesn't seem right."

"Can we at least take their money?" asked Nightshade.

"Sure," said Fred.

"Of course," said Mak-Thar.

"We're adventurers," said Helen. "That's what we do."

"Okay," said Nightshade. "So I take all their money and send them on their way."

"Great," said the spokescleric. "That is very shrewd of you. I'm sure your deities will reward you. Now in exchange for our money, you have to give us your talking mule."

CHAPTER TWENTY-SIX: IN WHICH OUR HEROES LEAVE THE DESERT AND EXPLORE THE HILLS.

FRED DECIDED NOT to hand Mak-Thar over to the evil clerics. Of all the decisions he had made since promising he would be in charge, this was the decision he was most sure of.

However, the spokescleric had laid out an interesting argument: The three dead clerics were now harmless. If the bodies were returned to the evil temple, they could be raised from the dead. Therefore, leaving the corpses in the desert was equivalent to killing harmless prisoners. Therefore, Fred had to help the living clerics carry the dead ones. Therefore, Fred had to give up his mule.

Fred, however, did not own Mak-Thar, so he was not persuaded on this last point. But the other points kind of made sense to him. In the end, they agreed that Mak-Thar would haul the bodies to a drop-off point, and the clerics would be responsible for hauling them the rest of the way. Also, the clerics had to give Fred's party a six-hour head start.

The clerics were actually willing to give Fred's party a 24-hour head start, because they had to rest up from things like getting kicked in the chest by Mak-Thar. The evil clerics didn't have anyone in the party who could miraculously heal people, and Fred was now beginning to see what Mak-Thar meant about the uselessness of Cause Light Wounds.

As soon as negotiations were over, Nightshade fell asleep. The deal almost broke down, then. Mak-Thar could carry three dead bodies, but Nightshade put him over his weight limit.

However, Mak-Thar remembered that Fred had once carried Nightshade down from a tree. Therefore, Fred could carry her across the desert, and everything would be fine.

Fred thought the elf was going to be somewhat awkward to carry across an entire desert. He was at the point of asking the clerics to carry one of their dead bodies themselves when they offered him a sack that was big enough to hold an entire person. (Fred offered to buy it, but the cleric said, "I give you this sack purely out of the evilness of my heart.")

This solved the problem. Fred was used to walking around with a hundred and sixty pounds of gold on his shoulder, so carrying a sack full of elf was actually no big deal. And thanks to the grace of Selene, his knee was no longer hurting him, so he tramped across the sandy plain quite cheerfully.

"This is a little embarrassing to be mentioning now," said Twilight. "But I just realized that we've been traveling in the hottest part of the day."

"Yeah," said Fred. "It *is* kind of hot. I think that's because the sun is up."

"Savvy desert travelers should travel at night," said Twilight.

"I'm savage," said Helen, "and *I* travel by day."

"I said 'savvy'," said Twilight. "It means knowledgeable."

"Mak-Thar's knowledgeable," said Helen, "and he travels by day, too."

"But we shouldn't," said Twilight. "During the day, we should seek shelter from the desert heat."

"We *could*, I suppose," Mak-Thar acknowledged. "But we are not required to do so. The encounter tables in *The Adventurer's Guide* assume we are traveling by day and camping at night. If we were to reverse this, we would doubtless suffer penalties."

"What about baking your brain in the hot desert sun?" asked Twilight. "Doesn't that cause you to suffer penalties?"

"It sounds like one of those problems that doesn't exist until someone mentions it," said Mak-Thar.

"So now we're back to your superstitious game worship."

"I'm not a game worshipper," said Mak-Thar. "I'm neutral. But I've spent my entire career believing that it's bad to give the GM ideas, and the habit is difficult to break, even though I now know there is no GM."

"Wait," said Fred. "You don't believe in the GM anymore?"

"Of course he doesn't," said Twilight. "Mak-Thar has been dead, remember?"

"So what did you see when you were dead?" asked Fred.

"Nothing," said Mak-Thar. "I expected that I would at least get to look at my character sheet, but nothing like that happened. One moment I was dying, trying in vain to draw my dagger. The next moment I was tethered to a tree and chewing grass. I had a sense that some time passed in between, but it was a brief time of nothingness. The experience was very much like waking up from a short nap."

"Did you see Selene?" asked Fred.

"No," said Mak-Thar. "But I do have a vague memory of a woman saying, 'Ha! Gotcha!'"

Fred was confused. "But if you know that life isn't a game, why do you keep telling us the rules?"

"Lots of things that aren't games have rules," said Mak-Thar. "Like spelling and grammar and arithmetic."

"You know," said Twilight, "when a servant of Selene says that life has rules, we mean that Selene is pleased when we act in certain ways."

"Yes, well, when I say that life has rules, I mean that scholars have done research and recorded their findings in *The Adventurer's Guide*."

"Were their findings peer-reviewed?" asked Twilight.

"Of course," said Mak-Thar.

Twilight snorted.

"Yes?" asked Mak-Thar. "Why do you snort at me?"

"I was not snorting," said Twilight. "I was merely sniffing because some sand got in my nose."

"I'm a mule," said Mak-Thar. "I know a snort when I hear one."

Helen snorted.

Twilight said, "I just find it ridiculous that someone might do a scientific experiment to calculate a fighter's hit points and armor class."

"As I understand it," said Mak-Thar, "the procedure is more like a study than an experiment. Counting a fighter's hit points under controlled conditions would probably be unethical."

"Ah," said Twilight. "So you might, for example, record the outcomes of multiple naturally occurring battles …"

"Yes," said Mak-Thar. "And then you would hypothesize a number of models and recommend the one that best fit the data."

"I'm pretty sure I would never do any such thing," said Helen. "Because I don't even know what that is."

Mak-Thar continued, "I'm sure that's how I would go about making a random encounter table. I would want data from many adventures, and then I would simply record the distribution."

Twilight frowned thoughtfully. "So what you're saying is that the Wilderness Encounter Table is actually a zoological survey."

"Yes. Of course."

"That makes so much more sense," said Twilight. "Are evil clerics found on the Wilderness Encounter Table?"

"Evil clerics could be listed either as 'Acolytes' or as 'NPM Party'," said Mak-Thar. "But I don't know if they are found in deserts. Let's check."

There was a brief pause while Twilight found Mak-Thar's *Adventurer's Guide*. As they resumed walking, Mak-Thar helped Twilight find the appropriate page.

"Here it is," said Twilight. " 'NPM Party'. What does that mean? A party entirely made up of people who don't belong to it?"

"It means a party of people who don't belong to *our* party," said Mak-Thar. "Which actually describes the majority of adventuring parties."

"So are we an NPM party to someone else?" asked Fred.

"I suppose we must be," said Mak-Thar. "Although you could really mess up your data if you allowed two surveys to each count the other survey team as an NPM party."

"Are you sure?" asked Twilight. "Maybe you mess up the data if you forget to count *yourself* as an NPM Party."

There were several seconds of silence as they trudged through the hot sand.

Finally Mak-Thar said, "I hope they have enough data points that you can safely ignore your own party. Anyway, you're always certain to encounter yourself, with probability one."

"Eh, I'm not sure they have enough data points on the desert table," said Twilight. "According to this, our chances of seeing a blue dragon are the same as our chances of seeing a hawk. That doesn't sound right."

"Hmm …" said Mak-Thar. "I agree. We should assume the table is an accurate representation of what is out here, but the published distribution may be inaccurate."

"Mak-Thar?" asked Fred. "Did you just say something in *The Adventurer's Guide* could be inaccurate?"

"Well, it's still accurate enough for most strategic purposes," said Mak-Thar. "If it were not, they would revise it."

"Of course," said Fred.

Twilight grinned. And inside, Fred grinned with him. Mak-Thar was beginning to see that there might be more to the world than what was written down.

* * *

Two days later, they left the desert and entered a country of low hills. Not long after, they came to a road. There, in accordance with their agreement, they left the three dead bodies.

Then Fred handed off Nightshade to Mak-Thar, and they continued on along the road.

After a mile or so, Twilight said, "So I may be revealing my inexperience again, but is it normal to haul dead bodies across the desert like that?"

"No," said Helen.

"Sometimes," said Mak-Thar.

"I've been in parties where we hauled our *own* dead," said Helen, "if we knew a place they could be resurrected. But this is the first time I've ever been in a party that hauled people they killed just to be nice to a band of evil clerics."

"It seemed like the reasonable thing to do," said Fred. "And it wasn't out of our way."

"I just hope our good deeds don't come back to haunt us," said Helen.

"Was that even good?" asked Twilight. "We don't know what evil we may have enabled."

"I just hope our morally amphibious deeds don't come back to haunt us," said Helen.

"Well, it's done now," said Mak-Thar. "Unless we want to go back and cremate them before the three survivors show up."

No one wanted to go back and cremate them.

After walking along the road for a while, Twilight asked, "Is anyone else unsettled by the assumption that they will have an easy trip to their evil temple?"

Fred said, "I thought they were going to tie the bodies to poles and drag them or carry them along the road, but I'm not seeing a lot of trees for making poles."

"Nor am I," said Twilight. "But I am seeing a lot of wagon tracks. If this is an evil cleric road …"

"Then we're about to get into a lot of fun?" suggested Helen.

"I was hoping you would offer to lead us on secret paths that avoid the main road's traffic," said Twilight.

"I am in agreement with the elf," said Mak-Thar. "I had hoped our encounter in the desert was merely random, but it seems to have raised questions that linger. What are the consequences of carrying bodies for them? Why do they believe their dead will be raised if they are left beside this road?"

"Why is there a temple in a swamp?" asked Twilight. "And how does this relate to the rumors of refugees and evil temples that people were monging in Basetown?"

"It *is* a mystery," admitted Helen.

"Yes," said Mak-Thar. "We have just enough answers to make us think that a little investigation will tell us more. Before we know it, we could be deeply enmeshed in a side quest. Let us not risk that. Nightshade is once more unconscious. I am still a mule. So I ask that we avoid learning any more, if possible. We do not need such distractions at this time."

Fred could tell that Helen *really* wanted those distractions. And he knew that following Helen into battle against the entire blob-chested religion would be lots of fun. But ... "Mak-Thar would be a big help against that evil temple if he could cast fireballs again."

Helen smiled, with a twinge of regret. "It's okay. I know what adventure I signed up for. I'll find a way through the hills that avoids the main road."

CHAPTER TWENTY-SEVEN: IN WHICH OUR HEROES BARGAIN FOR CHILI POWDER.

FOR THREE DAYS, they clambered through the scrubland. Every so often, Helen would scout ahead to make sure their path was clear. She returned with reports of wagons filled with grain moving along the road, heading in the direction of the temple in the swamp.

"That makes no sense," said Twilight.

"Plundering villages is what evil temples do," said Helen.

"But it's far too early to be harvesting grain," said Twilight.

"What if people had a lot of grain saved up?" asked Helen.

"Then they would need it in case of crop failure," said Twilight.

"Not if everybody died," said Helen.

"It's a side quest," said Mak-Thar. "Please ignore it."

So they ignored it. Helen continued to scout ahead, though, because that was the only way to be sure they weren't marching headlong into a side quest. If she found more pieces of the story, she kept them to herself.

Whenever she returned from a scouting mission, Fred noticed how difficult she was to notice. Her hair and skin seemed to blend with the colors of the scrub brush, and she could be quite close before Fred saw her. Even her armor was difficult to see. It had been scratched and dulled by the desert sand so that it looked like the rocks on the scrubby slopes.

"When I'm in the scrublands," said Helen, "I'm practically invisible. And when I wear Nycadaemon Knickers, so are my panty lines."

"Is that a problem a lot of women have?" Twilight asked. "Panty lines in their armor?"

"Mock me if you want," said Helen. "That slogan sells knickers."

The country was rough and travel was hard, but it was also invigorating. Fred felt good to be out of the shifting sand. Helen found them lots of rabbits, and they never had to fall back on their leftover supply of dried frogs.

Mak-Thar, too, had a change of diet. Instead of cattail husks, he suddenly had fresh grasses and shrubs to eat. It was the best forage he'd had on the journey so far. He said that Evenstar thought fresh shrubs were even better than oats.

So our brave heroes were in high spirits when they finally reached a little village nestled among the hills. Cozy wooden cottages with thatched roofs were clustered around a stone-lined well. Farmers in simple clothing worked in terraced gardens on the slopes.

"This must be the place," said Helen.

"It doesn't look like any village *I've* ever seen," said Mak-Thar skeptically. "What are they doing on the hills?"

"Agriculture," said Twilight.

"Why?"

"Because not everyone can make a living catering to adventurers," said Twilight. "Some people in the world have to grow food."

"It's suspicious," said Mak-Thar.

"It's a village," said Twilight.

"Why is no one wearing armor?" asked Mak-Thar.

"Because they're farmers," said Twilight.

"Most farmers are retired fighters," said Mak-Thar. "They should all have armor."

Twilight rolled his eyes. "Let's just go down and buy some chili powder, shall we?"

"What if it's not the right village?" asked Mak-Thar. "Check the map."

So they checked the map. This did not work so well. Helen knew where they were, but she was kind of fuzzy about how maps worked. Mak-Thar knew where Mucho Caliente was on the map, but he was kind of fuzzy about how real life worked. They couldn't make the map and real life line up.

Fred offered to go into the village and ask, but Mak-Thar feared that could lead to side quests. Eventually, they agreed that Helen would sneak down to the village and copy the letters on the sign at the edge of town.

Helen wrote kind of big, so she was only able to bring back the first three letters. But these letters were *M-U-C*, so Mak-Thar decided they would risk it. "Although I do hope we aren't walking into Muckberg."

* * *

It wasn't Muckberg. The sign said *Mucho Caliente.*

A dusty road led to a dusty patch of ground with a well in the middle. Houses huddled around the well and climbed up the surrounding slopes. Here and there, scraggly juniper trees added a touch of green. Brightly colored flowers grew in the flower beds.

Dogs barked. Children played. There were even a few chickens scratching the dust to find bugs.

"This feels like home," said Fred.

"It feels suspiciously well detailed," said Mak-Thar. "What kind of village has chickens but no shops?"

"A real kind of village?" Twilight suggested.

"I don't see any advertising anywhere," said Mak-Thar.

"How are we going to get chili powder?"

"We could ask someone," said Twilight. "We seem to have their attention."

It was true. The girls at the well had stopped their gossiping. A small boy ran up the road shouting that strangers had arrived. In nearby houses, people leaned out their windows. Farther away, men and women in dusty clothing left their work to stand in the street and stare.

"What's going on?" Fred asked Helen.

"I don't know," she said. "Maybe they've never seen a talking mule before."

"But I'm not talking," said Mak-Thar. "And they're not just staring at me. They're staring at all of us."

"They're staring at *me!*" said Twilight. He was delighted.

Twilight raised his voice and called out, "Greetings, friends! Do not be alarmed. I am indeed one of those magical people whom you know as the elves, but my intentions are honorable. I promise that I mean you no harm."

"Um," said Helen, "and I'm one of those muscular people whom you know as barbarians, but— Fred, do I have to do all that, too?"

"Hi," said Fred. "I'm Fred."

"I'm Helen," said Helen.

"And I am Mak-Thar the talking mule."

A middle-aged man with a black felt hat and a face like gravel stepped forward from the growing crowd and asked, "Who is your prisoner?"

"Prisoner?" asked Twilight. "We have no prisoner."

The man in the black hat frowned. "You have an unconscious woman on the mule's back. And the one who claims to be Fred holds a sack large enough to hold a human body."

"It's empty now," said Fred.

"The unconscious woman claims to be an elf," said Twilight. "Her name is Nightshade. She is not our prisoner, but rather our traveling companion."

"Right. 'Traveling companion.' Uh huh." The man in the

black hat seemed hostile, but he did not draw a weapon. He
didn't have one.

Fred looked around at the people who were staring at them.
None of them had weapons. What kind of village *was* this?

"She has fallen under some sort of spell," said Twilight. "But
she is unharmed. You may examine her yourself to verify the
truth of my words."

"Hey!" said Helen. "No one is going to be 'examining' any-
body. If we say she's unharmed, then they're just going to believe
us. That's the way it's going to go."

Have you heard of body language? Helen's body was a threat.
Her muscles gleamed in the afternoon sun.

A woman in a gray apron stepped up beside the man in the
black hat. Her forehead was so broad that it could win a head-
butting contest just by showing up. She demanded, "What do
you know of those who wear the green snake's head?"

"How did you know it was supposed to be a snake's head?"
asked Fred. "It sure looks like a beetle to me."

"Beetles don't have forked tongues," said the woman.

"I thought those were feelers," said Fred.

The man and the woman exchanged glances. The man relaxed a little bit, so that his face looked less like gravel and more
like pebbly sand. "Perhaps I misjudged you. When I saw the
body over your mule's back, I assumed you were evil clerics
from the evil temple."

Helen relaxed a little bit, too. "Nope. We're just adventurers
passing through town. Can you tell us where the tavern is?"

"We have no tavern."

Fred was stunned. Words like that should have been followed by a roar of thunder. At least. They were the sort of dire
words that could easily have been the cue for everyone in the
village to change into werewolves. But everyone just continued
to stand in the street and stare, as though the shocking words
had not been spoken.

"What about a provisioner?" asked Mak-Thar. "Do you have
a provisioner?"

"What's a provisioner?" asked the pebble-faced man.

"We have reached the edge of the earth," said Mak-Thar.

Twilight asked, "Do you have any businesses that cater to adventurers at all?"

"No," said the woman with the forehead.

"This is wonderful!" said Twilight.

"It's unnatural," said Mak-Thar, the talking mule.

"We are simple farmers," said the man. "My name is Roark, which means 'He who talks when he should be farming.' Our village is called 'Mucho Caliente'—"

"We read the sign," said Fred.

"—which means 'Place of terraced hillside agriculture.' "

"Um," said Twilight, "I don't think that's what 'Mucho Caliente' means."

"I'm pretty sure," said Roark. He looked around at the other villagers. They nodded in agreement with him. "Yes. Terraced hillside agriculture. We live a simple life. We have no need for swords or bows or talking mules. We believed the conflicts of the world would always pass us by. But now, with the arrival of the evil clerics ..." Roark shook his head.

"Have you had many dealings with the evil clerics?" asked Twilight.

"No," said the woman. "Not yet. But we fear they will come. The troubles started—"

"If I may interrupt," said Mak-Thar, "I would just like to point out that we are not here to rescue any villages from evil temples."

"I was only going to tell you a story," said the woman. Her expansive forehead wrinkled into a frown.

"Yes," said Mak-Thar. "And then you would have our sympathies. And then my kind-hearted friends would ask if there was anything we could do. And suddenly we'd find that we were committed to a side quest. But we are not here to commit to side quests. We are here to purchase chili powder. Twilight, tell them."

"I think you just told them, Mak-Thar."

"Yes, but you get reaction bonuses."

"If it is chili powder you seek," said Roark, "then you have come to the right place. How much do you need?"

"Enough to get past the white dragon," said Mak-Thar.

"I'll get a bottle," said the woman.

Roark smiled. "Why don't we invite them in? It is nearly meal time, and I'm sure they are hungry."

"No!" said Mak-Thar. "Don't eat the food!"

"That's just a myth," said Twilight. "And the myth is about *elven* food, not about the food in remote villages with terraced hillside agriculture."

"If you go inside for dinner, they'll ask you to sit down," said Mak-Thar. "When you're sitting down, they'll want to talk. Then they'll tell you they need our help, and then we'll be trapped in the evil-temple side quest."

Roark said, "Your talking mule is one strange duck."

"He is his own talking mule," said Twilight. "And I'm afraid he's in a bit of a hurry. Unless your village is in such dire straits that only a band of heroic adventurers can help, we'd prefer to just buy some chili powder and move on."

"I understand," said Roark.

"No hard feelings?" asked Fred.

"Of course not," said Roark. "We all have our troubles. Besides, I can't imagine a situation in which we could be saved only by the intervention of two fighters, an elf, and their talking mule."

"Two elves," said Helen. "One conscious and one un."

"Un? Oh, I see."

During this debate, the woman with the broad forehead returned with a bottle of red powder. It was only three inches high.

"That looks more like a vial than a bottle," said Mak-Thar.

"Yes," agreed the woman. "It really is much more than you need, but we cannot sell it in smaller quantities. Do you have ten copper pieces?"

"That's it?" asked Mak-Thar. "Ten copper pieces?"

"How much does it cost where you come from?"

"Um ..." said Mak-Thar, "... let's assume it costs ten copper pieces."

"Forgive me for charging so much," said the woman. "But you seem to be wealthy, and I must seize this chance to acquire copper for our village."

"Interesting," said Mak-Thar. "So you want the coins just for the metal?"

"Yes."

"Well, really, ten coins *is* a pound of copper," said Mak-Thar. "Looked at that way, we're actually paying her quite a bit."

"Yeah," said Twilight. "I was wondering about that. In Basetown, if you want to buy a cup of tea, you have to give the tavern wench enough copper to build the kettle. Something is wrong there."

"Well, we have the copper pieces," said Mak-Thar. "In fact, we can add a ten percent gratuity to show our gratitude for avoiding the side quest."

So Twilight fetched Mak-Thar's pouch of copper pieces, and they bought a vial of chili powder. The vial was secured in one of Mak-Thar's saddle bags, and Twilight was about to put away the coin pouch as well, when Helen stopped him.

"We need to arrange lodging for Nightshade," said Helen. "It's time for her to leave the party."

CHAPTER TWENTY-EIGHT: IN WHICH NIGHTSHADE LEAVES THE PARTY.

"EXCUSE US," SAID TWILIGHT to the crowd. "We need to discuss something in private."

"Of course," said Roark.

The villagers continued to stand there and stare, but they allowed Fred and his friends to move a discreet distance away.

"She's really not that heavy," said Mak-Thar. "I don't mind

carrying her—unless you think we are likely to find sixteen hundred coins of treasure at the end of this adventure."

"At the end of this adventure," said Helen, "you won't be a mule anymore, remember?"

"Ah," said Mak-Thar. "Quite right. I had not considered that."

"I can carry her," said Fred. "I've done it before."

"You carried her because you had to," said Helen. "But now we're in a village. And even if there's no tavern, we might be able to convince someone to take her in. It's not like she eats much."

That was true. Nightshade didn't even need a bed.

"But is it safe to leave her here?" Fred asked. "What if the green-blob priests show up?"

"If we really thought this village was in danger," said Helen, "we wouldn't be leaving now, would we?"

Well, no. Fred wouldn't want to abandon the unarmed villagers if they were in danger. So since he was planning to leave, that meant … the village was safe? That kind of made sense.

"The logistics of carrying her become quite complicated when we come back across the bridge," said Mak-Thar. "If I am not a mule, I will no longer be able to carry her and Fred. In fact, I will need someone who is not a man to carry *me*."

"Nightshade and I could stay beside the bridge and let you guys cross without us," said Fred.

"Then you'd be sitting out there all alone in the wilderness with an unconscious body," said Helen.

"Maybe she'll wake up," said Fred.

"She's just a liability," Helen insisted.

"I have to agree," said Twilight. "It's a shame, really. Nightshade had almost learned to be bearable. But she's been unconscious for days, and we have no way of knowing when she'll come back."

"Or *if* she'll come back," said Helen. "Remember that guy from the Bloody Axe."

Could they just leave Nightshade in Mucho Caliente? It didn't seem right. You should never leave a wounded buddy behind.

But she wasn't exactly wounded, was she? She just had more important stuff to do. It still wasn't clear whether she chose to fall asleep or whether it was something that happened to her, but either way, it meant that she wasn't on her feet helping her friends win battles.

Fred wanted to be nice. He had invited her along, so he had a responsibility to be sure she had a fun adventure. But he had promised he would lead. Maybe leading was not only about helping people get along with each other. Maybe he sometimes had to decide what was best for the party.

Nightshade was no longer helping the party. And Fred had told her she could leave as soon as they found a safe place. "I guess you're right. I think she's learning to be a good adventurer, but she's not being a good adventurer right now. And we need to focus on getting Mak-Thar unmuled. I guess Nightshade stays here."

* * *

Fred helped Roark and his wife stow Nightshade on a little platform they made by laying some boards across the rafters of their chicken coop. Fred was sure that was the best place to keep her. The building was designed to protect sleeping chickens, so it should also be good at protecting a sleeping elf.

While Fred made sure that Nightshade's sleeping place was secure, Mak-Thar divided the treasure. Nobody's share came to very much, so they decided that Nightshade would not have to pay out of her own pocket for coop rental. Instead, they all chipped in, paying a price equivalent to thirty days at an inn. Really, though, Nightshade wouldn't be any trouble as long as her snores didn't disturb the chickens.

Despite all these efforts, Fred felt guilty about walking out of Mucho Caliente and leaving Nightshade behind. The worst part was he didn't know whether he was wronging Nightshade or the villagers.

* * *

They followed a road that wound through the hills, heading up to higher elevations. It was now late spring and everything was green.

After a few miles, Mak-Thar said, "Well, it seems we have everything in place now. Twilight has finished the wombat parkas. We know the secret of the Cursed Bridge. And we have a vial of fine red powder which is supposed to protect us from white dragons—although I recommend that we also consider a backup plan."

"We could kill it," said Helen.

"Isn't that always a barbarian's backup plan?" asked Twilight.

"It's usually our frontup plan," said Helen.

"It does seem odd that the easiest part of our quest came last," said Twilight.

"You think this is over?" Helen shook her head. "Nah. It's all just beginning."

"Too bad Nightshade will miss it," said Fred.

"She was there for a lot of it, really," said Twilight. "She was instrumental in obtaining the wombat parkas, and she was at least present when we negotiated with Herman and his owlbears."

"Yeah, that's what I was doing," said Helen. "I was *negotiating* with those owlbears."

"It was easier to negotiate with the owlbears than with Herman," said Fred.

"Yes," said Twilight. "One must expect hermits to be eccentric. And perhaps even cantankerous. But demanding that one of us be sacrificed to feed his owlbears was simply rude."

"My thoughts have often been returning to the hermit," Mak-Thar admitted. "I keep trying to think of what I would have done in that situation. In theory, a neutral person shouldn't care if his pets eat an adventuring party. But somehow, it just seems wrong."

"That's because it's wrong," said Twilight.

"And yet," continued Mak-Thar, "I don't think Herman was evil. He wasn't threatening us because he enjoyed our suffering. He simply wanted to feed his pets."

"Well," said Helen, "I wasn't ready to star in a pet food commercial."

Mak-Thar swished his tail. "You asked me why I thought Paul was evil and Herman was just being neutral; I think it's because Paul killed me for fun."

Twilight shook his head. "He looked nervous and guilty. He didn't look like he was having fun."

"People always think evil is more fun," said Helen. "Then they try it and find out they were very, very wrong."

"That's it," said Mak-Thar. "Only the deities know for certain whether Paul was neutral or evil, but he *wanted* to be evil. Or at least, he had decided it was time to try it out."

Twilight said, "I still think it's wrong to let another sentient being die simply to feed some monsters you spliced together. That's a lot worse than just being reluctant to fight for higher principles."

"Who's reluctant to fight for higher principles?" asked Fred.

Twilight said, "I was thinking of Mak-Thar—"

"Me?"

"—but really the entire adventuring business seems to ignore the good in favor of the gold."

"I've been on plenty of adventures that paid way better than this," said Helen. "If you think I'm in it for the gold, you haven't been paying attention."

Twilight said, "You and Fred are both strong and beautiful enough to lead righteous armies against the forces of darkness. Instead, you join adventuring parties for fun—like it was some sort of bowling team."

"Bowling team?" asked Fred.

"That's a great idea!" said Helen. "We should start a Fighters' Guild bowling team."

"I don't bowl," said Fred.

"We could learn," said Helen.

"And don't let me be hypocritical," said Twilight. "I myself have a sacred duty to my family and my people, which I have been completely ignoring."

"You're on a heroic quest," said Fred. "You'll return the amulet when you get time."

"Yes," agreed Twilight. "When I get time. The return to my people doesn't seem as heroic as a quest to a magic spring, so I'll do my sacred duty later."

"We're on this quest to help our friend," said Fred. "Sometimes, when our friends need us, they become family."

"I'm just suggesting that people may not fall out into evil, neutral, and good," said Twilight. "It seems like there are lots of places in between."

"I was raised to believe that the GM graphs our alignment on a line segment," said Mak-Thar. "Evil is one endpoint, good is the other. True neutrality is the point in the middle."

"Your religion has a geometrical mythology?" asked Twilight.

"My former religion," said Mak-Thar. "Now I'm beginning to wonder if life is not the process of graphing oneself."

Twilight said, "You're the only person I know who expects to find the path to enlightenment sketched on a piece of graph paper."

"You don't need graph paper to graph alignment," said Mak-Thar. "You can just draw a line. Alignment is one dimensional, so it only needs one axis. ... Unless ... What if those new religions are a second axis?"

"Are you saying that morality has axles?" asked Fred.

"The number of axles determines whether your morality is a cart or a wagon," said Helen. "And if your morality is also a boat, then you're morally amphibious."

"That's a weird religion," said Fred.

"I'll stick with animism," said Helen.

"You believe that every object has a spirit?" asked Twilight.

"I believe that when I die I'll become an animated cartoon," said Helen. "But only if I'm very good."

"Are you good?" asked Mak-Thar. "I thought you said you were neutral."

"I'm—" Movement in the sky caught Helen's eye. "I'm ready

for the backup plan. It looks like we've found the dragon."

"We don't have a backup plan!" said Mak-Thar. "We don't even have a frontup plan!"

CHAPTER TWENTY-NINE: IN WHICH OUR HEROES DO NOT HAVE TIME TO MAKE A PLAN FOR FIGHTING THE WHITE DRAGON.

FRED REALLY HADN'T EXPECTED to run into the dragon so soon. Everything else on this adventure had been days or weeks apart, and yet here was the white dragon only an hour from the red-powder village.

But they had the red powder, so that meant they were going to win, right?

"Get the powder!" yelled Mak-Thar. "Get the powder!"

"Okay," said Twilight. He fished the small glass vial out of Mak-Thar's saddle bag. "But what do we do with it?"

"Throw it at the dragon!"

Twilight looked up into the sky, where the dragon was making a wide circle over their heads. "I can't really throw that high."

"Can you shoot an arrow that high?" asked Mak-Thar.

"I don't know."

"Let's see," said Mak-Thar. "A shortbow has a range of one hundred fifty yards. That assumes an optimal launch angle of forty-five degrees. Acceleration due to gravity is about ten meters per second squared, and a yard is about a meter, so …"

"You could just shoot an arrow and find out," said Helen.

"I fear that shooting arrows at the dragon may provoke an attack," said Twilight.

The dragon tucked in its wings and went into a dive.

"I wouldn't worry about provoking an attack," said Helen.

"It looks like you won't have to worry about range," said Fred.

"Watch out!" cried Mak-Thar. "A dragon's first attack is always its breath weapon!"

Helen left the road and started running up the slope. Fred left the road and started running down.

Twilight caught up to Fred and pointed at the bushy trees in the bottom of the draw. "Are we hoping to hide ourselves in the underbrush?"

"We're hoping to scatter the party so that only one of us gets hit with the dragon breath!"

"Oh," said Twilight, who was not scattered at all.

There was a sound like a twenty-minute ice storm falling on the hillside all at once. The armored joints at Fred's shoulders froze up. His foot hit a patch of ice, and Fred went sprawling across the ground.

The cold penetrated his armor a moment later. First his skin screamed, as though it had been burned. Then a damp chill like ice water in a cold cellar seeped into his bones. His blood felt thick and slow. His skull felt like it was too small for his brain.

Fred opened his eyes, and his eyelids made a quiet crinkling sound like someone crumpling a small piece of paper. Twilight was standing above him, holding the vial of chili powder, an expression of horror frozen onto his face.

Well, honestly, everything about Twilight was frozen. His cape appeared to billow out behind him, even though he was now standing still. His eyes did not blink. His chest did not rise and fall.

The vial of chili powder was unstoppered, and he seemed to be frozen in the act of raising the vial to his lips … or perhaps in the act of lowering the vial afterwards. A bit of the chili powder was missing.

From between Twilight's frosty blue lips, a red tongue poked out. Where the tongue touched, frost melted. Twilight drew in a breath.

Without moving his jaw, Twilight said, "Hot. Hot."

Then steam rose from his body, his face regained its natural color, and the elf could move once more.

"Fred! Are you all right?"

Fred was all right. He couldn't say he was all right because he couldn't move anything except his eyes, but he was probably all right. He could just lie here on the ground and wait for the sun to thaw him out.

Twilight knelt at Fred's side. The glass vial clinked against Fred's frozen lips.

Something warm filled Fred's mouth. The heat spread into his sinus cavities, and his head began to melt from the inside out. Saliva sloshed in, and the heat intensified, burning Fred's tongue. Fred swallowed, and his stomach shouted, "Hey! What's the big idea?!" (Not really.)

The miraculous powder melted his bones and spread outward. After a few seconds, Fred was able to rise to his feet.

"That stuff tastes terrible!" he said.

"I believe I shall be sick," said Twilight.

"A dragon's breath does damage equal to its hit points," called Mak-Thar, who was still standing on the road above. "If you have both survived, that means it has fewer hit points than you do."

Fred wasn't so sure about that. In Fred's opinion, Twilight had just saved his life. "Good herbalism, Twilight."

"Ingesting unknown powders is not herbalism," said Twilight. "It's desperation. Any idea how we get this stuff inside the dragon?"

"You know," said Fred, "I'm not really the idea guy."

"It's coming in for another run!" yelled Helen. "Give me the powder!"

"This could be intense," said Mak-Thar. "It still has two breath attacks left, and there is a fifty percent chance it will use one of them instead of closing for melee."

"Number, number, number!" shouted Helen. She was running down the slope to Twilight.

Twilight ran up the slope to Helen. When he met her, he handed off the vial and kept on running until he got to Mak-Thar.

Helen returned to the road and took a position about thirty yards in front of the mule. As the dragon soared down the canyon, Helen was between it and Mak-Thar. Helen raised the chili powder defiantly.

Twilight undid some saddle strings, and a pile of parkas fell to the ground. "Mak-Thar, get down!"

The mule dropped to its knees. Twilight covered Mak-Thar in the special mule-sized parka and then rolled underneath it.

The dragon swooped in. Helen tossed the vial of chili powder into the air and jumped off the road.

As Helen tumbled downhill and rolled through the rocks, the white dragon opened its hideous mouth and let loose a blast of frost. The road and Mak-Thar's parka were coated with ice.

As the blast of frost ended, the vial of chili powder disappeared inside the dragon's open mouth. The jaws snapped shut. The dragon swallowed. A lump moved down the monster's snaky throat as it soared away into the sky.

And … that was pretty much all that happened. The dragon circled around, gaining altitude for another dive.

"Ohhh!" said Helen. "Cleric. Need cleric."

Fred scrambled up the slope toward her voice.

With crunching noises, the mule-sized wombat parka was pulled free of the places where it had frozen to the road. Mak-Thar stood up. Twilight came dashing out from underneath the parka, running toward Helen's call.

Helen had successfully evaded the dragon's breath, but after rolling through the rocks and brush, she was scraped all over. Fred and Twilight reached her at the same time.

"Is something broken?" asked Twilight.

"No," Helen groaned. "But my whole body stings."

"You just skinned your knees," said Fred. "And your shoulders. And your elbows. And your nose. And—"

"Thanks Fred," said Helen. "That's enough."

"Well, it's certainly a lot," said Fred. "The nice thing is, because of your armor, you only skinned the mentionable parts of your body."

"I have some ointment," said Twilight. "It will probably take an hour to clean and disinfect all your wounds. Normally, I wouldn't mind—I'm immortal, so I can be patient—but right now we're being attacked by a dragon and our secret weapon has been used up, so ..."

"Right," said Helen. She rose to her feet and pulled a small, sharp branch out of her forearm. "Time for heroic barbarian stuff."

Yellin' Helen drew her humongous sword out of its back scabbard and charged up the hill yelling, "When I'm done with you, you'll be draggin' your sorry tail back to your cave! Get it? Dragging? Dragon? It's a pun!"

Mak-Thar said, "According to *The Adventurer's Guide*, white dragons have only a ten percent chance of understanding puns."

"We should go help her," said Twilight.

"We should stay spread out," said Fred. "But let's go help her anyway."

"I'll fetch her a parka!" said Twilight. "Those things really work!"

And so it was that Fred and Twilight and Helen met the dragon's next dive standing side by side with swords raised. (They would have stood shoulder to shoulder, but the wombat quills made it difficult to stand so close together.)

As the dragon came in, Mak-Thar shouted inspiring words: "This round, there's a fifty percent chance that it will forgo using its final breath attack and just try to maul us."

The dragon was fast. It had a large toothy mouth. Its claws were sharp. Fred suspected the dragon could do quite a bit of mauling.

Perhaps it was, as Mak-Thar insisted, simple random chance. Or perhaps it was the sight of three brave warriors standing with blades drawn. Perhaps it was the realization that the warriors had killed wombats. For whatever reason, the dragon did not swoop low enough to maul and be mauled. Instead, while it was still a safe distance away, it opened up its mouth to loose its final frosty breath for the day.

204 JASON A. HOLT

Fred, Twilight, and Helen braced themselves as the ferocious beast unleashed a blast of swirling mist.

The dragon swerved out of reach and soared again into the sky.

"Mist?" Fred blinked the water droplets from his eyelashes. "Did it just breathe mist?"

"Sage was right!" said Twilight. "It's been neutralized!"

"BLORP!" said the dragon, a hundred feet directly over their heads.

"Look out!" shouted Mak-Thar.

Chili-flavored dragon puke rained from the sky. Fred dove for cover.

SPLAT!

"It burns! It burns!" shouted Helen.

"No fair," said Mak-Thar. "In the first place, dragons get only three breath attacks per day. In the second place, white dragons aren't allowed to breathe acid."

"It only has a ten percent chance of being able to read *The Adventurer's Guide!*" said Twilight.

"Good point," said Mak-Thar.

Fortunately, most of the dragon puke fell on Helen's wombat parka. If she hadn't scraped up so much of her body, she might have been completely unharmed. Unfortunately, some of her wounds were unprotected and they were stinging fiercely.

"It burrrrns!"

Twilight rushed to her side with a gauze pad. "I hope the acid is a disinfectant. If it's not, that means there's an infection tough enough to live in a dragon's stomach, and anything like that is just going to laugh at my cute little elf ointments."

"Owwwwww!" Helen waved her sword at the sky. "Let me kill it!"

"It's going away!" said Mak-Thar. "I think we've driven it off."

"Twilight," said Fred, "I know your healing skills are a sacred miracle, but how fast do you think you and Selene can get Helen ready to move out? I would like to be very gone before the dragon returns."

CHAPTER THIRTY: IN WHICH OUR HEROES COME TO THAT BRIDGE AND HAVE TO CROSS IT.

"YOU KNOW," SAID TWILIGHT, "I may have complained that certain adventures fell short of the heroic ideal or that certain battles lacked narrative significance. But right now, I'm actually glad that adventuring is not like the stories I read as a youth."

"Really?" asked Fred.

"Yes," said Twilight. "In a fairy tale adventure, if we had to face three challenges, each would be more difficult than the last. But right now, after bandaging and disinfecting thirty-seven distinct wounds, I'm looking forward to simple tasks like 'cross a bridge' and 'climb a mountain.'"

They had already gained quite a bit of elevation. The rocky slope below the road had grown steeper and steeper until now it was nearly a cliff face above a deep canyon.

"Was it really thirty-seven distinct wounds?" asked Mak-Thar. "Because, assuming each wound is one hit point, that would imply—"

Helen said, "It's a lot of wounds, Mak-Thar. But they were just scrapes."

"And bruises," said Twilight.

"And a few bruises," Helen agreed. "I'll still be able to fight for you guys."

Twilight had used up all his remaining bandages, and Helen looked like she was about halfway to mummification. Fred wondered if she might not think about wearing more armor—or at least a leather jacket.

"I have no doubt that you can fight," said Mak-Thar. "I just want to be certain you can survive."

"Well, aren't we almost at the end?" asked Helen. "I think that's the mountain we're supposed to climb." She pointed across the canyon.

Maybe "canyon" was not the correct word for the space

between the two mountains. Maybe it was a "gorge" or a "ravine". Was a ravine steeper than a gorge? Fred didn't know. Whatever was steepest, that's what it was.

"The map is somewhat vague," said Mak-Thar. "The bridge is certainly between these two hexes, but because of the scale, I can't tell if the bridge is supposed to be close to Mucho Caliente or far away."

In fact, the bridge was not far away at all. After about a hundred paces, they saw it ahead of them, connecting their road to the face of the opposite mountain, just above the place where the mountain turned into a sheer cliff.

"It bothers me that we cannot see the bottom of the valley below," said Twilight.

Fred was sure that "valley" was too tame a word to describe the canyon. It was probably a gorge. "Gorge" reminded Fred of words like "gargantuan" and "gorgon". Words with lots of *G*s are scary.

"It certainly is a long way down," said Helen.

"Who built the bridge?" asked Twilight. "And why?"

"Well, there seems to be no reason to run a trade route through this region," said Mak-Thar. "So apparently the bridge is here simply for those who need to reach the magic spring."

"It could be a local nature club," Fred suggested.

"What?" asked Helen.

"Well, it's a pretty mountain," said Fred. "So maybe someone thought there should be a nice bridge to it."

"They forgot to put up interpretive signs," said Mak-Thar.

"Maybe the dragon ate them," said Twilight.

Fred wasn't exactly sure what "interpretive signs" were supposed to be. He suspected that Twilight and Mak-Thar were mocking his idea.

He was as surprised as everyone else when they did find two signs. The signs were nailed to a post beside the bridge.

The first sign said: *Weight limit 10,000 coins.**

Below it was a sign that said, in much smaller print: **Also, this bridge is cursed. See Herman the Hermit for details.*

Twilight read the signs aloud, for Helen's benefit, and then commented, "I'd hate to be the poor hiker who gets this far before he discovers he has to go back to the desert to find out how to cross the bridge."

Mak-Thar said, "Herman didn't tell us about the weight limit!"

Helen shrugged. "I think ten thousand is a pretty big number. We should be fine."

"You think *seven* is a pretty big number," said Mak-Thar.

"Okay. You got me."

Twilight frowned. "Do we need to go one at a time?"

"Can I go at all?" Mak-Thar asked. "That's the real question. Get *The Adventurer's Guide*. We have to find out how much mules weigh."

But you know—it was a funny thing—for some reason, *The Adventurer's Guide* didn't say how much mules weigh. It said how much mules can *carry*. It said how much party members of various races might weigh. But there was no statistic giving the weight of the average mule.

Fred was kind of surprised. Twilight said it made sense—that the guide was adventurer-centric and would only list the weights of things adventurers were likely to carry—but Fred knew adventurers. There were probably *lots* of parties that had tried to put their mule in a treasure sack.

If the weight of a mule wasn't listed, it wasn't because no one had ever tried to pick one up. It was because no one had ever succeeded.

"That's ridiculous," said Mak-Thar. "It *has* to tell us how much a mule weighs. What if you want to haul one in a wagon?"

"Or in a cart," said Twilight.

"Exactly."

"Or on another mule," said Twilight.

"Well, that might be a little ridiculous," said Mak-Thar.

"And yet," said Twilight, "if you'll recall ..."

He pointed out a rule in the rulebook.

"Oh, yes," said Mak-Thar. "That's right. A cart can carry only

4,000 coins, which is the same as the weight allowance of a single mule. Hmm …" Mak-Thar swished his tail. "So if we assume a mule cannot carry a mule, then we must conclude that a mule weighs more than 4,000 coins."

Helen looked him up and down. "I'd say you weigh more than the three of us put together."

"I can't be that heavy," said Mak-Thar. "I have only two hit dice. Something is not adding up."

"Well, I don't think we have to worry about it," said Helen.

"*You* don't have to worry because *you* don't weigh 10,000 coins," said Mak-Thar.

"But you probably don't, either. Look, the bridge is wide enough for a mule. Mules probably go back and forth all the time."

"What size of probable mules?" asked Mak-Thar. "Twilight, as mules go, would you say I am petite or plus size?"

"Honestly, I just liked the star on your forehead. I really don't know how big you are compared with other mules."

"Well," said Helen, "it's not like we can weigh you, so—"

"That's it!" said Mak-Thar. "We'll build a scale and weigh me."

"Build a scale," said Twilight.

"Yes," said Mak-Thar.

"Out here in the wilderness," said Twilight.

"I don't think we should go back to the village for construction supplies," said Fred. He was kind of afraid of that dragon.

"There is no need to go back," said Mak-Thar. "The bridge has nice long planks, and I brought a crowbar."

Twilight gazed into Mak-Thar's eyes. "So you want to tear apart the bridge, so we can build a scale, so we can weigh you, so we can see whether the bridge is structurally strong enough to hold you?"

"Yes," said Mak-Thar.

"Sounds like a good plan," said Helen. "Where's your crowbar?"

* * *

A scale is really a simple thing: You put a weight on one end, you put a weight on the other, and you see which is heavier.

Mak-Thar found a way to make it more complex than that. He stood on one end of the plank and had Twilight measure to be sure the other end of the plank was ten times longer. (There was a rock under the plank, and most of the plank was on the non-Mak-Thar side of the rock.) Then he had them pile stuff on the far end until its total weight lifted him into the air. Since the weight of the stuff was listed in *The Adventurer's Guide*, Mak-Thar was able to calculate his own weight. He weighed about 9,000 coins, which left him with a 10 percent margin for error.

"Actually, it's an 11 percent margin for error, but not a 12 percent margin. That's what worries me."

Helen said it was close enough, but it was getting late and she preferred to rebuild the bridge in the morning. (Helen had been the one to take out the plank because she was the one who was most confident that she was immune to the curse.)

So Twilight shot them a rabbit, and they camped beside the bridge for the night. They stood watches as usual, except that Helen asked Twilight to wake them if they drifted too near the edge of the road.

"If you roll off the road in your sleep," she told Fred, "you'll never stop rolling."

During the night, they were attacked by a small group of goblins that had twenty-five electrum pieces. This battle had absolutely no impact on their quest. It was so inconsequential that Twilight didn't even comment on how inconsequential it was.

In the morning, everyone felt refreshed and ready to go, and Twilight didn't comment on how sore they should be after fighting a dragon the day before. Somewhere along the way, Twilight had become an adventurer.

Fred looked up at the mountain on the other side of the gorge. It looked tall. But they had all day to climb it, and everyone looked ready. They had come to the bridge, and now it was time to cross it.

Mak-Thar had brought plenty of iron spikes, so when Helen replaced the scale-plank, she pounded in a couple extra spikes, just to be sure.

"Good as new," she said. "Who wants to go first?"

"I suppose I must go first," said Mak-Thar. "Because if it collapses and sends me to my doom, I don't want any of you stranded on the far side. And if it collapses with one of you, I don't want to be stranded on *this* side."

They all agreed that was logical.

"The funny thing about logic," said Mak-Thar, "is that it doesn't move one's hooves."

"Would it make you feel better if I walked with you?" asked Twilight.

"No! Your extra weight would doom us both!"

"Oh, right."

Helen clapped Mak-Thar on the shoulder. "You know what they say, Mak-Thar."

"Yes. 'The longest journey begins with a single step.'"

"No," said Helen. "They say, 'Giddy up, mule! Time's a-wasting.'"

"Don't they say both things?" asked Fred.

"I hope these aren't my last words," said Mak-Thar. He placed his hoof on the bridge.

Nothing happened.

He shifted his weight and placed another hoof on the bridge.

"Doing great!" said Fred.

Clip. Clop. Clip. Clop. Clip, clop, clip, clop, clip, clop ...

Mak-Thar the mule clip-clopped across the bridge above the gorge.

"Watch for trolls!" Twilight called.

"That's not helping!" called Mak-Thar.

The bridge did not collapse. Mak-Thar reached the other side and turned around.

"Now we bring his stuff," said Helen.

Herman the Hermit had said, *Any man who sets foot on the Cursed Bridge shall fall to his doom unless his heart is pure.* Neither the woman nor the elf was a man, so they were able to cross in safety. Helen and Twilight made a few trips carrying Mak-Thar's saddle and all the equipment associated with it. This phase of the operation ended with Twilight on the opposite side, loading the mule, and Helen back with Fred.

She asked, "Are you ready?"

"Yes. Thank you for not asking, 'Ready, Freddie?'"

Helen grinned. He knew she'd been thinking it.

Now it was Fred's turn. It was possible that Fred would be able to walk across the bridge on his own two feet. He weighed less than 10,000 coins, and the curse would not affect a man whose heart was pure. But no one was quite sure what that meant.

Mak-Thar assumed it meant the curse did not affect anyone whose alignment was "good". But Fred wasn't sure he believed in alignments. And anyway, you couldn't interpret the rest of the riddle literally and assume that "heart is pure" was just a metaphor. So to be safe, they had decided Fred would not set foot on the bridge.

Fred lay down on his belly and did a push-up. Helen grabbed his ankles and lifted them up to her hips. Fred walked forward on his hands, and Helen followed along behind. The two friends had done a lot together on their various adventures, but this was the first time they had ever done this.

Slap, thump, slap, thump. Fred and Helen wheelbarrowed across the Cursed Bridge.

Chapter Thirty-One: In Which Mak-Thar Faces a Dilemma.

"My hands are sore," Fred admitted, when he had reached the other side. "Poor Mak-Thar. You've been walking on your hands for the entire adventure!"

"It's different for mules," said Twilight.

"Lots of things are different for mules," said Mak-Thar. "That's what I've learned." He sighed and looked up the mountain.

The slope was shrubby and rocky, dotted here and there with a tree or a tuft of grass. On this side of the gorge, there was no road, but a trail zigzagged up the mountain's face.

"I want to thank you all again," said Mak-Thar. "When we left Basetown, I hoped that the spare treasure we picked up from random encounters would compensate you for your time, but I must admit that it really hasn't."

"That's okay," said Twilight. "We're all in it for the experience points, anyway."

"Oh," said Mak-Thar. "Well, that's a relief. I assume the experience points have been adequate. You might even go up a level."

Fred said, "He was joking."

"Are you sure?"

Fred nodded. "We're here for you, Mak-Thar."

Mak-Thar swished his tail. "You can't go on an adventure just to help an NPM fulfill a personal quest. That's suboptimal gameplay."

"We're your friends," said Twilight. "Surely you've figured that out by now."

"But Helen's not my friend," said Mak-Thar. "She and I have nothing in common."

"Don't be such a dumb mule," said Helen. "Anyone who walks through a swamp with you is your friend—assuming you don't kill each other before you get out."

"Is that part of the unwritten code?" asked Mak-Thar.

"Yes," said Helen.

Twilight smiled. "Mak-Thar would understand friendship better if it had rules in *The Adventurer's Guide*."

"It *does* have rules in *The Adventurer's Guide*," said Mak-Thar. "But it's all based on racial bonuses and charisma scores, and I know I don't get plusses."

"Nonsense!" said Twilight. "You're a very attractive mule."

"Oh, that reminds me!" said Helen.

"Reminds you of what?" asked Fred.

"Could you guys take the lead going up the trail?"

"Sure," said Fred. "Are we ready to go?"

They were. The four of them set off up the trail, with Fred in the lead and Helen guarding the rear.

After three switchbacks, Helen said, "Twilight, you sure have a cute mule."

She giggled and shortcut the trail to get ahead of Fred. "Thanks. I've been waiting to use that one."

Twilight was incredulous. "You wanted us to go ahead just so you could make personal remarks?"

"So I could make one more mule pun!" said Helen. "Face it, this is my last chance."

"Well, it was still wrong to shortcut the trail," said Twilight. "That causes erosion, you know."

"Is erosion like dry, itchy skin?" Fred asked.

"No," said Twilight. "That's— Oh my. Look who's here." He stopped and pointed back toward the bridge.

They all stopped. Jogging across the bridge in silent elven boots was their on-again, off-again companion Nightshade.

"Hey guys? Guys?"

Twilight called, "Hail traveler, newly returned from the land of the sleeping!"

"Yeah, whatever," said Nightshade. "Wait up? Please?"

They were waiting. And since they were three switchbacks above her, Fred figured they were waiting up.

Nightshade ignored the trail and ran straight up the slope.

"Don't shortcut the trail!" said Twilight.

"It's okay," said Nightshade. "I've got killer stats. I'm not even winded."

"It causes erosion," Twilight mumbled.

Nightshade stopped on the switchback below them and said, "Okay, so I know Mak-Thar's in a big hurry to get changed back into a human, but this thing just came up."

"Not a side quest!" said Mak-Thar.

Helen said, "The thing that just came up is wearing cute, black tights."

Nightshade rolled her eyes.

"How did you get past the dragon?" asked Twilight.

"Invisibility spell," said Nightshade. "Good thing I had one left, too. She was pissed."

Twilight frowned.

"Oh," said Nightshade. "Elves don't say 'pissed'?"

Twilight shook his head.

"What do we say?"

" 'Upset'," said Twilight.

"Yeah," said Nightshade. "She was upset."

Helen smirked.

Twilight rolled his eyes. "I'm glad I've given you fodder for new jokes."

Helen blinked at him innocently.

"What jokes?" asked Nightshade. "Does Helen tell jokes?"

"We're glad you made it safely past the dragon," said Fred.

"Me too," said Nightshade.

"That dragon was pretty scary," said Helen. "So scary that Twilight upset his pants."

"Well, now that we have that out of the way ..." said Twilight.

"The village wants our help," said Nightshade.

"Mucho Caliente?" asked Mak-Thar.

"Gesundheit," said Helen.

"What is *with* her?" asked Nightshade.

"She's in a good mood because we're near the end of our adventure and we're all still alive," said Fred.

"Okay," said Nightshade. "If she can wear that many bandages and still be in a good mood, I guess that's cool. Is that a 'no' on helping the village, then?"

"No side quests," said Mak-Thar.

"We might be able to help them later," said Twilight. "What's the problem?"

"There's an evil army marching towards it. When I woke up— Oh, nice call, by the way. Chicken coop. Real classy, guys."

"Chicken coops are very safe," said Fred.

"They're stinky," said Nightshade.

Fred thought chicken coops smelled like home.

"Anyway, when I woke up, there were all these people outside my coop talking about undead armies and evil clerics, and I thought, 'Cool!' So I go outside, and they're all like, 'Hey, Nightshade, save us.' So then I thought, 'Uh oh.' So I say, 'Where's Fred and Helen and them?' and they say, 'You're the only one.' And I'm like, 'Hey, you know what? Maybe I'll just go find them.' And they're all like, 'Sure. Good plan.' So that's what I did, because I really didn't want to fight an evil army alone."

"How close is this army?" asked Helen. "It's gonna take us all day to hike up and down this mountain."

Nightshade shrugged. "I don't know."

Twilight asked, "Would it be possible to split up?"

Helen said, "You mean like two or three of us go up the mountain with Mak-Thar, and the rest of us go back and fight an evil army?"

"Never split the party," said Mak-Thar.

"Yeah," said Helen. "I'm not a numbers person, but even *I* know that any group you can count on your fingers is too small to fight an army."

"She's right," said Fred. "We had to run away from a few bugs. I don't think we have much chance against an entire army."

"We would have help from the villagers," said Twilight.

"That's what *I* was thinking," said Nightshade. "But then I saw their militia practicing with rakes and hoes, and I realized that it wasn't because they were keeping their swords clean."

"Well," said Helen, "if we power hike, we can finish the quest by midafternoon and get back in time to save the village tomorrow morning."

"Is a power hike like a forced march?" asked Mak-Thar.

"Do we have reason to believe that the village can wait until tomorrow morning?" asked Twilight.

Nightshade shrugged. "I don't know. They should be good, right? Unless the army attacks today, right?"

"We could send Nightshade back to tell them we're coming," said Twilight.

"That's still kind of splitting the party," said Fred.

"Never split the party," said Mak-Thar. "Hm. I guess I *do* know a few unwritten rules."

"Okay," said Fred. "It sounds like we're all agreed that we need to finish this adventure first before we try to help the village."

Twilight said, "It sounds like we're all agreed that helping the village is a suicide mission."

"Maybe," said Fred. "Or maybe not. We would need a brilliant plan. And right now, the guy who's in charge of plans is kind of distracted by being a mule."

"This is true," said Mak-Thar.

"So we should demule him," said Fred, "and if he comes up with any ideas for saving a village, we can use them tomorrow."

"If the village still exists," said Twilight.

"If the village doesn't exist," said Helen, "then we can come up with brilliant plans for infiltrating an evil army and overthrowing them from the inside."

"That sounds like fun," said Nightshade. "I mean, I'd feel bad for the villagers, of course, but I guess they're just a bunch of NPMs."

So they set off up the trail again. Nightshade offered to scout ahead. Helen pointed out that, because they were zigzagging across the face of the mountain, everyone could simultaneously guard the front and the rear just by watching their flanks. Fred thought that was a neat trick.

Twilight was frowning. Fred could tell that the decision to delay saving the village didn't sit right with him.

At the next switchback, Fred got a good look at Mak-Thar and saw that his head was sagging and his ears were drooping.

"Is this trail too steep?" Fred asked. "We could lighten your load." (Fred had no idea how they would carry all that stuff once Mak-Thar became a man again.)

"I'm just an NPM," said Mak-Thar.

"What's the matter?" asked Twilight.

Mak-Thar said it again, this time with different emphasis: "*I'm* just an NPM."

"Oh," said Twilight.

"I'm just like the villagers," said Mak-Thar. "I'm not truly a member of the party. You have no reason to help me."

"But we *are* helping you," said Fred. "Because you're our friend."

"Yes," said Mak-Thar. "You know me, so you picked my quest over theirs. But what if they need you more?"

"I'm sure they do need us more," said Twilight. "But we're going with you because … we don't know how to help them."

Mak-Thar asked, "So if we could, we would?"

"Sure," said Twilight. "I think. Wouldn't we, Fred?"

Fred tried to think about it. Fred realized they didn't have time for him to think about it, so he said the thing that popped into his head. "We'd probably do what Mak-Thar wanted us to do. It's *his* quest."

"But what if I don't want the right thing?" asked Mak-Thar. "I'm neutral. It's in character for me to be selfish."

Fred shrugged. "It's in character for me to go along with whatever the noisiest person wants."

"That's a terrible system!" said Mak-Thar. "We put you in charge because we can trust you to do what's right!"

"Really?" asked Fred.

"Yeah," said Helen.

"Yeah," said Nightshade.

"Of course," said Twilight.

"What makes you guys think I know what's right?" asked Fred.

"You're good," said Mak-Thar.

Was Fred good? He did not recall ever choosing an alignment. He had never dropped a copper piece into the offering box at the Temple of Good.

"I'm just Fred," he told Mak-Thar. "Would a good person let us abandon a village that needs our help?"

"But we don't know a way to save it," said Twilight.

"Oh, Mak-Thar could think up a way," said Fred. "And Helen is itching to do a sneak attack or a diversion attack or something. There's a way to stop that evil army. We just don't want to."

Twilight frowned and bit his lip. "You're right. I'm being a coward."

"I'm just guilty of lack of imagination," said Helen. "If one of you guys has an army-defeating plan, count me in."

"I'm going to do whatever Mak-Thar wants," said Fred. "It's *his* quest."

"But that's not fair!" said Mak-Thar. "Of course I want to do the selfish thing. Don't leave it up to me! You can't let those people die just because they're NPMs."

"So you want to go back and help the village?" Twilight asked.

"I don't know what I want," said Mak-Thar. "I know what a neutral person is *supposed* to want. But I'm starting to feel like we've ignored this side quest a little too long."

"He's right," said Helen. "It's not about us risking our lives now. It's about us risking the lives of other people."

"So we go back?" asked Fred.

"Yeah, we should," said Helen.

"Is this a suicide mission?" asked Twilight. "And please don't grin like that."

Helen put a hand over her face to hide her grin.

"It's not a suicide mission," said Fred. "Not if we have Mak-Thar."

"Wow," said Nightshade. "This is heavy."

Fred asked, "What do you say, Mak-Thar?"

"We have to go back," said Mak-Thar. "And we must hurry. But I'm going to say that you all talked me into it, because otherwise the decision might shift my alignment."

"Cool!" said Helen.

"Wonderful!" said Twilight. "Good thing we have five wombat parkas."

"Oh," said Helen. "I forgot about the dragon."

CHAPTER THIRTY-TWO: IN WHICH OUR HEROES STILL DO NOT HAVE TIME TO MAKE A PLAN FOR FIGHTING THE DRAGON.

THIS TIME WHEN THEY REACHED THE BRIDGE, Mak-Thar said, "We should leave all the equipment here."

Twilight, who was unpacking the mule so he could meet the bridge's weight limit asked, "What do you mean by 'leave'?"

"We take the wombat parkas," said Mak-Thar. "But that's it. Everything else stays here. It will just slow us down, and we need to hurry."

"Mak-Thar," said Twilight, "this is a far, far better thing that you do than you have ever done."

"I feel we should optimize for speed," said Mak-Thar. "Of course, I am trusting that the village will provide us with any supplies we need to use in their defense."

"What about your *Adventurer's Guide*?" asked Twilight.

"Oh, take that!" said Mak-Thar. "And take the flasks of oil, if you can do it in one trip. You can never have too much oil."

Twilight put *The Adventurer's Guide* and twenty flasks of oil in Fred's sack and carried them across the bridge. Once Fred and Helen had wheelbarrowed to the other side, Twilight handed

Mak-Thar's final baggage off to Fred. It was the first time Fred had ever carried an *Adventurer's Guide*.

As they hurried down the road, Mak-Thar said, "We need a plan for dealing with the dragon. Nightshade, can you make all of us invisible?"

"I can't even make myself invisible. That was my last Invisibility scroll."

"Wait," said Helen, "when you offered to be the party thief, didn't you tell us you had lots of Invisibility scrolls?"

"I said I had *some*," said Nightshade. "I wouldn't have said 'lots'."

"So how many did you have?" asked Helen.

"It turns out, I only had one."

Mak-Thar said, "You're lucky you had even one if you didn't write down your inventory. … My inventory! Does anyone have a piece of paper? We need to write down what Fred is carrying."

"He has twenty flasks of oil and *The Adventurer's Guide*," said Twilight.

"And if we lose track, I can open the sack and look," Fred explained patiently.

"Does you no good if you can't count to twenty," said Nightshade.

"Fred can count to twenty," said Helen. "Fred knows all kinds of numbers. Just because he's a fighter doesn't mean he's stupid."

"How many numbers do *you* know?" asked Nightshade.

Helen made a fist and waved it at Nightshade's nose. "This many."

"Okay," said Nightshade. "I guess that's a lot."

Fred said, "You two did walk through the swamp together, you know."

"Is that some sort of metaphor?" Nightshade asked.

"You had to be there," said Helen.

"I was there," said Nightshade. "It was swampy."

"Yes," said Fred. "You were both there. And now you're both out. So now you're friends."

"I'm allowed to tease my friends, Fred."

"Try to tease them without making fists," Fred suggested.

Twilight said, "I think we're all frustrated by the way Night-shade just drops out of the party and then drops back in."

"She's like a blink dog," said Mak-Thar.

Helen laughed.

"I have no idea what that is," said Twilight. "I was just trying to make the point—"

Nightshade asked, "Um, what was our plan for fighting the dragon again?"

"We don't have one," said Fred.

"Will the plan we don't have work five times?" asked Night-shade. "Because that's how many dragons there are." She pointed up the slope.

Four baby dragons were scampering down the hillside, coughing puffs of frost. The mama dragon was trying to cut them off. Whenever she got in front, they dodged behind her and clambered over her tail. Then they continued their awkward charge.

"That's adorable," said Twilight.

"I think we can take the babies," said Helen. "They don't seem to be flying. Is the big one still out of breath?"

"Unfortunately not," said Mak-Thar. "Her breath weapon will have recharged overnight."

"Well, we have our parkas," said Fred.

"Even with parkas we'll still look like prey," said Helen. "It's time to teach them respect for steel."

Twilight said, "I think killing the babies will make the big dragon angry. Then we will die."

"And the babies are cute," said Fred.

"But still big enough to bite your head off," said Helen.

"I have a plan," said Nightshade. "Let's run away really fast!"

"Good plan!" said Fred.

They all started running. It was easy for Fred to tell that everyone was running, because they all passed him.

On the slope above, the baby dragons continued their pursuit, leaping over rocks and crashing through shrubs.

"Wait!" said Mak-Thar, who had 360-degree vision. "This is a bad plan. Fred can't outrun the dragons."

Nightshade looked over her shoulder and called, "Run faster!"

"He can't!" said Mak-Thar. "A fighter in plate mail armor has a top running speed of sixty yards per round."

Nightshade stopped, turned to face Fred, and waved her arms in the air. Magic flew from her fingers to Fred's waist, and a buckle came undone. All of Fred's leg armor fell to his ankles. Fred tripped and sprawled across the road.

"Brilliant idea!" said Mak-Thar. "Can you unbuckle the top half, too?"

Fred sat up and kicked off his leg armor. Before he could stand, the elves were on either side of him, undoing all his buckles.

"Load it on my back!" said Mak-Thar.

"We left your saddle behind," said Twilight.

"Oh," said Mak-Thar. "Then perhaps we should stand and fight. Put Fred's armor back on."

Helen said, "We can all carry Fred's armor if everyone grabs a piece."

She picked up his left leg. Fred picked up his right. Well, actually he picked up the armor that had been on his leg, but it felt like he was holding his own leg, which was really weird.

The elves had Fred's breastplate and backplate, so Fred was now a lot lighter. They all took off down the road. After a few steps, Fred decided that carrying his leg and his treasure sack was awkward, so he put the leg in the sack and kept on running.

It was actually fun. Fred was used to running in armor, so now, with his legs removed, he felt like he was running on nothing. He had ghost legs, and his ghost legs could move really fast.

Everyone was running, and Fred could keep up! This had never happened to him before. He could run as fast as a mule! And since a mule is basically just a horse with donkey ears, Fred was running really fast.

After about a minute of running, Nightshade said, "I think we lost them."

"Keep running!" said Mak-Thar. "*The Adventurer's Guide* says we can sprint for five minutes."

"That seems unlikely," said Twilight. "We'd all be able to run four-minute miles."

Mak-Thar started mumbling in between breaths. "... 120 yards per round ... ten rounds is 1200 yards ... fifteen rounds is 1800 yards, that's over a mile ..."

The mumbling stopped, and Mak-Thar tossed his head in the way he did when he was feeling good about something. The running did not stop. They continued down the road to Mucho Caliente.

After a while, Helen said, "I think we can stop now."

"I'd like to rest," said Twilight.

"Elves don't sleep," said Nightshade.

"We *do* rest, though."

"Oh very well," said Mak-Thar, and they all came to a stop. "It would have been interesting to run the full five minutes, though."

Nightshade lay down in the middle of the road and pointed her toes at the sky. "I feel like I've been running forever."

"Is she falling asleep on us again?" Helen asked.

"Elves don't sleep," said Nightshade.

"You've spent most of the week asleep," said Helen.

"Oh really? I thought it was only one day."

"You'll be pleased to know," said Mak-Thar, "that we have just run a two-and-a-half-minute mile."

"That's impossible," said Twilight. "Except for you. There's no way the rest of us can keep up with a galloping mule for two-and-a-half minutes."

"According to *The Adventurer's Guide*," said Mak-Thar, "the sprinting speed of a mule is equal to that of an unencumbered adventurer."

"We weren't unencumbered," said Twilight. "We were carrying Fred's armor. Fred has a loaded sack!"

"If you have less than forty pounds, you are entitled to move at maximum speed, which is 120 yards per round."

"It's 120 *feet* per round," said Nightshade.

"In the dungeon, yes," said Mak-Thar. "But in the wilderness, we use yards."

Twilight was incredulous. "So we're three times faster than the last adventure just because we're outside?"

"Yes," said Mak-Thar. "If you like, you can pretend that being outdoors gives us a greater spiritual connection to all living things and this energy helps us run faster."

"Well, it certainly is a miracle that we outran the dragons," said Twilight.

"Not a miracle," said Mak-Thar. "The hatchlings could not fly, and the mother was afraid to leave them. Dragons move only ninety yards per round if earthbound."

"That rhymes!" said Fred.

"I think 120 yards per round was kind of fast for me," said Nightshade, still lying with her toes pointed at the sky.

Mak-Thar frowned. "Actually, you shouldn't have been able to do that in plate mail armor."

"It's special elf plate mail," said Nightshade.

"Oh right," said Mak-Thar. "You mentioned that before, but for some reason I didn't believe you."

"Never doubt my awesomeness," said Nightshade, still lying in the middle of the road.

"It's your consciousness we worry about," said Twilight.

"This would be a really dumb time to fall asleep again," said Helen.

"I'm just resting," said Nightshade.

"We all must rest," said Mak-Thar. "We have to sit here half an hour if we want to be able to fight without penalties."

Chapter Thirty-Three: In Which Our Heroes Commit to a Side Quest.

The village of Mucho Caliente was not burned to the ground. That was the first thing Fred noticed, and he felt very relieved.

Fred realized that he had been feeling guilty. These people had needed his help, and he'd just abandoned them because he had more important things to do. Something about that wasn't right. In fact, maybe abandoning people who needed his help was wrong.

Fred was pretty sure he shouldn't do things that were wrong. On the other hand, he had ignored the village's problems because he was committed to helping Mak-Thar, so maybe the situation was morally ambidextrous.

Well, it didn't matter, because they were here now. Fred had trusted other people to figure out what to do, and the one who had decided to do the right thing had been Mak-Thar, of all people. So maybe everything was going to work out in the end. They just had to defeat an evil army, save a village, and then get Mak-Thar a drink of magic water.

Yeah, Fred was pretty sure his friends could handle this.

No one in Mucho Caliente was doing agriculture when Fred and his friends strolled into town. Most of the able-bodied people were in the village's only flat space—which was the tiny patch of bare ground around the village well. A short, burly-armed man with a gardening trowel was trying to teach the villagers to use their rakes and hoes as pole arms.

"It's a little late for the training montage," said Twilight.

Roark was standing off to one side watching the training. As Fred and his friends neared the center of town, they caught Roark's eye. He left the militia and came over to meet them.

"Welcome back," said Roark. "I did not expect to see you again."

"Ha!" said Nightshade. "We're adventurers. We're not afraid of anything!"

"I know," said Roark. "That's why I assumed the dragon would eat you."

"Her eggs hatched, by the way," said Twilight. "There are five dragons now."

Roark rolled his eyes. "If it's not one thing, it's another."

"We would have been here sooner," said Mak-Thar, "but we had to rest for three turns to avoid a minus-two penalty on to-hit and damage rolls."

"I see," said Roark. "And this, um, thing has been avoided?"

"Yes," said Mak-Thar.

"Don't worry," said Helen. "We don't understand the mule, either."

Mak-Thar put his ears back.

Fred said, "Nightshade was telling us you had some trouble?"

"Not yet," said Roark. "But an army of inexpertly uniformed soldiers was encamped along the banks of Caliente Creek last night. The road from the valley leads only to our village. We have no doubt that we are their next target."

"They could be here any minute!" said Nightshade. "We came back just in time."

"Perhaps," said Roark. "When I sent Nightshade out to find you—"

"You were hoping the dragon would eat her, too?" asked Helen.

"No," said Roark. "I *assumed* the dragon would eat her. But on the off chance that you had all survived, I thought perhaps she would persuade you to return and help us. Now, however, after watching my people drill for most of the morning, I believe that our best hope is to flee like frightened ground squirrels."

"You have holes to hide in?" asked Twilight.

"No," said Roark. "It's just a figure of speech."

"The Place of Terraced Hillside Agriculture has such a colorful language," said Twilight.

"Well, no need to flee," said Fred. "We're here to save you. Right, guys?"

"Yep," said Helen.

"You betcha," said Nightshade.

"But what if flight is their best hope for survival?" asked Twilight. "I, too, wish to be heroic. But now that I see the lives that are at stake, perhaps it is better to be pragmatic."

Helen raised her hand.

"Yes, Helen?" asked Fred.

"Does 'pragmatic' mean 'pregnant automatically'?"

"It means 'practical'," said Twilight.

"Oh. Okay. That makes more sense, then."

Fred clasped Twilight's shoulder and met the elf's gaze. "We can do this. We're adventurers!"

"Right," said Helen. "Roark wouldn't offer us this quest if he thought we were going to lose."

"Actually," said Roark, "now that I'm talking to you in the flesh, I'm leaning toward Operation Ground Squirrel."

"Well it's too late now," said Mak-Thar. "We've accepted your side quest, so you'll just have to deal with us."

* * *

After watching the villagers train for a minute-and-a-half, Fred realized that any plan relying on a spirited and heroic stand would end with a lot of dead villagers and broken garden tools. That was too bad, because Fred rather liked spirited and heroic stands, and he was sure Helen and Twilight, at least, would be up for it.

Nonetheless, it was clear that the villagers had to avoid fighting. So Fred asked Mak-Thar, "Can you make this village disappear?"

"No," said Mak-Thar. "I'm only a mule."

"It doesn't have to *magically* disappear," said Fred. "We just need it to be unfindable when the evil army comes looking for it."

"I don't see how that's possible," said Mak-Thar.

"Suppose I give you half an hour to think about it," said Fred. "Do you think you would see how it's possible in half an hour?"

"I doubt I'd need more than ten minutes," said Mak-Thar.

"Great!" said Fred.

"But the plan I come up with might take an hour or two to implement."

"No problem," said Fred. "Because the other half of our plan is that Helen and I visit the clerics to buy you time."

"That's a terrible plan," said Mak-Thar.

"Is not," said Helen.

"Is too," said Mak-Thar. "Let's assume you find the army and ascertain that they are indeed on the march to the village. You'll convince Fred that the only way to stop them is if both of you charge right into the middle."

"Sneak attack always works," said Helen.

"Your surprise advantage lasts only one round," said Mak-Thar. "After that first round, you each have to fight half an army. They'll kill you in five rounds or less. Then, after resting for the remainder of the turn, they'll be on the march again. The two of you can delay them for at most ten minutes."

Mak-Thar was right. Fred needed to send Helen out of the village so that any spontaneous outbreaks of battle happened far away from the hapless villagers. But he and Helen could not defeat the entire army. Fred needed someone along who could really slow the army down.

"We'll take Twilight," said Fred.

Twilight raised his eyebrows. "Me?"

"Helen and I are fighters," said Fred. "But fights don't last very long. We need to buy time. You're the party's best talker."

"What about me?" asked Nightshade.

What about her? Fred had to admit that he had failed this little elf-girl. He really hadn't been able to help her fit into the party. And he couldn't rely on her, because she kept falling asleep.

The right thing to do would be to take her along and arrange things so that Helen and Nightshade came to understand and respect each other, forming unbreakable bonds that would make them lifetime friends. And if there hadn't been a village at stake, Fred would have tried it.

But he wasn't an amazing leader who could unlock the potential of even the flakiest elf-chick. He was just Fighter Fred. So he decided to leave Nightshade where she had the most chance of doing some good.

"I need you to help Mak-Thar. He might need to look up a rule. Or he might need oil poured somewhere. He might need something set on fire at a certain time. And Mak-Thar has no hands. Nightshade, you and Mak-Thar are really good at working together. Throughout our travels, you have been his hands. Please work with him now and save the village of Mucho Caliente."

Nightshade's eyes glistened with pride. "It will be an honor."

"Cool," said Helen. "Let's go kick some Mak-Thar."

"That's not the plan," said Fred, patiently. "The plan is for Twilight to find some way to stall them."

"All right," said Helen. "Let's go talk their Mak-Thars off."

CHAPTER THIRTY-FOUR: IN WHICH FRED, HELEN, AND TWILIGHT TAKE ON AN ENTIRE EVIL ARMY.

FRED, HELEN, AND TWILIGHT sat on a rocky hillside, plotting their next move. Helen had just returned from scouting.

"It's just a *little* army," she said. "We can take these guys."

"How big is little?" asked Twilight.

"Are you being mystical?" asked Helen.

"No," said Twilight. "I'm asking for a head count."

"Barbarians usually count heads after the battle."

Fred asked, "Do you think the number of soldiers is more than ten?"

"How many is ten?"

"Two hands."

Helen looked at her fingers and thought a moment.

"It's probably more than ten," said Twilight.

"They have only three supply wagons," said Helen. "And a light cavalry unit. And some pack mules."

"And soldiers?" asked Twilight.

"Yeah, lots of those," said Helen. "But it's still not what I'd call an 'army'. I think the word might be 'regiment'."

"I'm surprised you don't think the word is 'Vegemite'," muttered Twilight.

"What was that?"

"Nothing."

"I think we'll stick with Twilight's plan," said Fred. "If we kill the entire regiment ourselves, Mak-Thar and Nightshade will feel left out."

"All right," said Helen. "Anyway, the bad guys are on the other side of this hill."

This was much closer to Mucho Caliente than Fred would have liked. If their delay tactic failed, Mak-Thar would have at most twenty minutes to implement his plan—whatever it turned out to be.

"Before we go …" said Twilight.

Fred *knew* he had picked the right person for delay tactics.

"… I just want to say that I have enjoyed adventuring with you both. Helen, I appreciate that we have gone all this way and you have not teased me even one time about looking at your chest."

Helen laughed and slapped Twilight on the back.

"And Fred … that was amazing what you did with Mak-Thar on the mountain."

What had Fred done with Mak-Thar? He remembered not knowing whether to continue the quest or come back to help the village. He remembered asking Mak-Thar to decide. What did Twilight think he had done? "Oh, you liked that?"

"Of course! All this time, he's been fixated on being 'neutral'.

But when you put the decision in his hands, you forced him to confront the fact that he's basically good at heart."

Was that what Fred had done? If so, it had been pure luck and instinct. "Oh, I didn't think … anyone would notice."

"I noticed," said Twilight. "And it made me proud to have you as our leader."

Helen said, "Yeah, you've done great, Fred. But if this talking thing doesn't work out, I'm going to ignore everything you say and charge into the regiment of evil clerics."

Fred knew that was Helen's backup plan. He gave Twilight a meaningful look. And in Twilight's eyes, he saw understanding. If they did not want to die, they had to make sure this talking thing worked out.

* * *

On a dusty road that wound through scrub-brush hills, Twilight, Yellin' Helen, and Fighter Fred stepped into the path of a hundred evil soldiers. Their only defenses were their swords, their wits, and their wombat parkas.

Fred's parka smelled like dragon puke, chili powder, and wombat fat. The day was much too warm for the heavy pelt, but it was part of Twilight's plan.

Twilight mumbled, "If this doesn't work, I just want to say—"

"It will work," said Fred. "Just be you."

"I'm supposed to be an evil cleric," Twilight reminded him.

"Just be an evil cleric," said Fred. "We know you can handle this."

"And if you can't," said Helen, "we can all die gloriously."

"I should have been a fishmonger," said Twilight.

The enemy soldiers were now close enough that Fred could see individual faces. He had expected a malevolent glow in their eyes, but these men and women looked mostly like tired soldiers who had been marching half the day. Those in the front rank carried tension in their shoulders, as though they expected they would be given the order to attack Fred and his friends. Farther back, the soldiers' faces showed curiosity as they craned their necks to get a better look at what was blocking the road.

A man in front bearing a staff carved in the shape of a twisted snake gave the order to halt when the soldiers were well within bowshot range.

Twilight placed his hands on his hips and shouted, "Go no farther, Cultists of Toxia! The villages below may be yours, but these hills are the domain of the Dark Cult of the Wombat Skinners."

The man with the staff made a show of counting Fred, Twilight, and Helen. Then he glanced at his own troops.

"I believe we outnumber you."

"It is not meet that we should clash in arms," said Twilight. "Our aims are the same. We both seek to rid these lands of all that is good. Until that is accomplished, your soldiers and my cult must be allies."

"Toxia prefers allies who are somewhat powerful," said the man with the staff. "You appear easy to defeat."

"And yet we have skinned wombats," said Twilight. "Our powers go beyond what you can see."

The man with the staff offered Twilight a thin smile. "I assume, then, that you would be willing to let us test those powers. Clearly, if you place yourself before the might of my cohort, you have nothing to fear."

Helen murmured, " 'Cohort.' That's the word."

"A cohort of soldiers can conquer *people*," said Twilight. "But if the Cultists of Toxia would conquer this *wilderness*, they must learn to battle with the stones themselves."

"You battle with stones? Your swords must be quite blunt."

"Ah, but our minds are keen," said Twilight. "The Dark Cult of the Wombat Skinners has not conquered this wilderness with our blades. We conquer the land with our minds. Shall I demonstrate?"

The evil snake worshipper seemed amused. "Please."

"Command your people to bring forth a tall table and a dozen wooden cups," said Twilight.

"We aren't interested in seeing how much you can drink."

"You demonstrate your confidence by mocking me," said

Twilight. "But do you have the confidence to face me?"

"A challenge to single combat? I am no fool. My power is not in my staff but rather in the people I command. If it is battle you seek, you must fight all of us."

"I seek a game," said Twilight.

"A game?"

"A game of cups. My wits against yours."

"Oh, I see," said the man with the snake staff. "But no, thank you. We have villages to plunder."

"If you are so intent on plundering villages," asked Twilight, "why did you come to the wilderness? We have no villages here."

"The road must lead somewhere."

"It has led you to us," said Twilight. "Do you retreat from my challenge?"

"I really don't see what it would prove."

"It will prove who is fit to rule over these stones. If you win, I will acknowledge that you are powerful enough to oppress this land. If I win, you must take your army out of these hills and acknowledge that there are forces here you do not understand."

"Are you saying you will transfer control to me if I beat you at a game of cups?"

"Yes," said Twilight. "'Twill take but a moment of your time."

* * *

So Twilight actually convinced the leader of the evil cohort to play the game of cups—a game so simple that even Fred had played it once or twice.

The game was played with a dozen cups and a lot of tiny stones. Initially, there were five stones in each cup, but during play, the players would move the stones around and make various captures until there were no legal moves left. The winner was the one who captured more stones.

The enemy soldiers found a table and cups much faster than Twilight would have liked. He countered by insisting that the choice of stones was sacred to the Dark Cult of the

Wombat Skinners. Fred and Helen hunted about on the road for interesting-looking pebbles. They offered the pebbles to Twilight one at a time, and he rejected most of them as being unworthy. This ruse was good for about ten minutes of stalling time.

But the enemy captain eventually grew impatient and said, "I think this has gone far enough. Finish filling your cups now, or you shall have to play with what you have."

Twilight tossed away the pebble he had been examining and asked, with a gleam in his eye, "You would let me start with only twenty stones on my side?"

The captain's confidence wavered, then. He had assumed that starting with fewer stones would put Twilight at a disadvantage. If Twilight thought it was an advantage, then maybe the captain didn't know the game as well as he thought.

"Very well," said the captain. "Take your time. But be snappy about it."

They managed to drag out the stone-finding "ceremony" for five more minutes. Fred was glad that Twilight didn't go any longer. Evil clerics only have so much patience, and you don't want to try the patience of a man who can order an army to attack you.

In solemn tones, Twilight announced that he was ready to play. The evil captain demanded the right to make the first move. Twilight conceded this, and the game began.

The captain was much better at cups than Fred was. His opening moves were very successful. As the game developed, Twilight took longer and longer to analyze his position.

All too soon, they were in the endgame. In the final moves, Twilight made a number of surprising captures (well, Fred hadn't seen them coming) and when the stones were counted, Twilight was the winner.

"I have defeated you in head-to-head gamesmanship," Twilight declared. "Now, according to our agreement witnessed by all the evil people present, you must leave these hills and never return."

This wasn't going to work, Fred realized. The captain had a cohort of soldiers and he was evil. He had no reason to keep his word.

"Or," continued Twilight, "we could play double or nothing."

"Double or nothing?" asked the captain. "I am curious. How does one double 'never return'?"

"If you win," said Twilight, "the Dark Cult of the Wombat Skinners shall recognize your right to oppress these rocky hillsides. But if I win, you shall agree to never return, and you shall give me one of the villages you possess."

"Well, if you have your heart set on a dozen razed buildings and a heap of ashes," said the captain, "I suppose I have time for one more game."

* * *

Twilight really was quite good at cups. He managed to string the captain along for several games, raising the stakes each time, until thirty-two villages were at stake. Fred doubted the Cultists of Toxia actually controlled that many villages—they were an evil temple, not an evil kingdom— but the captain was still agreeing to the stakes with a straight face.

In this final game, Twilight spent a lot of extra time frowning and studying the cups.

"It's no use," the captain finally said. "You shan't find a way to win this time."

Two moves later, the captain captured a cup of five stones, and Twilight had clearly lost.

With a roar, Twilight grabbed the table and flipped it over, spilling cups and pebbles all over the road.

Fred was shocked. So was the captain. The nearby soldiers took a step back and exchanged surprised glances.

"I hate you!" said Twilight. "I'm never playing this stupid game again!" He turned away, stalked off the road, and headed up the hillside.

For a moment, Fred just stood there, not knowing what to do. Helen said, "Sorry. He's a sore loser."

"Is he ever!" said the captain.

"Please excuse us," said Helen. "Fred and I should go try to calm him down."

"Of course."

Fred and Helen hurried up the slope after Twilight. The bewildered captain and his soldiers just let them go.

* * *

When they caught up to Twilight, Fred asked, "Was that part of the plan?"

"I was improvising," Twilight admitted. "I needed a way to get us out of there. Win or lose, he was going to kill us. But I didn't think he was prepared for a rage quit."

"It was convincing," said Fred.

Twilight grinned. "Thank you. I've always wanted to flip a table. It was very satisfying."

CHAPTER THIRTY-FIVE: IN WHICH MAK-THAR AND NIGHTSHADE SAVE A VILLAGE.

AFTER THEIR THREE-HOUR CUPS BREAK, the Cultists of Toxia were well-rested and ready to march. They moved up the road quickly. They had been marching only a short while when they met another elf—a stylishly dressed elf maiden picking wild-flowers.

The elf maiden did not stop to challenge them to a game of cups. She shrieked and ran away up the road. The captain ordered a group of soldiers to pursue her, and the rest of his cohort trailed along behind.

Fred didn't see any of this, but Mak-Thar and Nightshade explained it to him that evening:

"I just kept running," Nightshade said. "And they kept

chasing me. But I'd left my armor in the village, so I was *way* faster than them."

"This was all technically under the combat rules," Mak-Thar explained. "So Nightshade was able to sprint for two miles."

Shortly after the soldiers encountered the elf maiden, the road they had been following began to narrow. Very soon, it was merely a path along the contours of the hills.

Mak-Thar explained the situation this way: "For the rest of the army, it was still wilderness travel. So they used up movement every time they crossed into a new hex."

After two miles, the path headed down a rocky draw, where it met the road again. The soldiers found themselves very near the point at which they had started marching that morning.

"Once Nightshade had rested," Mak-Thar said, "she was able to come back to the village using wilderness travel, but the bulk of the army was exhausted from their forced march. You see, we created a path that went around the point where three hexagons meet. Even though the army made only a three-mile loop, they have penalties for crossing three hexagons."

"Brilliant!" said Twilight.

"Thank you," said Mak-Thar.

"And definitely something only *you* would think of," said Twilight.

"Thank you again."

"So how did you make the path?" asked Helen. "And why didn't the army come marching up the road?"

"Well," said Mak-Thar, "while I was trying to think of a plan—it took me only seven minutes, by the way—I was watching the village's improvised militia. And I thought, these people swing their pole arms like they were hoes."

"That's because their pole arms are hoes," said Helen.

"Precisely," agreed Mak-Thar. "Watching their pitiful technique, I realized that a life of agriculture probably had not prepared them for combat. They are trained for hoeing. In other words, they are very good at moving earth."

"So the villagers built the new path," said Nightshade. "And they hoed up the old road and moved rocks onto it to make it look like the road was never there."

"You were lucky that the soldiers were not very observant," said Twilight. "I would think the lack of vegetation would have given it away."

"Yes," agreed Mak-Thar. "*You* would think that, my friend, because you notice plants. Most people don't."

"But people do notice a cute, little elf-chick," said Nightshade.

"And so they missed the road," said Mak-Thar. "I'm sure they are quite discouraged. What had seemed to be a road leading to another village has turned out to be an exhaustingly circular path. They now have no choice but to return whence they came and threaten Mucho Caliente no more."

CHAPTER THIRTY-SIX: IN WHICH OUR HEROES TRY TO COMPLETE MAK-THAR'S QUEST AGAIN.

THERE'S A CERTAIN SORT OF STORY that ends with the heroes drinking and dancing with the villagers they have saved. This was Fred's first time in a story like that, and he thought it was great!

Everyone was so happy. Young women seemed pleased when Fred asked them to dance.

Young men seemed alarmed when Helen asked them to dance, but that seemed to please Helen.

Twilight pulled out his flute and joined the band. Nightshade had too much to drink and tried to teach everyone a dance called "The Macarena". All the village children took turns petting Mak-Thar.

The next morning as they were once again walking along the road, Fred said, "That was fun. I want to do more adventures that save villages."

"As side quests go," said Mak-Thar, "it was quite enjoyable."

Helen said, "It's weird that everyone was so happy with us when all we did was tell them to destroy their road."

"We did lots more than that," said Nightshade. "I got to be a decoy. Twilight stalled an entire army. And I'm sure you and Fred were cool, too."

"We were ornamental," said Helen. "But it was still fun. I liked pretending to be in the evil wombat cult. Maybe I'll make that my new permanent religion."

"You can't be evil," protested Mak-Thar. "Not after all we've just been through."

Twilight said, "I'm sure she was jesting. Right?"

Helen smiled. "I'm glad you're finally starting to appreciate my sense of humor."

* * *

As a reward for services rendered, the villagers had given them a chest of chili powder. The chest was small—about the size of a loaf of bread—but it had all the chili powder Fred thought he would ever need.

When they reached the part of the road guarded by the white dragons, all they had to do was open the lid. The dragons maintained a respectful distance and allowed the party to continue on to the Cursed Bridge.

Fred once again wheelbarrowed to avoid setting foot on the bridge. He *did* wonder if his heart was pure, but he wasn't ready to fall to his doom finding out.

Mak-Thar and Twilight spent some time debating the relative merits of climbing the mountain with or without all of the gear they had left behind. Eventually, Mak-Thar decided to take it. The saddle certainly made it easier for him carry the wombat parkas and the chili chest.

As Twilight loaded Mak-Thar for the last time, he said, "I confess that I shall miss Evenstar."

Mak-Thar gave Twilight a solemn gaze. "I confess that I am quite worried about her. We are all hoping the magic spring can restore me to my true form, but we don't have a good model for predicting the outcome for Evenstar."

"You have me," said Helen. "And this model predicts that everything will work out all right."

"You always think that," said Mak-Thar.

"And I'm always right."

"Survivorship bias."

* * *

The only weird thing that happened on their hike up the mountain was that they did not need their wombat parkas. The air was somewhat cooler at the higher elevations, but certainly not so cold that any of them felt a strong desire to smell like a skinned wombat.

Eventually, they reached a sign that said *Magic Spring*.

"Maybe there really *is* a nature club," said Twilight.

Water trickled out of a small pool and ran down the mountain. The trail did not continue. It was obvious that their journey had finally come to an end.

CHAPTER THIRTY-SEVEN: IN WHICH SOME OF OUR HEROES REVEAL THEIR TRUE FORMS.

"SO THIS IS IT," SAID TWILIGHT. "The wombat skinning, the owlbear surgery, all those pointless random encounters—it all comes down to this."

"I don't know if I can do it," said Mak-Thar.

Helen sat down on a rock and shook her head. "You can lead a mule to water, but you can't make him drink."

Twilight put his hand on Mak-Thar's shoulder. "Selene put you into Evenstar's body for a reason. And the grace of the goddess is with us even now. If Evenstar is to be sacrificed so that you may regain your true form, then it is a sacrifice necessary for Nature's harmony. Birth and rebirth. Life and death. All are intertwined, Mak-Thar. We must accept this if we are to become our true selves."

"Wow," said Nightshade. "That's so poetic."

"I'm not *just* worried about Evenstar," said Mak-Thar. "I'm worried about my true form. Remember what you said, about taking the outer form that matches your inner self?"

"Yes."

"Well, what if my alignment has shifted?"

"What?"

"What if I'm not neutral anymore?" Mak-Thar asked. "Helping that village was almost a selfless act! What if my alignment spectrum has shifted too far toward good?"

Twilight shook his head. "I don't see how you could be too good, Mak-Thar."

"Can you cast Detect Good on me? I've got to know."

Helen's face wore a confused frown. "What? You're afraid the spring will make you too pretty or something?"

"Yes!" said Mak-Thar. "What if I'm now too good to be a mage?"

"Mages don't have to be neutral," said Nightshade. "We can be whatever we want."

"What if my true self is actually a cleric?" asked Mak-Thar. "I'll have to wear armor under my robes and learn to use a mace. I don't want to start over now. I've invested too many experience points!"

Fred said, "You know, Mak-Thar, we've all spent a lot of time helping you get to this spring. Some of us have splinters in our hands from wheelbarrowing across a bridge three times. There comes a point when you have to stop thinking about stuff. There comes a point when you are so committed to something that you just have to *do* it. You passed that point a long time ago."

Mak-Thar's ears lowered, and his head drooped. "I suppose you're right."

He ambled over to the pool and ... stood there a moment.

"Well?" asked Helen.

"I was hoping for one last look at Evenstar," said Mak-Thar. "But the pool is too ripply."

Mak-Thar heaved a sigh. Then the mule that was somehow both Mak-Thar and Evenstar put its lips into the water and took a big long slurp.

Fred was watching close, because he didn't want to miss it. You don't see one thing turn into another every day. Well, maybe you do, if you're a mage and you're practicing Polymorph spells, but *Fred* didn't see one thing turn into another every day.

He didn't see it today, either.

One moment, the mule was drinking. And the next moment, the mule was still drinking. Then some more moments passed, and Fred began to wonder if the spring was supposed to have some sort of delayed effect or something.

Actually, the problem was that Fred was too focused on the mule. Mak-Thar was standing behind her.

Fred didn't see him until the mage raised his scrawny arms. With a loud cry of magic words, Mak-Thar flung out a fireball that flew high into the afternoon sky and exploded.

Lit by the fiery glow of his own creation, the mage shouted, "Mak-Thar the Magnificent is back!"

Evenstar glanced at the fireball with one eye, then went back to drinking. She was thirsty.

Nightshade said, "His true form is probably naked, guys. We should turn our backs."

Mak-Thar stepped out from behind Evenstar. Fortunately, he was not naked. In fact, he was wearing his dingy robe, his overstuffed backpack, his belt with many pouches, and, coiled around his shoulders …

"You even have your rope!" said Fred.

"Three hundred feet of rope," said Twilight.

Mak-Thar reached into a pouch, pulled out his notebook, and flipped it open to the appropriate page. "According to my inventory, it's four hundred fifty feet of rope!"

Twilight blinked in confusion. "I was sure it was only three hundred in the Dungeon of Doom."

"But this is my *true form*!" said Mak-Thar.

"Ah," said Twilight. "So naturally, your true form has even more rope."

"Yes!" said Mak-Thar. "It's wonderful! I'm going to cast Edwin's Weird Dweomer."

"Not here!" said Twilight. "You'll start an avalanche."

"Do you really think so?" asked Mak-Thar.

"Yes," said Twilight.

Fred kind of wanted him to cast it. He'd never seen an avalanche.

"So no more mule jokes," said Helen. "Oh well. It was fun while it lasted."

"While you guys are all distracted by Mak-Thar, my elf takes a drink from the spring."

"Why would she do that?" asked Twilight. "I mean, why would you do that?"

"Well," said Nightshade, "I have this theory that her true form is really awesome. So this could be a quick way to level up."

Helen said, "The party's barbarian watches your elf because she wants to see you turn into a frog."

"Probably more like a hyperactive chipmunk," grumbled Twilight.

"Okay, cool. I drink."

And she did.

A magical mist swirled around Nightshade. Lights began to sparkle all over her body. She did not change height. She did not change shape. When the lights faded and the mist cleared, mostly what had changed was her equipment.

Gone were the shiny black armor and shapely black tights. Now she wore a suit of fine black leather. Her chain mail skirt had been replaced by leather pleats. She still had her sword, bow, and quiver of arrows, but her little backpack, though still cute, now looked somewhat travelworn.

"Oh no," said Nightshade. "Oh no!" She removed her backpack and rummaged through it frantically. "I've lost my scrolls! I've lost my Backpack of Holding!"

The joy faded from Mak-Thar's face as he heard these dire words. "Lost your Backpack of Holding? Oh, Nightshade!"

Fred had never seen Mak-Thar so overcome with sympathy for another human being. Well, technically Nightshade was an elven being. ... Or was she?

"Um," said Twilight, "that's not the only thing you lost." He raised a finger to the tip of one of his pointy ears.

"What?" Nightshade grabbed her ears. "I still have my ears, don't I? What happened? Am I hideous now?"

Twilight took his hand mirror out of his pack and showed Nightshade her face.

"Oh, that's a relief," she said. "I was afraid I didn't look cute and perky anymore."

"You're still cute and perky," said Twilight, "but I don't think you're an elf."

Nightshade checked herself out again. "Look at that cute nose. Definitely elfin."

"But the ears!" insisted Twilight.

"I know. They're round. I think they look nicer that way. Maybe my true self is a special race of round-eared elf."

"There are no round-eared elves!"

"How can you be sure?" asked Nightshade. "Maybe we just don't hang out with your kind."

"I think she's still Nightshade," said Fred.

Helen shook her head. "You had to make this about you, didn't you?"

"Excuse me?" asked Nightshade.

"You couldn't just sit back and enjoy Mak-Thar's big moment. You had to find some way to put yourself at the center."

"I was just trying to level up," said Nightshade. "It's what any smart adventurer would do."

"Well," said Mak-Thar, "instead of leveling up, you appear to have changed class."

Nightshade held out her arms and examined her leather sleeves. "Do you really think so?"

"Can you still cast spells?" asked Mak-Thar.

"Um ... maybe ... not?"

"That backpack is too small to hold a spellbook," said Mak-Thar.

"Yeah," said Nightshade. "I guess you're right. Oh, but look at this!" She reached into her backpack and pulled out a compact, pocket-sized *Adventurer's Guide*. "Isn't it cute?"

Mak-Thar frowned. "*The Adventurer's Guide* is not cute."

"I guess he's still Mak-Thar," said Fred. He'd been a little worried by all the displays of emotion.

"He is," agreed Twilight.

"I am," said Mak-Thar. "In fact, now that I can hold my notebook again, I feel more like myself than I have felt in a long time."

Fred asked, "And Nightshade is ...?"

"I'm a thief," admitted Nightshade.

Fred nodded. Leather armor. Sword and bow. Human ears. She looked like a thief.

"I guess it makes sense," said Nightshade. "Given my back story."

"Your super cool back story?" asked Twilight. "That's so cool you can't tell us what it is?"

"It has some secret plot hooks," said Nightshade. She looked at her leather sleeves again. "I didn't realize that a career change was one of them."

"Yes, you're very mysterious," said Helen. "But this was not supposed to be about you. This was supposed to be about Mak-Thar, and somehow you've managed to take a perfectly good adventure and steal the ending."

Twilight said, "Well, she *is* a thief."

"I wouldn't worry about it," said Fred. "This is a way better ending than my last adventure."

"Definitely," said Twilight.

"I concur," said Mak-Thar.

Helen sighed. This sigh meant—

Well, she told them all what it meant: "Okay. I'll let it go.

Nightshade, I'm glad you've found your true calling."

"But I didn't *want* this to be my true calling! I just wanted to be a sneaky mage."

"A sneaky mage with a sword and armor," said Twilight, "who was also really good with a bow."

"And whose petite little butt looks good in any outfit she chooses to wear," said Helen.

"What?" Nightshade tried to look at her own butt. "Do you really think so?"

"Yeah," said Helen. "Standing next to you, I feel like an owlbear."

"But you're a professional model!" said Nightshade.

"Oh forget it," grumbled Helen. "Pretend I never said anything. I'm going to pretend this adventure ended with Mak-Thar's fireball."

"That fireball does make a lovely ending," said Twilight. "But the dreary truth is that we've only reached the midpoint."

"Oh yeah," said Fred. "We still have to go all the way back."

"My thief knows a shortcut."

Twilight threw up his hands. "How can your thief know a shortcut? You've only been your thief for two minutes!"

"Yeah, okay. But when I was looking in your mirror, I saw this sign. Here. See for yourself."

Twilight took the mirror. "She's right. There's a second sign beside the spring. You can't see it until you look in the mirror."

They all crowded around—except for Evenstar, who was a much less active participant in the conversation now that Mak-Thar had moved out. The mirror-image sign said *Secret shortcut to Basetown.** And below that was a sign that said in smaller print **For details, visit Sage the Sage.*

Mak-Thar said, "I am beginning to resent the Sages' Guild's monopoly on travel information."

"The sign has an arrow on it," said Fred. "Could we just follow the arrow?"

"There's no trail," said Twilight. "And it's not the best footing. I'm not sure Evenstar can make it."

"Going downhill is hard on her knees," said Mak-Thar. "But she's not overloaded with rations now. I think she'll be fine."

* * *

After an hour of downhill walking, they saw a half-pint flying on a broom. Sage the Sage spotted them and came down for a landing. Evenstar eyed her suspiciously.

"Greetings, weary travelers!"

Mak-Thar scowled. "You could have told us there was a shortcut."

"It would have discouraged you," said Sage. "The shortcut goes only one way."

"How can a trail go only one way?" asked Twilight.

"Magic! Do you want me to show you the trail? Or do you want to continue going in this direction until you hit the scree slope above the Bottomless Gorge?"

"Well," said Twilight, "I believe I speak for all of us when I say we would prefer to avoid finding ourselves on a scree slope above a bottomless gorge."

"What's scree?" asked Nightshade.

"It's the sound you make as you slide down a slope of loose, flat stones," said Helen.

"My thief can climb it."

"I see you have added ladies to your party," said Sage. "Very wise of you."

"Yes," said Mak-Thar. "They are a pair of wise ... ladies."

"I'll give you the secret of the trail—" said Sage.

"Thank you," said Helen.

"I wasn't finished. I'll give you the secret of the trail in exchange for ..." Sage paused dramatically.

Helen rolled her eyes. "Oh. So *now* you're finished?"

"... your wombat parkas."

"I don't believe it," said Mak-Thar. "This entire adventure was just a side quest to bring you wombat parkas."

"Absolutely not," said Sage. "You would have needed them if a blizzard had come up."

"In late spring?" asked Mak-Thar.

"Actually," said Twilight, "spring blizzards are the worst. This high up, it can snow any time of the year. She was wise to tell us to be prepared."

"And we used the parkas a lot along the way," said Fred.

"See?" said Sage. "The secret of the one-way trail for only a few used wombat parkas. Pretty good deal, huh?"

"I suppose we have little choice," said Mak-Thar. "Very well, the parkas are yours. As are the rations, by the way. Herman sends them as his affiliate commission."

"Oh goody. I'll sell them to you for one gold piece per day."

"Really?" asked Mak-Thar. "That's less than half of list price!"

"I like you," said Sage. "Besides, you were about to dump the rations and tell me to haul them back myself. This way, you have to keep them."

"Shrewd," said Mak-Thar. He reached into his coin pouch. "You don't know how good it feels to be able to pay you myself."

When the deal was concluded, Sage said, "Okay, the secret to the trail is that the trail markers can be seen only in a mirror."

"Oh," said Mak-Thar. "I should have figured that out already!"

"That's how the trail can be only one way," said Sage. "The magic won't work if you try to climb the mountain from Basetown."

"So how short is the shortcut?" asked Helen.

"Real short," said Sage. "Basetown is about half a day due east."

"The map is in hexagons," said Mak-Thar. "We can't go due east."

"You can if you follow my secret trail."

* * *

And that's how Mak-Thar's heroic quest ended—with five brave adventurers and one unflappable mule following an imaginary line between hexagons. It was kind of a magey ending. And since it was Mak-Thar's quest, Fred thought a magey ending was just about right.

THE END

WHAT'S NEXT FOR FIGHTER FRED?

WILL OUR BRAVE HEROES now go their separate ways, or will Helen convince them to join forces and overthrow that evil temple? What's up with Nightshade's back story? And now that she's a thief, will Helen have more or less patience with her? Oh, and Twilight still has that Amulet of Spring. Will he ever get around to doing something about that?

These questions and more will be sort of answered in *Fighter Fred and the Evil Temple of Evil*!

ACKNOWLEDGMENTS

THE WOMBAT WILDERNESS would not exist without the inspiration of Gary Gygax's *Dungeons & Dragons*. In particular, this book was inspired by the 1981 edition of the expert rules edited by David Cook with Steve Marsh. I also looked at material from Kim Mohan's *Wilderness Survival Guide*, but except for the weather tables, everything was too realistic to be of much use.

Doug Hoover read an earlier draft of this novel and made many helpful comments. My family—Sierra, Zora, and Linden—were my first readers, and this book could not have been published without their support.

The studious reader will note that mules do not actually say "HEE-HAW!" the way donkeys do, but apparently Mak-Thar doesn't know that. Furthermore, it is possible that this book includes an inaccurate portrayal of wombats.

ABOUT THE AUTHOR

JASON A. HOLT writes from the viewpoint of Fighter Fred, but in real life, he likes rulebooks as much as Mak-Thar does. Jason has worked on over forty-two board games. In particular, he designed the English-language word list for Codenames and translated the rulebook for Galaxy Trucker.

His first game-based novel was *Galaxy Trucker: Rocky Road*, and he also writes the Edgewhen® fantasy adventure series. You can find out more at Edgewhen.com.

When Jason isn't writing, he's usually sleeping or eating. When the weather is nice, he'll go for a long run. Sounds kinda boring, but the fact is, it's hard to find a hobby that's more fun than writing Fighter Fred.

You can find out more about Jason at JasonAHolt.com. He even has a mailing list that will tell you when you can expect his next book.

CPSIA information can be obtained
at www.ICGtesting.com
Printed in the USA
FSHW011357300820
73415FS